UNAUTHORIZED EXPERIMENT

"Lookit those things!" Lt. Thurmond shouted. The coils were beginning to glow with a light like huge firefly tails, illuminating things in the engineering department basement—

And one of the things was crawling into the aisle.

It was four legged and ten feet long, with olive-drab skin as slimy as a frog's. Two eyes glittered beneath brow ridges, while in the center of the creature's flat forehead was a pearly iridescence which might also have been an eye of sorts. It opened its mouth with a glitter of conelike teeth and bellowed— but the sound was lost in the roar of the pillars.

Officers Robertson and Thurmond thumbed the hammers of their weapons. Then there was a soundless blue flash. The pillars burped light in a sort of afterthought. Then they began to cool. The basement full of unguessably complex hardware no longer held any large animals.

The creature had vanished in the flash.

But so had both policemen.

D1041216

Tor Books by David Drake

*Forthcoming

DAVID DRAKE

BRIDGEHEAD

A TOM DOHERTY ASSOCIATES BOOK
NEW YORK

BRIDGEHEAD

Copyright © 1986 by David Drake

A Tor Book
Published by Tom Doherty Associates, LLC
175 Fifth Avenue
New York, NY 10010

Cover art by Wayne Barlowe

ISBN-13: 978-0-765-35647-5
ISBN-10: 0-765-35647-3

First Edition: February 1986
Second Edition: January 2007

Printed in the United States of America

0 9 8 7 6 5 4 3 2 1

Dedication

For Bernadette Bosky, who helped with the book from before its inception.

The blue glare flooded briefly through the ranks of basement windows.

Officer Bus Robertson cursed, though it was what he had half-expected. Had been waiting for, really, for the past five minutes. He keyed his microphone and said, "Lieutenant, it's happened again. Over."

The radio burped static and the voice of Lieutenant Thurmond asking, "You're still at engineering, Robertson?"

"Yessir. In front."

"All right," said the radio after a hissing pause, "hold one. Over and out."

Robertson hung his mike on the dash hook. After a moment's hesitation, he switched off the patrol car's ignition. The night was already pouring through the open

windows. Its softness took over the car completely when
the whine of the air conditioner ceased. The lack of mechanical noise was a comfort to Robertson as he studied
the building beside him.

Engineering dated back to the original foundation of the
campus in the 1920s. Here on Science Drive, however,
there had been none of the neo-Gothic architecture which
had turned the liberal arts and administrative center of the
university into a showpiece. The engineering building was
of red brick only mildly ornamented with concrete swags
and casements. The windows were large, but each was
made up of a dozen rectangular panes set in a common
sash. The central mass of the building rose four stories
above the street level, but the wings to either side were
lower by a story or two. The hillside fell away sharply
enough from the street that the south wall of the basement
level was glazed for eight feet above the ground.

It was through that wall that the night had been lit by a
silent blue explosion.

Bus Robertson got out on the curb side. He could reach
his radio if it called him through the open window. When
he had first joined the university police, the buildings on
Science Drive had been pleasantly reminiscent of the high
school from which he had graduated five years before—
solid and unpretentious, a reminder that there were values
beyond those of the preppies . . . whose tuition nonetheless was the ultimate source of Robertson's salary.

There had followed six months of increasing strangeness, however, focusing finally down to the rare gouts of
light from the engineering building. There had been several reports from students walking late at night, but nothing was ever actually wrong, no signs of fire or the ozone
harshness of arcing components. Then a week ago, Robertson had seen the glare himself, and for the first time he

understood why the previous flashes had aroused as much comment as they had on a campus where much of the student body would have ignored a rape; there were people paid to take care of things like that, weren't there? And anyway, Daddy said it was better not to get involved.

The light was different even at a distance too great to pinpoint its source, its color too deeply saturated to be confused with that of the mercury-vapor streetlights. Even apart from its richness, the light was closer to the violet end of the spectrum than a germicidal lamp. It was frightening only for the reason that a swift object making ninety-degree turns in the distant sky is frightening: the glare did not appear to belong on Earth.

A car approached fast on the silent street, fast enough that Robertson's eyes narrowed in a frown. Then the light in front of the mathematics and physics building glittered on the vehicle's blue bar light: Lieutenant Thurmond, and not wasting any time about it.

The second cruiser swung across the empty traffic lane and pulled up nose to nose with Robertson's car. Its exhaust continued to poom for a moment; then the engine cut to silence and the headlights died to only brief orange afterimages of their filaments. There was a squawk from Robertson's radio as his superior reported in curtly. Lieutenant Thurmond got out of the car, settling his portable unit into the holster on the left side of his belt, where it balanced the revolver.

"Down there in the basement, sir," Robertson said. He was taller than Thurmond, but the black lieutenant was built with the squat power of a bulldog. At times, Thurmond could be intimidating, but right at the moment, Robertson was more than glad of the lieutenant's presence.

Not that anything was really wrong.

"Looks quiet enough now," Thurmond said.

"Just the one flash," Robertson agreed, "but it lighted up the whole floor." There had been nothing in his superior's voice to suggest doubt about the event; only a statement, a datum to be weighed. "I guess it's just some experiment or other, nothing to worry about now we seen it," Robertson added after a moment's silence.

"Hell," Thurmond said without a clear referent. He hunched his shoulders, loosening the dark blue fabric of his uniform. He had boxed professionally twenty years before. The way he shrugged his torso forward when he made a decision was one of the holdovers from that time. "They might have let somebody know, mightn't they?" he said. "It's not like it hasn't been in the papers about the funny light on West Campus. Let's go take a look. Maybe we can find out who the hell's in charge."

The squat man began walking toward the main door of the building. Robertson noticed that the lieutenant's left hand had already isolated one of the passkeys on his belt-chained ring.

The air in the lobby was still innocent of any odor beyond that of sweeping compound on the dark asphalt tile. There would be a fire door between him and any short circuit or overheated machinery in the basement, Robertson knew. The narrow beam of Thurmond's flashlight bobbed across the bulletin boards, the empty hallway, the chromed stand with a card advertising for blood donors. The lieutenant held his light out at arm's length to his left side, probably by habit rather than in anticipation of need, but . . .

"I could find the switches," suggested Bus Robertson.

"This'll do," Thurmond replied.

Robertson unsheathed his own flashlight as he followed his superior. That gave him something to do with his hands besides play nervously with the strap of his holster.

Thurmond's laconic style was making his subordinate uneasy, even in a situation without apparent danger.

The first stairway led up only. The building was something of a labyrinth even without the office addition of glass and stucco yoked by walkways to the back of the original structure. A turn past darkened, silent rooms brought the officers to a second red Exit sign. The concrete stairs beyond this one led down as well as up. The lights demanded by the building code in fire exits were a quick passage back to the real world for Bus Robertson. He relaxed, and it was only in that moment that he realized quite how taut he had been.

Lieutenant Thurmond did not seem any different when he pushed open the lower fire door, but Robertson had only his own nervousness to suggest that the older man had been tense in the first place. The banks of fluorescents in the basement's sixteen-foot ceiling were not lit. There were scores of lighted instrument dials, however. While their green or yellow glows did not illuminate the huge room, they did limit and demarcate it as stars do the night sky. There was an unexpected tinge to the atmosphere, an organic odor rather than the electrical sharpness for which Robertson had been prepared. Machinery hummed in placid unconcern.

"It must have been over there," said Robertson. He gestured toward the apparatus behind the chain-link partition separating half the enormous room. "It was through those windows, at least." He switched on his own flashlight as a pointer and drew it across the enclosure. The woven-wire fencing glittered in the beam's oval. The glass of the outer wall reflected the light in varying facets as it skipped from one pane to the next.

The narrow beam hid the fenced-off equipment rather than illuminating it, however. Like the basement itself, the apparatus was large, sprawling, and messy. Festoons of wire connected breadboard circuitry. There were scores of crackle-finished chaisses, which appeared from the excrescences bolted to them to have been adapted to service beyond that originally intended. The flashlight could blur a range of colors in a ribbon of control wires; in the diodes and solder of a circuit board; in the spiral shadows of an armored conduit. The pair of campus police could no more grasp the arrangement of the apparatus than they could its purpose.

"Doesn't seem to be a damn soul around, does there?" said Thurmond as he paced down the aisle with his own light turned purposelessly inward. He rattled the partition with his free hand. It was supported by a frame of heavy angle iron. The whole made a sullen clatter that mortised well with the lieutenant's mood. "Shouldn't have something like this running and nobody around to watch it, should they?"

Actually, there did not at the moment seem to be any reason why the hardware should not have been left to itself. Bus Robertson was feeling more than a little silly. He did not understand the apparatus past which he walked with his superior, but that did not concern him. Robertson had spent four years in the navy as a damage control crewman on an aircraft carrier. He was used to being around extraordinarily complex hardware whose function was beyond his estimate.

The light *had* been different. It was *weird*, and it was impinging on the normal world as it flooded even the clouds overhead in its brief intensity. The light was now a thing of the past, also. Memory can only store unusual data by reference to things known and accepted. Bus was trying to remember why he had been disturbed by a hue, sort of the shade of the summer sky, only richer. . . .

There were several rooms walled off on the south side of the basement. One of them was a lab with a radiation-hazard sticker beneath the glazed portion of its door. That gave Robertson a momentary tremor; but nobody was building an atomic pile down here, they weren't *that* crazy.

The side rooms had false ceilings, so the concrete beams and pillars of the basement proper lowered over them. The wood-and-glass enclosures were containers, boxes to hold people and human endeavors. The chain-link fence across the aisle from them was by contrast an integral part of the great room, as was the hulking tangle of apparatus set off by the partition.

"Lieutenant, I hear something," Robertson said. They were nearing the end of the long aisle. Bus flicked his flashlight beam across bulletin boards with dusty notices.

"That buzzing, you mean?" said Lieutenant Thurmond. His own beam prodded impalpably at the two huge pillars at the end of the enclosure. The light scattered on the fencing between the men and the pillars and again when Thurmond's aim drifted away from the pillars and let the beam touch the cross partition which closed the fenced area to the north wall of the basement.

Where the light played over the pillars themselves, it was mirrored back in its yellowish tinge from the surface. Only at the edges of the narrow beam were the interior construction of the pillars visible: fine-gauge wire had been wound on cores a yard in diameter. The sheen of its lacquer insulation was darker and more purple than the copper itself would have been. The cylindrical windings, very nearly as high as the twelve-foot partition setting off the work area, were encased in square-section boxes of clear plastic. It was this sheathing which made the windings so difficult to see. The plastic gave a measure of mechanical and dust protection, but it was clearly not intended to be airtight. One side of each box was hinged to be swung away.

The pillars seemed to be about as far apart as they were high, ten or twelve feet. Within the enclosure, where it would form the third point of an isosceles triangle with the pillars, was a circle painted on the floor. An array of instruments including a computer terminal stood across the circle from the pillars—which themselves seemed to be buzzing, as the lieutenant had said.

But it was not the buzzing that Robertson had really meant when he'd said he heard something. It was more—

"Hey, lookit those goddamn things!" Thurmond shouted. The clear reflection of his flashlight had vanished from the protective sheathing because the coils within were themselves beginning to glow with a light that had no particular color as yet. Its average intensity was less than that of a firefly's tail. When multiplied by the entire surface of the windings, the glow illuminated things in the basement which the flashlights had missed.

One of the things was crawling around the back of the enclosure, into the aisle.

It was ten feet long and looked more like forty. The skin was as slimy as a frog's, drab-colored but perhaps a shade lighter on the throat and the inner side of four broadly splayed legs. Two eyes glittered beneath brow ridges, while in the center of the creature's flat forehead was a pearly iridescence which might also have been an eye of sorts.

The creature squirmed another step into the aisle. It opened its mouth with a glitter of conelike teeth and the swampy effluvium—still water and rotting fish—which Robertson had noticed as soon as he'd entered the basement. The throat was probably bellowing something also, but the sound was lost in the roar of the pillars.

Lieutenant Thurmond was in a crouch, his right hand sweeping out the revolver he had never before had occasion to draw as a member of the university police. Bus Robertson held his flashlight out with both hands as if its narrow beam were a pole to fend off the monster which took another splayed footstep toward them. The beam could not be seen against the increasing glow of the pillars. Thurmond thumbed back the hammer of his weapon. There was a soundless blue flash—*the* flash.

For an instant, Bus Robertson could see nothing but the retinal afterimage of the blazing pillars and the egg-shaped splotch of his flashlight beam on the bare floor. The basement was so silent that Lieutenant Thurmond's hoarse breathing was the most of what sound there was. The smell of the toad-squat, toad-faced creature was gone; and the creature was gone as well.

As Robertson's vision returned, he could see that there were marks of sorts on the gritty dust of the floor. They might have been left by the wet, webbed feet that Robertson remembered; but even the traces of dampness had now disappeared.

"What the hell?" Thurmond was saying. He jumped around the corner. Robertson followed with his revolver out and his heart pounding. The cross aisle to the boiler-room door was empty except for the tracks. "What the hell?"

The lieutenant spun very abruptly, as if he suspected that something was crawling down the aisle behind them now with its fangs bared. There was nothing there, either.

The pillars burped light in a sort of afterthought. Then they began to cool. The room of unguessably complex hardware no longer held any large animal—human or otherwise.

Certainly neither of the policemen were anywhere to be seen.

"We've got a flow," said Selve. The instruments on his console had been flat, as they should be during shutdown. Now the readouts were making their second automatic log-twelve jump, and the peaks were still rising. Strictly speaking there was no alarm, but the rising whine of the recorders was enough to warn the three Contact Members.

"Well, just a leakage," said Keyliss as she jumped to the console herself; the words were a prayer. "A bit of trash in the coils here, in synchrony with—"

"It's no surge, it's a full-scale run," Astor shouted as she, too, riffled her glance along the instruments. "Selve, you were supposed to clear the boards after the run this afternoon. Now we'll have to go in early and see what damage this has done!" Astor was taller and more powerfully built than either of her companions, a fact that colored the formal equality of the members of the Contact Team.

"I *did* clear and balance the systems—" Selve snapped.

Simultaneously, Keyliss said, "Look, Astor, if there *is* a flow—"

"Of *course* there's a flow! Can't you read the dials?"

"—then it's because you insisted we go back to Portal Eleven and check out the anomaly last week. That's what's set everything askew. And now you want to do it again."

"Don't be ridiculous," said Astor. "We all agreed that we'd brought the systems back in balance after that." But her voice was lower and perhaps a trifle apologetic for the initial outburst. It was easy to lash out in frustration at whoever was nearest. The anomalies seemed insoluble. While they were minor in themselves, they might indirectly lead to—

To the end of the world.

Keyliss was willing to bury the hatchet as well. She turned back to the console and asked—to change the subject and not because she could not have read out the information for herself—"What's the other terminus?"

"Thirty-seven, I think," said Selve as he adjusted a pair of controls. "Short duration, I'd say. No more than twenty minutes."

"Carboniferous," translated Astor. "And no way of telling if there was a real transport without going downline and checking ourselves."

"And increasing the likelihood of more backflows in the future, and worse ones," Keyliss noted tartly. "After all, what real harm will twenty minutes from the Carboniferous do? At worst?"

Selve looked up from his console. There was a low trembling, more imagined than truly sensed, coming from the sealed black pillars of their drive coils thirty feet away. A ghost memory in its own circuits was responding to the activity in the device to which it had recently been coupled. "The unit was cleared this afternoon," Selve said, "and now it's not. Gustafson couldn't have activated it if he wanted to, so long as we kept it locked here." His index finger tapped the console beside a switch thrown firmly to the off position. "I don't understand, I just don't understand."

Keyliss took a deep breath. "All right," she said, "we won't inspect the site until we're scheduled to tomorrow." After a moment she added, "Sometimes I feel like I'm juggling bombs. Some are duds and some aren't. If one starts to get away, I can catch it again—but maybe then another one falls instead. And you never know which is the dud."

*   *   *

His pencil had remained poised above the paper ever since he heard the tea kettle begin to sing in the kitchen, seven minutes before. Mrs. Hitchings's tap on the jamb of the open door was only the culmination of the process, the dawn that is the certain result of the Earth's rotation. "I've made you a pot of tea, Louis," said Mrs. Hitchings. She carried in the tray without request, now that she had received Professor Gustafson's formal attention.

"Thank you, Eva," Gustafson said. His desk was untidy, but.he had learned from experience to leave clear a portion the size of a tea tray on the corner nearest the door. If he worked to eleven P.M. in his room, his landlady would appear with the full panoply: teapot in a knitted cozy; a single cup and saucer (Mrs. Hitchings never attempted to turn her interruptions into social events); milk pitcher; sugar bowl, holding cubes and an ornately clawed pair of tongs; and a matching dish with lemon slices laid in a neat, overlapping pattern. Gustafson used milk to cut the acidity of the tea. In twenty-three years as Eva Hitchings's tenant, he had never taken a sugar cube or lemon slice from the tray.

"Don't stay up too long, now," Mrs. Hitchings said as she exited the room. "We're not as young as we once were, Louis."

Well, that was no more than the truth, Louis Gustafson thought as he poured his tea. The bergamot odor of Earl Grey sweetened the air. When he had been younger, he drove to his office at night in order to avoid interruptions. No one came down into the basement of the engineering building after hours. His was the only office there, just as he was the only professor with continuing research going on among the pipes and concrete.

Gustafson's night vision was no longer up to after-dark drives from the center of town to the campus and tiredly back, however. Besides, the disruption of going to the office was easily—and obviously—as great as that of Mrs. Hitchings's clockwork kindnesses. Gustafson had finally decided that when he had something difficult to put on paper, his mind would refuse to get on with the task until he had been interrupted a time or two.

His glasses had fogged when he poured the tea. He took them off and cleared them by holding them carefully above the ventilation holes of his incandescent desk lamp. Then, as his tea cooled, he began to write in a neat, draftsman's hand.

The sentences came easily now. The delay had shown a portion of his mind that there was no need to lie after all. He did not have to claim equations which had been offered him complete by Keyliss, Astor, and Selve.

"The notes and worksheets which this letter accompanies," Professor Gustafson wrote, "will make it possible to reconstruct my work, even in the event that portions of the equipment are destroyed during testing tomorrow."

The pencil hesitated, then canceled the last word. He resumed, "The errors which have led to this letter becoming public are mine alone. Furthermore, the fact that I intended to apply an Army Research Office grant for matter transmission research to this use was known by only me." That was a lie: his two American assistants, Arlene and Michael, had drawn up the grant proposal for Gustafson when his own mind refused to function in even so well-intentioned a deceit. "In translating theories into reality, however, I was immeasurably helped by my graduate assistants, Arlene Myaschensky, Michael Gardner, and Mustafa Bayar."

The pencil waited again, then wrote the concluding sentence: "These three are no less responsible than I for the fact that mechanical transference in time will become possible in our century.''

''Health!'' said Charles Eisley in Turkish, and took a drink. Mustafa Bayar echoed the toast, while Sue Schlicter, the tallest of the three in the living room of Eisley's home, merely drank.

The tall, black-haired woman looked down at her glass. ''Anisette?'' she said. ''But you know, Charles, I'd swear it was more than the fifty proof on the bottle.''

Eisley smiled broadly as he rotated the bottle on the glass-topped table. He had brought two gallons of Jeni Raki back from his most recent post, Ankara—the Foreign Service encourages a specialist interest in liquor. It was not until he met Mustafa Bayar, a Turkish national on the campus at which Eisley taught a course in international relations as diplomat in residence—until State found a post suitable for his senior rank—that he had reason to congratulate himself on his foresight in providing a drink otherwise unobtainable here.

Now he pointed to the figure Sue had seen on the label: 50°. ''This, you mean?'' he said. ''I was surprised, too, till I saw some whiskey bottled in Turkey that said 40°. That's not proof—even imperial proof. It's percent. What you're drinking''—he nodded to the glass—''is one-half absolute alcohol.''

Sue pursed her lips approvingly and tossed off the rest of her raki.

''Sorry, Mustafa,'' Eisley said. ''I don't suppose you came with an intention of being lectured on your national drink. How can I help you?''

Mustafa Bayar was stocky and dark with a bushy mustache. He laced his hands around his own empty glass. He was glaring at it with the fervor of one of his Ottoman forebears surveying the smoldering ruins of Constantinople. Abruptly he looked up again in blank concern. "I am"—he glanced from his host to Sue Schlicter, then back again—"I am interrupting, Dr. Eisley. I should not be here."

Eisley reached out a hand to the younger man's shoulder to keep Bayar from getting up and leaving as suddenly as he had come. Whatever had brought the Turk out at this hour had to be more serious than the whiff of beer on his breath could alone explain.

"Besides," said Sue, "you aren't interrupting anything that won't keep. Hey, Charles?" She grinned wickedly and stretched one of her incredibly long, booted legs over the arm of the couch on which she was sitting.

Bayar blinked, more with the amazement of meeting a creature from mythology than in active disapproval. Turks were not Arabs, and their women had been forbidden to go veiled since the 1922 revolution. But it was still the culture from which the word seraglio—*sarai*—had come; and for that matter, lanky, six-foot women like Sue were uncommon anywhere. "Ah," Bayar said. He focused his eyes on Eisley again and got a grip on his thoughts. "You see, Dr. Eisley, not my classwork, but—"

The other two people waited, both subconsciously expecting some variation on 'a woman.' Instead the young Turk said, "The project I am working on, you see. For Dr. Gustafson. I come to you not only as a friend"—Eisley nodded slowly in the pause, to keep the narrative coming now that it had begun—"but because you are part of the government. Of the embassy."

Eisley would be appointed as deputy chief of mission when a suitable post opened, but he was not attached to an embassy at present. He did not bother to correct the technical misstatement, however. Jumping to what he suspected was the heart of the problem, he said, "You're afraid that an unfavorable report by Professor Gustafson will affect your student visa, Mustafa?"

"Yes, that is—" Bayar agreed with a shake of his head and chopping motions of both hands. Droplets of raki glittered in the air. "Not an unfavorable report, no, but—Dr. Gustafson is a fine man, very brilliant. I am honored to know him. But . . ."

Sue was still on the couch, but as she watched Bayar now she had the cool concentration of a cat which has sighted movement. Eisley himself kept his face sympathetic but without further emotion or suggestion of concern. He did not blink as he met his guest's eyes.

"You see," Bayar went on as his own gaze fell, "Dr. Gustafson is lying to the government. Your government. He has grant money, from the army even, and he is not spending it to transport matter the way he says."

Without speaking, Eisley filled Bayar's glass and his own. He raised an eyebrow to Sue, but she shook her head briefly so as not to disturb the statement.

Mustafa raised his eyes. "When they learn, perhaps nothing will happen to Dr. Gustafson. He is an important man, respected. They will think he has gone mad, of course." The young man tossed back his glass of clear liquor. His shudder seemed more a response to his plight than a physical reaction to the raki. "What will they do to a foreigner, hey? A terrible Turk who has stolen money from the government? I did not know, at first—but who will believe that?"

He stared glumly into his empty glass.

Sue got up smoothly and took the bottle. "I think, Mustafa," she said mildly as she poured and added ice for all of them, "that you'd better tell us what your boss is doing with the money and why they'll think he's a candidate for the funny farm. Sorry, why he's crazy.''

"Dr. Gustafson," the Turk said, "thinks he has met persons from another time. Our future. They call themselves Travelers. A man named Selve and two women with him." Mustafa frowned, because his words did not properly indicate Selve's position in the hierarchy, even according to Moslem perceptions. He continued regardless, "Dr. Gustafson thinks he has been told how to build a, a time transport. He has used funds from his grant and he has done so. Built it. We have built it." Mustafa drew a tight circle around his heart with an index finger.

"I think," said Charles Eisley, "that there are some avenues that can be profitably attempted. To present the data in a fashion that minimizes the danger to your, ah, status, Mustafa."

He swirled the ice and raki in the bottom of his glass, but he kept his eyes candidly, disarmingly, on those of the young man consulting him. He had met Bayar as a friend. Both men had been lonely for things which were simply alien to most of the people with whom they came in contact, even at a cosmopolitan university. Now, however, the Turk was presenting himself as a "case"; and Eisley's reflexes were taking over whether he liked it or not. "It's to nobody's benefit to have a major flap about this, after all. . . . A respected professor losing, ah, touch as he gets older. Outsiders, perhaps cultists of some sort, taking advantage of him."

Eisley stood up, sucking in his gut as was his recent practice. He had not been conscious of his body before he met Sue. He knew that he was soft and that he carried thirty pounds of which the weight charts would not approve; but diplomacy is a sedentary occupation, and Charles looked well enough in tailored suits against the men he

met on the embassy cocktail circuit. It had hit him like a
sledgehammer when his wife left him—not that there was
any love lost by then, but the change.

Which did not mean that Eisley began taking care of his
body, only that he began drinking more. Then he met Sue,
and there was now an exercise bench hidden from her in
the room that had only been box storage until then. He
would have changed his will sooner if he had known
spirits as joyous as Sue Schlicter lurked in lawyers' offices.

"So for embarrassment," said Mustafa Bayar, a gleam
of puppyish hope in his eyes, "you think they will not
wish to make examples of the others and even me?"

"It would make no sense to do so," said Eisley, aged
forty-six and trying to shrink his waistline a decade for his
thirty-year-old mistress. His words were true, but what his
mind really meant was that as a diplomat, a negotiator, he
could see no sense in publicity. He would have felt the
same way at learning the Russians were basing nuclear
weapons in Greece: get them out quietly, and for God's
sake don't let the media learn and start a flap. He knew
also that many people—and the Army Research Office
might take a typically army attitude to diplomatic questions—
did not think the way Foreign Service officers were expected to think.   ·

Sue poured more raki all around. Her face broadened in
a slow smile. "You know," she said, "that may be the
best way to cover Mustafa's ass. But it seems to me that it
could cause problems in another way."

Eisley pursed his lips but said nothing until he could
gather more data. Bayar, the only one of the trio still
seated, raised an eyebrow. "Miss Schlicter?" he prompted
politely.

"You say Gustafson's good, that he's got a good track
record," the woman said, meeting the Turk's eyes. "What

happens if you blow the whistle—and Gustafson turns out to have been right this time, too?''

The question hung over the clink of ice cubes as Charles Eisley swirled his drink.

The Saab cocked halfway up the curb with its motor running warned Dr. Alexis Market subconsciously. Without having to think, she stepped clear as Isaac Hoperin banged open the door of the physics and mathematics building at a dead run.

"Oh! I'm sorry, Lexie!" Dr. Hoperin blurted. He glanced down at the briefcase swinging furiously in his left hand. Hoperin's eyes were black and bright. Lexie had always thought of her colleague as a manic vole, despite the long hair that trailed behind his prematurely high forehead. Fortunately, she had managed to avoid saying that even in the depths of her frequent migraines.

"Ah," Hoperin was saying, "I managed to leave this in my office last night, can you believe that?" He waggled the briefcase deliberately. Then, as if it were a starter's flag, he bolted into his car. The Saab lurched off the curb so abruptly that the engine almost died. Hoperin straightened his course and racketed out of the parking lot. Fortunately, it was early enough in the morning that there were no other cars to contend with.

Market did not think further about the incident as she climbed the stairs. Ike Hoperin had the office next to hers on the third floor, but they had no social contact beyond departmental meetings. The stairs were enough to think about this morning. Some days Lexie thought that she should make a point of running the four flights to and from the basement several times a day. It should be a quick way to shed the extra ten—be honest: fifteen—pounds she carried. Thirty-two-year-old women didn't long stay in acceptable shape if they let themselves go. This morning, though . . . if the old building had an elevator, she would have used it. She massaged her left wrist.

The door of Hoperin's office was open. He really had been in a hurry. Within, a drawer of the locking file cabinet was also open, but it must have held only the briefcase. Market started to close the door when it struck her that Ike might very well have left his keys inside. Market had no use for the sort of officiousness which caused trouble for other people while smugly claiming to be helpful. She drew the door partway closed but did not latch it.

Market locked her own door from the inside. She needed time to think. Even if someone saw her car in the lot, she could still be in the lounge or the ladies' room. Instead of turning on a light, Lexie ran up the shade of her north-facing window.

Ike Hoperin's Saab had just pulled into the parking lot of the engineering building next door. It would have been faster for him to simply walk between buildings; though when you're in a hurry, you often misjudge a situation. What on earth did Ike have going at the engineering building that had him in such a bounding hurry?

Lexie continued to massage her wrist. Not that she had any reason to think about bizarre behavior on the part of her colleagues. The silk scarf with which she had tied herself to the bedposts had not abraded the skin or bruised her, even when Steve departed considerably from the ex-pected program. She seemed to have pulled something, however, before she forced herself into flaccid dissociation from anything that was happening to her body.

Funny how people could surprise you on the levels at which you thought you knew them. There was Ike Hoperin, more excited than anybody had seen him since the Sixth

Fleet took out El Djem. And there was Steve last night
. . . a matter which for the moment seemed far more
important than whatever was going on in the engineering
building.

There was a sound between a hiss and a gasp, like the
air brakes of a bus releasing. The docking area within the
enclosure, the circle painted on the floor, held three con-
servatively dressed figures and an ordinary locker where
nothing had been a moment before. The pillars were cold
and black with darkness reflected from their Lucite cover-
ings. A few of the instruments in the hollow basement
registered, but there was no major reaction from the apparatus which Professor Gustafson and his students had built.

"Unbefucking-lievable!" said Isaac Hoperin, standing
beside the seated Gustafson. The physics professor's left
hand was wound into the wires of the chain-link partition.
His grip was fiercer than he would have found bearable if
he had noticed it. Hoperin had never seen the event before.
Even in this ambiance of concrete and secondhand hardware, the way the figures appeared had the slick, phony
quality of stage magic.

Gustafson looked at the younger professor with relief
and a touch of wry amusement. "You see," he said to
Hoperin, "the calculations you are helping with have a
definite real-world application after all, Isaac."

"Damn, but we will get it to work, won't we?" said
Arlene Myaschensky. She was a big woman, too heavy to
be conventionally attractive, with lustrous auburn hair. Her
bovine appearance made her easy to discount until one saw
her at work—conducting every test with an obsessive rigor
which simply did not allow the use of a fudge factor.
Arlene had done most of the work on the desktop unit the
students had decided to build secretly in a laboratory

upstairs—and she had remained cheerful despite the repeated failure of that small unit which was built precisely
to the specifications which the Travelers had provided.

Myaschensky, Bayar, and Mike Gardner were on the
far side of the docking area. Light from the windows was
bright enough to fuzz the outlines of the students' heads
and shoulders instead of silhouetting them to eyes across
the enclosure. Louis Gustafson was a kindly man, but
there was nonetheless a reserve about him—a matter more
of age than of personal temperament—which made it clear
he was a full professor and they were graduate students. At
times like this, when tension was high but the apparatus
was not involved, Gustafson and the clump of his students
stood separate. Hoperin, an associate professor and a
colleague by rank, was with Gustafson as a part of the
natural order of things. The two of them stepped into the
painted circle to greet the newcomers.

Mustafa Bayar grunted. In a tone of surprise, he said,
"This is the first time I watched them"—he snapped his
fingers—"poof, appear, and thought to myself that it might
be real, everything we have been told. It makes it very
different to see." He paused and added in seeming incon-
sequence, "I have a headache, too. A hangover."

"How are you doing, Mike?" Myaschensky asked, perhaps prompted by the Turk's last comment.

Mike Gardner was a little above average height and a
little less than average weight, in normal times a pleasant-
looking man with a frequent smile. At the moment, his
face was frozen into a worried expression as he stared at
the figures within the painted circle. He was wearing
ordinary street clothes, jeans and a sport shirt, but he
carried a quilted nylon parka as well. It was out of place
here on a summer morning, but Selve had said the weather—

across the Portal—was uncertain. Gardner's hands were gripping the jacket as if it were a rope above an abyss.

"Mike?" Arlene repeated. She touched his shoulder.

"Jeez," Gardner said softly. He turned and managed a smile for the woman's worried eyes. He had been listening, he now realized; but the fact that the words were directed to him had not penetrated until they were emphasized by Arlene's touch. "I guess I'm like Mustafa," Gardner explained. "It wasn't till maybe just now that I felt it . . . was going to happen. Really. Suppose your husband'd like the honor of the first test for himself?"

Mustafa and Arlene, who would not be part of the first human test of the apparatus, looked at one another to avoid looking at Gardner. Myaschensky, trying to keep her voice light, said, "Machines are something Dave uses. He turns them on and they work, and that's all he thinks about them. That's a good attitude for an entomologist." She patted Mike Gardner's shoulder again. "That's probably a good attitude for all of us to take about this. We may not know what they're really doing"—she gestured with her chin toward the two women and the man who had just blurred into sight—"but they've gone to too much trouble themselves for this not to work."

And as she watched the group in the docking area, she thought, Easy for you to say, Myaschensky.

Months ago, Mike Gardner had lined off the docking area using white latex-base paint and no special skill or tools. The line wavered in course and thickness. Where the concrete had not been swept clean enough, the paint was already lifting up its yellow-gray underside.

Like the breadboard circuitry comprising much of the equipment, though, the lines were sufficient to their purpose. When the device Gustafson had built was activated, everything within the lined area would be moved and replaced by something filling a similar volume elsewhere.

The same was true of the Travelers' own apparatus. When Astor, Keyliss, and Selve appeared, odors and qualities within the basement of the building changed because of the volume of air transferred with them. To be accidentally within the docking area during such a transfer would mean an unplanned excursion—and hinted problems at the far end. Bidirectional transfers would take place, but in— good time. Keyliss had laughed at the joke on time travel. Her colleagues and the students joined in, after a moment. Professor Gustafson had simply continued to blink at the trio who claimed to be the descendents, three hundred generations removed, of twentieth-century man.

But the lined-off area was to prevent awkwardness, not danger. The edges of the transport field were soft. The event took place by integral units on a go/no go basis. There was no chance of a left arm being snatched elsewhere while its owner screamed. The broom-finished concrete floor, effectively one with the building and the fabric of the Earth itself, did not gape into concavity during operations.

Astor now stalked across the twenty-foot circle as if it were an arena and Louis Gustafson her opponent. "What is he?" she demanded in perfect English. Her hand gestured out at Hoperin as if the physicist were a mess of dog vomit. "This is your responsibility, Louis. Why is he here?" Astor spoke with obvious, hissing rage, but her voice was pitched too low to draw the students from their deferential place by the wall.

"Yes," said Gustafson, who did not comprehend or even fully recognize the anger. "We needed help determining the layer spacings of the coils." He pointed at the copper pillars, a mild gesture and not a slashing attack on circumstances as the woman's hand had made. "My friend, Dr. Hoperin, gave us that help. Now he very properly wants to see the results of his work and ours."

Astor's six-foot height made her an inch or two taller than anyone else in the basement. As stocky as Mustafa Bayar, she was formidable both in body and in personality. Fifteen years before, while an undergraduate, Isaac Hoperin had chanted, "We shall overcome," as he lay down in the path of a tank transporter at the main gate of Fort Bragg. He now clutched his briefcase with white knuckles, but he was not about to run from this confrontation, either.

"You were told, Louis," Astor began, "how necessary secrecy is to—"

Hoperin cut her off. "What government department are you with?" he asked sharply. "You obviously think your rank takes precedence to natural law. What *are* you?"

Astor stopped, nonplussed. Keyliss stepped forward with a trace of a smile. She extended her hand to shake Hoperin's and said, "Astor is part of the Contact Unit, Doctor. You prefer to be called 'Doctor'? As am I, Keyliss, and Selve here as well, all equals."

Selve moved past Astor on the other side and also held out a hand—his left, since Keyliss was shaking Hoperin's right. It was now Hoperin's turn to be taken aback. He started to set down his briefcase. Then he curved his index finger up from the handle to return Selve's grip.

All three of the Travelers wore outfits of charcoal gray. The women were dressed in skirts to midcalf, jackets, and white blouses. Selve wore trousers, jacket, and a bowtie with incongruous black polka dots on a white ground at the throat of his plain white shirt. The trio had the slightly skewed look of a comedy team. Their uniformity of dress did not disguise their individual personalities, however.

"I—" Hoperin said in a less belligerent voice. Remembering that the big woman, Astor, had called Gustafson by his first name, the physicist said, "Well, I suppose Isaac. Or Hoperin. But not Doctor, no."

"The tolerances weren't that close," muttered Astor, who had been responsible for transmitting that portion of the data. "At worst we could have modulated the main coils with a small external unit. . . ." She did not meet the eyes of her colleagues or the two professors.

"Isaac," said Keyliss, "this project is very important to our times. If Louis believes you're necessary to its success, then we all welcome you. But perhaps—Louis, is there a place where we can sit down and talk before we proceed? The five of us?"

"Well, my office," said Gustafson. He turned his head to indicate a paneled cubicle on the other side of the fencing. "I don't know about chairs. . . ." With sudden focus, the white-haired man looked back at Astor and said, "This is my responsibility, you know. One of my students will be taking part in the test today. If I'm uncertain as to how to meet design parameters with the available materials, I will enlist necessary help. Isaac is very trustworthy and very able." He touched the physicist's arm in a gesture of association.

"You have our full confidence, Louis," said Astor with a touch of bitterness. "But perhaps yes, a discussion with Isaac here directly would be in order."

Professor Gustafson paused at the doorway of the mesh enclosure. "Michael," he called to the student who would accompany him on the first test, "we should not be long, I trust."

As the professors and the visitors trailed out of the enclosure, Selve said more or less aloud, "This is a secret that mustn't get out until we've been successful, after all.''

The stairwell door was locked. The sign on it read: Experiment in Progress. Please Do Not Disturb.

Sara Jean Layberg thought she recognized Mike's hand in the precise lettering. With a little sigh, she turned back up the stairs. She patted her hair, which, like the spodumene she used as a pottery glaze, held myriad variations on the general theme of brown . . . and some white still scarcely visible unless she stared into a mirror and thought about life more than she ought to do.

The locked door was both a relief and a disappointment. Sara Jean had visited the school several times when Mike had begun helping her with the design and construction of her kiln. That had been before Gardner became her lover, however. Her husband, Henry, could have built the kiln, but his duties as internist at the university medical center kept him too busy for that—or for much of anything else involving Sara Jean.

She hadn't wanted to come back to the engineering building, but it seemed the only way to be sure that the two of them could meet. For a talk. She had steeled herself to walk in on Mike in the basement laboratory. Since she couldn't do that, she would wait upstairs, where the intrusion would have less reason to make Mike angry. They were so busy with this experiment, after all.

Layberg stumbled as her unguided foot took one more step than there was in the flight. She had not seen or heard from Mike in twenty-four days. He wasn't that busy.

"Hi, Sara Jean," called a familiar voice. "How's your kiln doing?"

Sara Jean's face was already brightening into the proper social lines when her eyes cleared enough from grim introspection to focus on the speaker: a well-knit man of moderate height, hair graying but his mustache still a rich brown. He wore slacks and a dress shirt but no tie. In his right hand was the carafe of an automatic coffee maker, which he had just filled in the men's room. Danny, of course. It was one of the paradoxes of Alcoholics Anonymous, where they had met, that neither of them knew the other's last name.

"Oh, it's fine, Danny," she said aloud. "I, ah—I've been thinking of a salt kiln, too. I thought I'd see Mike, but they've got the doors locked for an experiment, it says. Ah, you can't use the same kiln for regular glazes as well as salt, you know."

"I don't know a thing about it," the man said cheerfully, "but I did know that Mike was the person to help with a job that took using a wrench as well as knowing the theory. Look"—Danny glanced down at the carafe as if he had just become aware of it—"come on back to the office while I make a pot of coffee. I'm the EE chairman's secretary now, Dr. Shroyer's, and he always wants a cup as soon as he comes in, no matter how hot it is."

Danny fluttered his shirt collar with his free hand, though actually the interior of the old building was comfortable despite the lack of air conditioning. "Then we can wait in Lab Three." He gestured vaguely down the hall. "It wasn't going to be used during summer session, so the students on Professor Gustafson's project pretty well took it over. I'm sure they'll come up there when they're finished in those dungeons downstairs."

"Well, I—" Sara Jean said. She looked at her watch, then her purse, without actually seeing either one of them. Then she smiled forcefully and said, "Well, yes, Danny, that would be a good idea. How do you like working for a department chairman now instead of being in the dean's office?'' As she walked beside the taller man, her heels clicked sharply on the tile floor.

"I think this will be simplest, Isaac," said Keyliss as she closed the glazed office door, "if you first give us your understanding of the project you have joined." She nodded toward Gustafson to blur any impression that she was criticizing him.

There was a swivel chair behind the desk. Gustafson walked around to it but did not sit down. The small room's three straight chairs had been pressed into service as bookshelves. Their stacks of heavy volumes were neat continuations of the rows filling the shelves proper.

Isaac Hoperin cleared a corner of the desk with less care than his host would have chosen. The physicist then sat down with his back to Gustafson alone. He opened his mouth but hesitated while tact replaced 'I've been told . . .' with the phrase that actually came out: "As it's been described to me, you—the three of you—are from the distant future. Our future. You purportedly came here through a . . . well, there's no other word for it, is there? Through a time machine. And you want to build a time machine here and now, in the twentieth century, I understand."

"We want Louis to build a time machine here and now," Astor corrected. "Because, you see, he did build one in our age. In our history."

"Effects don't normally predate causes, do they? Well, that's only one of the things I don't understand," Hoperin said. He took out a cigarette and tapped it twice on the crystal of his watch to pack the tobacco, then lit it. Unseen behind him, Gustafson winced.

"And I'll be very honest with you," the physicist went on, flicking his eyes across the Travelers again when his cigarette glowed and puffed, "I've seen the formulae you've provided Louis here, and I can't imagine how such an apparatus could possibly have the effect you claim—especially with the power requirements you specify. If you're working in a Gödel manifold, creating timelike loops, then *where* are you getting the one over radical two c's worth of power you'd need to drive it? Not from what I've seen in there, not the numbers, not the hardware. And if it's Dobbs-like phasetime—well . . . It's as ridiculous as those claims for solar-power satellites—though at least those"—he poked his cigarette toward the pillars visible through the office window—"won't be spraying high-energy microwaves through the chromosomes of everybody on Earth."

"You should think of what you see only as the controls, Isaac," Selve said.

Astor clenched her fist and glared at her male colleague. Keyliss was frowning also, but she put a hand on Astor's arm. "There are two questions," Keyliss said. "Whether or not the apparatus works"—she nodded in a reference to the hardware in the enclosure—"and why we are—why our age is acting as it is. The first question"—her voice rose slightly and her fingers clamped tighter as Astor started to speak—"will very simply be answered when you see the demonstration."

Astor relaxed with a grimace. Keyliss released her and continued, "It is crucially important that you understand what we are about, however, so that you will also understand the need for secrecy. I—"

She broke off in a series of high-pitched sneezes as a tendril of smoke licked her face. Calmly, Astor said, "We, too, realize that the principles of time transport are unknown to your age. That was a matter of great concern to scientists of our time, who believe that actions in the past can change reality in the future, in our present. Historically, time transport was developed in your age . . . which, as you say, is incapable of grasping the equations even when it is handed them."

Hoperin glared and inhaled so deeply that the tube of his cigarette rolled back toward his lips in an angry glow. Astor was unconcerned with the effect of her insult, if she even noticed it. She went on, "If you did not develop time transport, then we do not exist. In a form we would recognize, surely; and perhaps not at all. There would have been instead a world-destroying war. . . ."

Selve muttered what could only have been a prayer and looked at the floor. Even Astor seemed more tense as she continued, "At any rate, we have been sent here to make sure that you do develop the technique on which our age depends. All the credit will be yours—your age's—because that is what your future knows."

"It is absolutely critical," interjected Keyliss at a pause, "that few people know what is really being done. If your government were to become involved, there would be no way to hide our role, our age's interference in your age. We would have made certain the disaster of a changed future that we were sent to avoid."

Hoperin crushed out his cigarette on the metal edge of the desktop, thinking about the Nobel Prize for physics and his seminal contribution to come: the Hoperin deterministic spacetime manifold. He dropped the stub on the floor with the ashes, in lieu of an ashtray. "Look," he said, "I'm helping Louis because he's a friend and because I'm, well, interested, even if this is a load of hokum you're pitching. As for the government learning anything, not from me. Or not unless the ones they have tapping my phones and reading my mail off and on are a lot smarter than those I've met were."

Selve and Keyliss exchanged glances. Astor's expression did not change. None of the Travelers interrupted the physicist as he went on. "But what you've described, this bootstrapping—that's surely impossible, isn't it? I grant you the potential of hardware whose principles I am incapable of grasping"—his tone became a partly conscious mimicking of the powerful female's—"but there you're talking not about principles but about sheer common sense."

Each dark-clad female opened her mouth to reply and paused at the first syllable from the other. Selve inserted his voice into the gap, saying, "Isaac, we're technical personnel, rather like Louis. We are not theoreticians. We've been very carefully prepared for our duties by assimilating as much of the languages and cultures of your age as was possible in ours, but we cannot describe to you the—bases of the problems foreseen by the theoreticians of our day. You would not understand them, and we do not understand them."

"I'm sure that when our part of the project has been successfully concluded," Astor put in, "there will be opportunities for you—as an insider, of course, and still in secrecy—to discuss matters with more knowledgeable persons than us."

Selve's face lost all expression. He looked at his colleague without speaking. Astor, startled, also stopped speaking.

"It remains to convince Isaac that there's a secret to keep, doesn't it?" Keyliss said smoothly. "And perhaps you have doubts also, Louis?" she added with a smile, which Gustafson echoed tightly. "Shall we proceed with the demonstration?"

She opened the door with a flourish. Hoperin looked at a fresh cigarette, then shot it back into the pack. "Sure," he said. "That's what we came for."

*   *   *

Cooper, thought Sara Jean Layberg. The plastic name-plate on the desk read "Daniel R. Cooper." The desk return held a typewriter, but deeper in the office there was a computer terminal hooked to a printer.

A man in his early thirties turned as Sara Jean and the secretary entered. He was in sport coat and tie, very good looking and dressed with a flair that suggested he knew it. "Oh, hello, Danny," he said. "Couldn't find you or Marge. Any notion whether Dr. Shroyer might be in this afternoon?"

"She's on vacation this week, Dr. Rice," Danny said. He stepped into the left room of the three-room suite and poured his carafe of water into the tank of the coffee maker. "But Dr. Shroyer ought to be in any time. Going to be in your office? I can buzz you when he gets here."

"Umm," Rice said. "Look, if it's all the same, I'll just wait in his office. I need to discuss some matters with him before the students get back."

"Sure," said Cooper, flipping his hand toward the farthest room of the interconnected trio. "Look, if he gets in before I'm back, tell him I'm just running Mrs. Layberg here"—of course Danny had known her full name, she'd given it to him at the meeting to pass on to the grad student he thought could help her set up the kiln—"down to Lab Three."

"Ah, Mrs. Layberg?" Rice said. "I'm Barry Rice, one of the Young Turks here on the faculty." He extended his hand.

Rice's eyes had taken in the tailored quality of Sara Jean's beige dress and very possibly the fact that her wristwatch was a Rolex. Sara Jean had been uncertain as to what she should wear. She was more comfortable in slacks and a pullover shirt, but dresses enhanced her looks

. . . and that had been the deciding factor. Now she took Rice's hand, but she said noncommittally, "Yes, my husband's on the faculty, too. Not here, of course; he's an internist at the medical center." Sara Jean had met men before who first-named their secretaries but expected those secretaries to address them as "Doctor." It was not an attitude toward which she warmed. "Mr. Cooper," she continued as she turned to Danny, "I can probably find—"

"Oh, it won't take a minute, and nothing's happening now anyway," Danny interrupted lightly. Over his shoulder he called, "I won't be long, Dr. Rice."

As the two of them strode down the hall, Danny threw Sara Jean a conspiratorial wink. It brightened her day more than anything else thus far had done.

"God," Sue Schlicter said as she made it to a standing position. The sheet trailed back to Eisley and the bed like the wake of the shock waves in her head. She began walking carefully toward the liquor cabinet. Her eyes were slitted. The sun that made her wince also glowed on her body hair. "Charles," she said, "I haven't been this sick since I was in high school. When I got up to call in, I thought I was going to barf in your wastebasket."

Eisley had been watching her slim figure from behind in a reverie. Driven now by contrition, he sat up more quickly than he should have even with his acquired tolerance for raki. "Oh, Lord, Sue, I should have warned you," he said. "Raki can really do that the morning after, and you can't ignore it because the taste stays with you all day."

"I'm a big girl," Sue said as she uncapped a bottle of Scotch. "Daddy doesn't have to hold my hand when I cross the street. And I'm going to work on the taste right

now. . . ." She splashed whiskey into a highball glass.
"Want one yourself?"

"Oh. Sure," Eisley said. He watched her step into the
kitchen with the glasses. She moved as smoothly as a
Nereid in a still lake. She could not possibly know how
"Daddy" shredded her lover's guts when he heard it . . .
and she was here, anyway, that was all that mattered
really. . . .

The tall woman paced back with a glass in each hand.
The ice clinked, but she kept her eyes on her footing rather
than on the drinks. "What are you going to do about
Mustafa?" she asked.

Eisley's stomach twisted as if he had physically shifted
too abruptly. "Well, I suppose I'll have to minute it to the
department," he said. He took the Scotch and sipped it,
more for the pause it gave him than for the taste. "It's . . .
well, one really has to have the record available to point to
if some question is raised later."

Sue's expression was partly a result of her swizzling the
Scotch around to clear her mouth. Then she swallowed. It
was still a moment before her lips unpursed. "Cover your
ass, huh?" she said. Her glance and her lover's both
slipped toward the phrase's literal referent. She smiled. He
did not. His paunch was all too evident and as pale as a
fish belly in the hard sunlight. "Thing is," Sue continued
as Eisley kept his face blank against a flash of self-
revulsion, "that doesn't do much for Mustafa, does it? He
came looking for help, after all."

"And he came to a senior officer of the United States
Foreign Service," Eisley said sharply.

"He probably thought he was coming to the only friend
he had in North Carolina, Charles," the woman replied.
Her voice was as thin as the light glancing from the ice in

her drink. "Is that a reason to saw the branch off behind him?"

The bed sagged as Schlicter sat on the end of it. Her back was straight, and her eyes were straight on Eisley's as she sipped more of her liquor.

Eisley felt like a worm on a hook. There was none of the diplomatic indirection that he was used to hearing, even when someone was being fired. His wife had never pressed him that way. When she left, the first notification of the fact had been a letter from her attorney. "Well, Sue," he said with a practiced smile and a practiced unction, "the good thing about a formal minute is that nobody's really going to read it until after something happens. There's not the least chance that it will cause Mustafa additional problems."

"He came for help," she said with even more of an edge than before. "Not lowering the boom on him—maybe— doesn't seem like the sort of help I'd expect from a friend."

And so they were talking about something else after all, Eisley thought with a grim satisfaction. He would be offered an overseas post within the next six months . . . and while a wife might be a valuable adjunct to his duties, there was no way he could carry his mistress with him, say, to Nouakchott or Mogadishu. Sue was not a safe choice for the diplomatic round, even as a wife. . . .

"All right," Eisley said. Now that the terms were clear to him, he spoke as if to a professional equal: with reserve, but without patronizing. "I would have said that Mustafa primarily wanted a shoulder to cry on, and we gave him that. What do you see as the practical help which I can offer him now?"

"You can recruit him as a source," she said simply. "Mustafa comes from an important family, or they wouldn't be able to send him here. And he's good, or he wouldn't be working on something like this, even if it's crackpot. So he's going to be a valuable source of information when he goes home. If he's well disposed to the U.S. And if nothing happens to turn this valuable friend into an enemy of America."

Eisley got out of bed slowly. He took the woman's empty glass and carried it with his part-full one to the liquor cabinet. Just before he spoke, Sue added, "And while you're making sure that Mustafa Bayar is on file as an important national resource, I'll see what I can learn about what's really going on. After all, Mustafa isn't in a position to give a very clear account of things."

"Neither are you," said Eisley as he poured more Scotch. He hadn't really intended to refill his own glass. "They certainly won't tell you anything they didn't tell Mustafa, either—Gustafson or the people who seem to be taking advantage of him."

"Sure they will," said Schlicter from unexpectedly nearby. Her arms wrapped Eisley gently, pressing her breasts and the bony arc of her pelvis against his softer flesh. "Whether they're on the level or not, they're afraid to have this business out in the open. If I insist, and they see I mean it, they don't have any choice but to put me right in the middle of what they're doing."

She was grinning like a summer dawn when the diplomat eased around to face her. "I wonder what it's like to ride a time machine," she said, partially as a joke.

"Michael," called Keyliss as she walked out of Gustafson's office, "are you ready for your first experience of time transport? And Arlene and Mustafa, ready to terminate the test if any of the equipment seems on the verge of failure?"

The students turned with a furtive surprise from the locker they had been examining while the meeting went on. The Travelers' locker was standard in appearance: two feet deep, four wide, and almost eight feet from top to bottom. It had a gray finish, vents stamped along either sidewall, and a double-leaf door across the front. At a glance or a short distance, it in no way differed from scores of heavy-duty lockers throughout the building.

It was not metal, though. When Mike rapped it with a fingertip, the material flexed and rang no more than a concrete block would have done. The padlock through the door hasp had no keyhole or any other clue as to how it was meant to be opened. Mustafa had bent to look up through the ventilating slots; without a light, he could see nothing. The students' curiosity was reasonable, but they all felt like boys peeping into the girls' shower when the principals in the project spilled out of the office.

"Ah, ready anytime," Gardner said. He was amused to find that the embarrassment had driven out the fears which had chased themselves through his head since four in the morning. He was reacting now like a subordinate afraid of censure rather than as a test pilot chancing a very long stall.

"Here," said Astor as she walked to the locker herself. "We won't need this during the secondary transport—that is, from your present to the Carboniferous. Give me a hand and we'll get it out of the affected area."

"I'm ready to watch," Arlene Myaschensky said, "but I do worry about the hardware—letting you down somewhere." The euphemism made her blush slightly. "It's mostly either old or hand-built, and—you know."

"Heave," said Astor as she and the three grad students put their weight against the locker. It was not as heavy as it appeared—no heavier than an empty steel unit of the size—and it skidded easily.

"There's really nothing to worry about, Arlene," said Selve over the sound of the locker on concrete. "Either it will transport us or it won't. The return transport is a one-for-one rebound occurring without fail when the duration dialed in here"—he pointed to the rank of instruments facing the tall pillars—"has been reached. If everything here is destroyed while we're gone, we still return. Just as we—the three of us—will return to our present in"—she did not look at any timing device—"an hour thirty-one and a half minutes."

The locker cleared the painted line by a foot and a half. "Good," said Astor as she straightened. With a smirk toward the students, she gripped the barrel of the padlock and pulled it down. The lock's shackle released and straightened with a liquid flexibility. Still smirking, the big female opened the doors wide.

"So you claim to be able to travel in time from our future," said Isaac Hoperin, "and then you claim to travel from now back to another—period of time?" Hoperin was not geologist enough to know precisely what "the Carboniferous" implied, and he was far too much a scientist to simply guess.

"Yes," called Astor over her shoulder, "we do. And you claim to be representative of your age's technical experts?"

"You did see us arrive," added Keyliss, more mildly but to the same effect. "And in a moment you'll see the apparatus here transport us again."

Selve said, "The reason to shut down the equipment, Arlene, is that it will add to the time till completion— operational completion—if things burn up during testing. Better to rebuild a weak spot in the circuitry than to spend weeks repairing the damage done by a successful test. But no danger.''

Astor handed him a weapon out of the locker.

The basic lines of a gun are going to be the same no matter what the principle or the details: handgrips and a shoulder stock, so that the business end can be steadied for use. The Travelers' weapons—Keyliss took hers and Astor drew out the third for herself—even had a rod resembling a barrel projecting from a larger cylinder that took the place of a carbine's receiver. The barrel was solid, however.

Keyliss did something with a control, and the barrel of her weapon flared into a twenty-degree cone. "We don't really need these for, for the period, but we certainly don't need tight focus.''

"For water,'' Astor said to Mike and Arlene, who were noting the suits remaining in the locker. Mustafa, whose home city was now patrolled by soldiers with Thompson submachine guns, was more interested in the weapons. Head-covering suits of slick orange fabric hung from the three walls. The face-pieces were amber and as flexible as the remainder of the garments.

"All right,'' said Isaac Hoperin, "I want to go along.''

"Isaac,'' said Professor Gustafson, "I really don't—''

"Well, it may cut a few minutes off the planned duration,'' said Selve, "but I suppose we could recalibrate. . . .'' He frowned as he looked toward the linked circuitry extending almost a hundred feet into the distance of the enclosure.

"What possible difference does twenty minutes or fifteen make?'' Astor said sharply. "We could make two separate transports in the time it would take us to adjust that mess without affecting the preset.''

"Shut up, you idiot,'' said Keyliss in the Travelers' common language. Use of the birth tongue while on Contact duties was a serious violation of protocol. Keyliss had been shocked into the outburst. Similar shock had frozen both her colleagues when their minds caught up with Astor's tongue.

"It's not what happens to the experiment," Gustafson said, unaware in the crystal stillness. "It's what might happen to you, Isaac. There's no need to risk—"

"Louis," said Selve with a rare touch of asperity, "the risk is technical—that everything will sit and buzz. Not physical. There is no physical risk."

"You know," said Mike Gardner to the floor, "nothing's going to change until we do it. So I think we may as well do it."

Everyone looked at the young man. He had retrieved his parka. He held it with tense fingers which belied the calm of his face.

Astor banged shut the locker. She slid the shackle back through the hasp but did not bother to relock it. "Yes," she said neutrally. "Those who are taking part in the transport, please stand near the center of the docking area. Others please stay beyond the line."

Hoperin put a friendly arm around Gustafson's shoulders. As an afterthought, the physicist tossed away the unlighted cigarette he held. The two faculty members walked farther into the circle.

Arlene Myaschensky smiled brightly and squeezed Mike's hand. Somewhat to the surprise of everyone else, Mustafa Bayar seized Mike and kissed him on both cheeks. He then pounded the American on the arm and said, "Go with God, brother."

While the locals positioned themselves as Astor had directed, Selve said softly to Keyliss, "Do you think it wise to take the technical person?" He spoke in his birth tongue, both for secrecy and to express approval for what the woman had done a moment before.

Keyliss continued to stare at Astor's back. The taller female had not met the eyes of either colleague since her rebuke. "Yes, I think it's all right. They're very narrow, that sort, ours as well as here. Isaac will be observant only in his field: and there's far too much detail available there for him to correlate it in the time he has."

"Yes," agreed Selve, "there is very little time. For any of us."

"Good morning, Bob, can I grab a little of your time before the students get back?" said the determinedly cheery voice before Robert Shroyer was fully into the central office.

"Oh, hello, Barry," the department chairman said with considerably less enthusiasm. "Well, let me get my coffee first. Will you have a cup?"

The coffee maker in the side office was just gurgling to a halt. Shroyer's mug was set out with sugar and creamer already spooned into it. The mail today included the two fat volumes of the latest *Fisher Scientific* catalog and a letter from a former colleague at MIT. Shroyer wondered what Rice would be complaining about this time. Good mind, but . . .

"I think your secretary went off with a Mrs. Layberg," Rice volunteered so that he did not have to refuse the chairman's offer. About the last thing his blood pressure needed was that he start slurping coffee, for Christ's sake! But it wouldn't do to—

"Sara Jean?" Shroyer said with more interest than he had displayed to Rice thus far. "Oh, yes, I'm having dinner there tonight. What did she want?"

Barry Rice trailed his superior across the center office

again. "Oh," he said, "I—to tell the truth, I thought she was visiting Danny. You know her, then?"

"Her husband and I were roommates at Michigan," Shroyer said as he seated himself. Returns on both ends made his desk a squared-off U. Stacks of paperwork were spaced across the entire surface, neatly organized despite their volume.

"Oh," Rice repeated. He sat down in one of the upholstered chairs, but he did so gingerly. Shroyer had rather pointedly not swiveled his own chair to face the younger man. "Actually, what I wanted to see you about is a bit delicate. Do you have any idea of what Professor Gustafson and his students are doing?"

Shroyer sighed. He supposed he was about to learn.

"I don't understand how anybody can make sense of this, Danny," said Sara Jean Layberg. She touched the tarpaulin which covered the apparatus on the desk in the center of the lab. Along the walls was additional equipment arrayed on tables, filing cabinets, and sometimes on the floor itself. Not all of it was interconnected; but a great deal of it was, and even the individual units were as meaningless as cuneiform tablets to Sara Jean. She was comfortable with her intelligence and with her education. She had taught young children with a level of success that never failed to net her praises from their parents at year's end. But this clutter in which Mike functioned with the certainty of a fish in water was simply and completely beyond her.

"Oh, there's not very much to that," the secretary said. He moved the paint can—Solar Cold, a property rather than a color—which held down one corner of the tarp. "When I was sound man with a news crew in Washington, we used all sorts of hardware that was probably as sophisticated as any of this. You can get a long way knowing what happens and not worrying about the why.''

Grinning wryly, he raised the corner of the tarp. "That was a good job, you know? Probably the best one I ever drank myself out of.''

"So you understand this, then?" Sara Jean said in mild wonder. Her fingers idly traced a pair of cables from a floor duct toward the desk.

"No, but you could if you had any need to," Danny explained. He pulled the tarp farther back. A pair of wire-wound tubes stood up from a base of aluminum sheeting. The tubes were no more than a foot high, shorter than the transformer and the rack of diodes feeding them. The strands of cables Mrs. Layberg had been touching were splayed colorfully onto connectors on the diode boards as well. "You know," Danny went on, "what this does look like is the economy version of the thing they're building in the basement." He laughed. "Whatever that is.''

There was a muted pop from the connection strip, although the switch marked POWER with a strip of red tapes was clearly off.

"Preparing to engage," called Mustafa Bayar as he watched the dials rise toward their programmed levels. His deep voice could barely be heard in the docking circle over the hum of the apparatus.

"It's taking too long," Selve shouted into Keyliss's ear. "We're getting a cross feed from our own unit, it's got to be!"

Astor was shouting in parallel rather than in reply, "Their equipment just has a high specific moment. The resistances are higher than we calcu—"

"Now!"

Arlene Myaschensky hiccoughed as the gauges dropped back. The blue flash from the pillars swallowed the noise and the daylight together. It poured over and through the figures in the docking area, dissolving them like mannequins in an alkahest.

Then they were gone. The air was bright with moisture condensing and the wings of insects, fluttering in the absence of the leaves on which they had rested moments before.

The vibration was making the pressure tanks of the oxyacetylene torch in the corner ring like a demented glockenspiel. "I don't see—" Danny Cooper cried as in desperation he rocked the power switch back and forth. The humming from the apparatus continued, and it continued to redouble itself through the sounding board of the reinforced concrete floor. "It can't be something we've done!"

Sara Jean was poised with her hand on the feed cables. The sheathing trembled. The burnt-cinnamon odor of hot insulation radiated from the coils. "Cover it up again," the woman said suddenly. She snatched at the edge of the tarp Danny had folded back.

"That can't help!" Danny replied, but he grasped the other corner. He was no more willing than Sara Jean to rip connections loose; and despite his words, he was sure to the sick core of his belly that he had triggered the event by uncovering the apparatus.

As the two frightened outsiders raised the tarpaulin to throw it back over the buzzing coils, their world disappeared in a blue flash.

Mike Gardner had put out a hand reflexively to steady himself on Professor Gustafson's shoulder. Instead he touched a smooth-barked tree. Gustafson gasped in delight from the other side of it. The air was wet and warm and had a faintly acid tang.

"Astor," the professor cried, "Isaac! We did it! Dear God, we really did it!" Tears were running down the old man's cheeks as he tried to clasp everyone around him.

Dear God, thought Mike Gardner, we did do it.

They all stood on land firm enough to be called dry, but the brown mud squelched beneath their weight. There was open water within a yard of Mike's shoes. It slapped in ripples as something slid off a fallen log before anyone's eyes could focus on it. Keyliss turned sharply, but she did not put the weapon to her shoulder.

Isaac Hoperin touched, then pushed hard against the scaly trunk beside him. It was thicker than he was tall, and the bole shot up over a hundred feet before it exploded into a fan of leaves like a gigantic feather duster. "We—" the physicist began. He turned more specifically toward Selve, the visitor nearest to him. "What would have happened if I had"—his lips pursed while he considered alternative words—"appeared within this tree instead of beside it?" he asked.

Astor replied, "You couldn't. The tree's too big to transport, so you couldn't replace its volume. This is a unit effect, not simply volume, and the control is in the sending apparatus, not the target."

Everything was green and brown and black. The water was obsidian except where floating debris or the reflected sky gave it a color besides that of ebony. Mike had followed Hoperin's gaze up the column of the great tree. There was very little sky to be seen. None of the foliage spreading toward the sunlight looked like the leaves and needles with which he was vaguely familiar. Tendrils like those of weeping willows—or ferns, of course; or ferns—

sprang directly from the top of many trunks and fell back toward the ground. There was no breeze to stir them. On their undersides gleamed jewels of water condensed despite the enervating heat. Back slightly from the rush-choked margin was a clump of slimmer trees whose stranded foliage hung thin and limp as a slattern's hair.

"I don't like that seven-second delay," Selve said to Keyliss in English, but also in a whisper.

She frowned and did not face him directly. "I checked the linking circuits myself before the test," she said coolly. "They were disconnected."

"My goodness, is that a bird?" cried Professor Gustafson. He had taken off his steamed glasses to wipe them just as a great, bright shape drummed over the water, saw the standing figures, and reversed to disappear the way it had come.

Mike Gardner saw only a little more than his professor: a chitinous body; wings spanning a yard, their beats strong enough to leave a memory in the water's surface; eyes that were the same fiery orange as the tips of the mandibles beneath them. No bird, and if he had somehow suspected this was a stage set and not—

"Not a bird, Louis," said Astor more sharply than the correction seemed to require. "There are no birds in this age. That must have been an insect."

"I'm not blaming you, Keyliss," said Selve. The pair of them were edging away from the others. Leaf mold covered the soggy ground beyond the circle cleared by the transport. "But it's like that backflow last night. There's something wrong with the system. We can't report it ready for use until we've found the fault."

Keyliss swallowed. She stared at the landscape of marsh and giant trees, but she saw something very different in her mind's eye. "Yes," she said, "we'll only get one chance. It's . . . I've come to like Louis and the others."

"Our return isn't affected by where we are in the target age," said Astor, "so there's no reason you shouldn't walk around." Her colleagues were not her ostensible audience, but she shot a dirty look at their backs. "Try to keep at least one of us in sight, though, not that the animal life here is any real danger."

Professional again, Keyliss turned and walked back to the main group. "Yes," she said, "there should be more than five minutes before the—"

The air is humming, thought Mike Gardner. But it was not the air. It was a pair of worlds being superimposed upon one another at a frequency which slowed to a—

Blue flash.

Sara Jean knew she had to be falling because there was nothing around her except the blue light. Her hand grabbed for the cables she had let go of—the tarp had disappeared, draining out of her fingers like wave-sucked sand. The cable was not there, either. She stumbled on the solid floor, not because it had moved, but because panic had thrown her own body into motion.

She recognized nothing in the silent room except Danny Cooper. His goggled-eyed wonder was almost certainly a mirror of her own expression. "Danny," she said, "I don't know where the cover went." She could speak about the tarpaulin while her brain still refused to deal with anything else.

They were in a large room. It had walls of pastel green with faired edges like the front of a squash court rather than right-angle meetings. There were four doors but no windows. The style of furnishing and decoration was as alien to Sara Jean as the equipment in Mike's lab had been a moment before.

"Those," said Danny Cooper. He pointed toward the black pillars at the end of the room. "That's what did it, Sara. It's like the ones down in the basement and the little ones we . . ."

He walked gingerly toward the paired objects. They were coldly silent and, so far as Sara Jean could tell, were architectural rather than mechanical contrivances. They certainly had none of the wire-wound busyness of the coils which had hummed and . . .

The two of them had to be in the laboratory.

If they weren't, where in God's name were they?

The curved and scalloped objects in the center of the room could be instrument consoles. She tapped one with her blunt fingers. The units had a plasticity of line that was far more surprising to Sara Jean than the fact that they appeared to be made of synthetics and not metal. A display on the wall caught her eye. She walked over to it. Danny called something as he inspected the pillars. The thirty-yard distance and Mrs. Layberg's own bemusement kept Cooper's words from registering.

It was a rack of pottery. Not a rack, precisely, because the peg supports seemed to be integral to the wall. There were several bowls, but most of the dozen objects were narrow-necked vases. Their curves were as perfect and delicate as those of a swimming otter. The basic color was brown, but their surfaces were marked by black striations which twisted instead of angling as surface crazing would have done.

"Sara Jean," Danny called loudly. "I'm going to open this door."

The brown-haired woman turned. Danny was pointing at the door beyond the pillars. The other three doors were in the wall on which the pottery was displayed, but there did not seem to be any distinctions among them. Mauve crescents at waist height were presumably the latches.

"All right," Sara Jean replied. She picked up one of the vases. At once she decided that she had been wrong. It had to be plastic and not pottery at all. The vase was about ten inches high and very slim overall. Even so, it should have weighed far more than it did. The closest equivalent in mass to what she held was a single long-stemmed rose; a comparison which occurred to Sara Jean because she had been thinking how well such a rose—a white one—would have set the vase off.

"Sara, come here!" Danny shouted from the open doorway. "Sara!" There was more pure excitement in his voice than fear, but the fear was there as well.

Sara Jean ran to her companion as quickly as her high heels and the vase in her hand permitted. The vase was not as fragile as its paper-thin walls made it appear. The surfaces were not synthetically slick; rather, they had the texture of weathered fir. She should have put the object down, but it was too lovely to be broken by haste—and Danny's summons required haste.

Cooper still clung to the door with one hand. It opened inward from a road or extended balcony. That surface was ten feet wide with no railing . . . and she and Danny looked out at midheight on the buildings across from them, every one of them a thousand feet high or more.

"We can't really be . . ." the woman said. She walked toward the edge of the balcony. The slick underside of another layer projected above her like a roof. Danny was following now, a pace behind. The buildings Sara Jean could see were no more uniform than so many termite mounds studding the Serengeti Plain. As she walked forward, her wedge of vision broadened vertically. All the buildings were tall; but she could look down on a few, while the spires of the highest were hidden by distance even now that the upper balcony did not block her view.

"There aren't this many people on Earth," Danny whispered. The air that should have boiled through these artificial canyons was still. It had a metallic taste, which had been present inside but seemed more noticeable in the context of a landscape.

The implications in terms of human numbers had not occurred to Sara Jean before her companion spoke. There was motion visible, though the distance hid details and the very scale made it difficult to think of the quivering activity as having anything to do with men. All the buildings were stratified by balconies like the one on which she and Danny stood. Vehicles and smaller blurs which must have been individuals scudded brightly across the faces of mountainous structures. Nowhere was there a crowd or even an apparent grouping, but the total number of figures in the panorama would have populated a small town.

Sara Jean leaned over to peer down without coming too close to the edge of the balcony. Danny said, "I—" in a gurgling voice and tugged at her arm.

"Don't," she said in irritation as she looked up. "I'll drop this— Oh." She saw the figure that swelled as it raced toward them down the surface on which they stood.

Sara Jean straightened. She started to run back to the door, but she realized that the figure was approaching very fast. Her free hand clamped Danny's shoulder as if he were a grade-schooler at a street crossing. If they stood still, the figure could easily pass them. If they moved, they might merely dodge into its path. She felt like a squirrel on the highway. Danny gave a startled bleat. He did not try to move. The fingers that held him could extrude clay between them like the jaws of a hydraulic press.

For an instant, the figure was in sharp focus. Then it was a man-sized blur, decelerating from sixty or seventy miles per hour without a vehicle. The air roiled by its speed buffeted the teacher and secretary, making Danny gasp with memory of the drop a pace behind him.

There was a vehicle of sorts after all. The figure stood on a disk the size of a serving tray and gripped a T-shaped handle. With one hand the figure flipped up—her—face shield. Wisps of silky black hair fluttered at the edges of her helmet. She began shouting something. Danny stepped toward her with his hands out in contrition, but there was no sense at all to the sounds the local woman was speaking. Her garment was a puffy suit of cream-and-purple mottlings. When she had been moving, the fabric had molded her form without the fluttering that air resistance would have caused.

Doors popped along the balcony. They disgorged men—no, women most of them and most of them with guns pointed. Sara Jean felt that she was becoming dizzy. She still saw everything with diamond clarity. The women with guns wore uniforms of the same pale green as the walls of the room with the pillars. On them, the soothing color had a frog-belly wrongness. They were shouting also, past the muzzles of their weapons, and there were no words, only terrible noises.

Two men and a woman scurried out of the room in which Layberg and Cooper had themselves appeared. The new trio wore mauve and ocher. Their clothing appeared to be randomly printed until the identity of the three suits became apparent. One of the men pointed toward Sara Jean with his whole hand. He spoke as the other gabble stilled. With the wonder of a witness to a theophany, Sara Jean realized he was saying in English, ''Why have you come here?''

"We haven't come," she cried. She held out the vase in her hand toward the speaker. "We don't know—"

Like a nightmare repeating, the balcony began to shudder as the world had when it flung them into madness. Sara Jean crossed her forearms over her eyes, but there was nothing at all around her—

Except the blue glare.

"All right, Barry," Chairman Shroyer said, "I'll talk to Louis about the possibility—"

Rice leaned forward in his chair, opening his mouth to speak. Shroyer rode his own voice firmly over the coming protest, repeating, "The possibility that you can get into the basement when they have an experiment under way. But I don't see—"

Rice had closed the door to the connecting office. Danny Cooper flung it inward so forcefully that it banged the corner of Rice's chair. "B-Bob," the secretary gasped, "something . . ."

"Now what the hell?" snapped Rice.

"Cooper, are you all right?" Shroyer demanded. Danny slumped against the chairman's desk. He was disheveled and breathing hard. Shroyer offered an ineffectual hand over the width of the desk return. Then he pushed around the furniture and Rice as well to get to where he could support his secretary. "Rice," he said out of the corner of his mouth, "maybe you'd better phone the Rescue Squad."

"Oh, no," Cooper said. "I'm—" He shook himself, then straightened from the desk. "We touched a, a machine in Lab Three. Sara Jean was there. It wasn't the— I mean, it wasn't just me. It made us see things." Straightening even more stiffly, Cooper added, "Dr. Shroyer, I think it sent us somewhere. The machine Professor Gustafson made."

"Here, why don't you sit down, Danny," said Barry Rice. He toed one of the padded chairs and touched Cooper on the elbow to guide him down onto it. Chairman Shroyer pursed his lips in doubt as the secretary settled away from him. Giving his superior a knowing look, Rice continued, "I think you need to tell the chairman and me just what Gustafson's experiment did to you."

Danny had run out of the laboratory as soon as he recognized the solid walls around him. Sara Jean gripped the table for a moment to steady herself. She remembered screaming or thought she did. The deep breath she took now choked her on burnt insulation. It swam in gray swirls above the hot equipment. There was a pair of scorch marks on the tarpaulin where it covered the cylindrical coils.

She walked out of the room quickly and with her face set. It made her look stern, but there were no signs of the panic very close beneath the surface. Years of teaching preschoolers had trained Sara Jean never to show panic. You kept a stolid expression while you got help from the nearest source available.

The stair treads were concrete. They had no rebound whatever, even when Sara Jean began taking them two at a time. The fire door into the basement was locked, as her mind had absolutely refused to remember it would be.

Her control did not crack. Rather, it burned away in fury at unintelligible constraints on what had been a normal world. Sara Jean began to pound on the door with the heel of her hand. The stair tower reverberated. She continued hammering. The sound by now had become an end in itself, a pulse that drank her frustration like surf washing ramparts of sand.

The door opened. Sara Jean pitched into the arms of the figure within. It was some moments before she realized it was Mike Gardner on whose embarrassed shoulder she sobbed.

"Now will you believe there's something wrong with the system, Astor?" snarled Keyliss to the bigger woman's back.

Astor turned with a snarl of her own. "Does that make you so happy, then? Maybe it's even something you were planning?"

Arlene and Mustafa slid from the instruments they had been watching and converged on Mike Gardner. His shirt, his hair, and the neck of his jacket, which he still gripped, were dark with sweat. "Did it?" Arlene demanded. She pumped her colleague's arm in what had to be congratulations on getting back alive.

"Everything here was all right," put in Mustafa, "though there was some overheating in the main rectifiers."

"I think you really . . ." Isaac Hoperin said to Selve as the Traveler frowned. "It seems that you were able to do what you told Louis you could, though I don't see . . ."

"I suppose it would have looked all right," Selve replied. He walked away from the physicist in abstraction rather than discourtesy. There were electronic recorders which would give detailed information on the run, but for the moment he just wanted to check the frequencies indicated by the three-pen paper tape unit hooked to the output board. Over his shoulder he added, "The location Portal was all right, but the duration was much too short. Even with the transfer mass increased by one person. . . ."

Someone began pounding on the door to the nearest stairwell.

"Astor," said Keyliss in a deadly voice, "if you suspect treason affecting the project, then you'd better bring formal charges, hadn't you?'' Her spine was stiff as the gun she held at high port.

''Your device,'' said Professor Gustafson as he took the hands of both Keyliss and Astor, ''has been successful beyond my dreams.'' Tears of joy were close to brimming down his cheeks. He had not been listening to the tense interchange between the Travelers. ''You have, you have given our world a focus beyond war and weapons, you three. You have saved our time and yours together.''

''I thought it worked,'' said Gardner with a doubtful nod toward the Travelers. ''It, there wasn't any hurt, we got back and—'' He looked at his shoes, which should have been muddy and leaf-stained. They were not, though the perspiration from his own body had traveled back—forward?—with him. ''Ah, Professor, should I get the door?''

''Yes, of course get it!'' Astor said. ''What sort of incident will there be if you don't?''

Keyliss, equally willing to find a subject which did not involve treason and failure, said, ''There shouldn't have been any effects outside the immediate area, unless— Do you use cesium oscillation for lighting? Ah—in this age?''

''Perhaps I should—'' Professor Gustafson said.

Before he more than turned, however, the graduate student had reached the door and opened it himself. The various emotions which had hung in the air of the basement became brittle for the instant of the latch clicking. Sara Jean's stumbling entry was a surprise and anticlimax to everyone.

Mike Gardner was too shocked to swear, even under his breath. The others—Gustafson and the other students, at least—had met Mrs. Layberg a time or two, but they almost certainly did not recognize her in this context of panic and confusion. God, he was in trouble. . . . "Sara Jean," he said aloud, "what's the matter?"

The woman took charge of herself in a way that went beyond standing straighter and brushing a wisp of hair out of her face. "I'm sorry for the way I . . ." she said. She stepped a little apart from Gardner, though she kept one hand on his waist. Loudly enough to be heard by all those watching, Sara Jean went on, "Upstairs something happened, and I was—with people in another cit—" Her eyes, scanning her audience, froze on the weapon which Keyliss still held at her side.

Sara Jean's recovered composure broke again. She pointed and screamed, "Mike, oh, my God, they had guns like that, and they— What's happening here?"

Astor snatched Keyliss's weapon and thrust it back into the locker in which she had already stowed her own. Selve's gun was leaned idly against a rack of instruments, out of the interloper's sight, at least. . . .

"The anomalies!" Selve cried with the joy of Archimedes leaping from his bath. "Astor, the feedback, everything— there's something similar enough to a transport unit upstairs that we modulate it between this one and our own!"

"Madam, are you all right?" asked Louis Gustafson as he moved toward Mrs. Layberg. He collided at the enclosure doorway with Astor. In his determination to reach a person whom he might have injured with his experiment, the old professor shouldered the Traveler aside.

"Where were you when you transferred?" demanded Astor, a half pace behind Gustafson now but no less intent on Sara Jean Layberg. The big Traveler did not have to ask about the Portal to which the woman had been transported: the circumstances which she had already blurted identified that adequately. Only at the home Portal would there have been armed guards—and the possibility of a stranger returning alive.

"Oh, shit," said Arlene Myaschensky. Her hand closed on Bayar's wrist for support, though she did not look at the Turk. "The test unit we built in the lab. Oh, shit."

"We were in Laboratory, I think it was Three," Sara Jean said in a clear voice. She seemed to be under control again, though close examination would have shown that her eyes were not focused on anything in the basement. "Danny Cooper had taken me there to wait for"—her arm moved from Mike's waist to return demurely to the woman's side—"Mr. Gardner. Something on a table started, I don't know, buzzing."

Mustafa and Arlene had been edging closer while Mrs. Layberg spoke. Now Arlene repeated, "Oh, shit," under her breath.

"We were in a, a huge city," Sara Jean continued. "Then there were women"—she nodded fiercely toward Astor—"with guns, like the ones y-you have. Where have I been? Where have you s-sent me?"

Gustafson had stopped a stride away from Sara Jean when he saw she was physically all right. Keyliss put a hand on the professor's shoulder to edge by him. "Sara," the Traveler said, "through an error which will be corrected at once, you have visited twelve thousand A.D." Keyliss took a deep breath. "Perhaps we can arrange another visit under more pleasant circumstances."

"Come, Sara, please," said Astor, with more firmness than respect. "Take me to where the event occurred at once." She reached out as if to bodily turn Sara Jean toward the stairwell.

Mike Gardner interposed his body, though it brought him almost chest to chest with the big Traveler. "I know where it is," he said flatly. "We built a tabletop unit to spec to see if we could get the same results. I'll take you to it.''

Astor stepped back. ''All right, Michael,'' she said. ''So long as we know.'' She gestured toward the stairs with a flourish that lay between suggestion and imperiousness.

The two female Travelers flanked Gardner as he walked away. Professor Gustafson moved with them, almost in step. He said, ''How did you duplicate all the apparatus on your own, Michael? I don't see . . .''

''We took feeds from the digital signal generators down here,'' said Mustafa to the professor's back.

Gardner had his own problems now. His two fellows wobbled with unexpressed relief, however, since the potential disaster of their own experiment seemed to be greeted with interest rather than censure. ''But all the power was turned off,'' added Arlene, beside Bayar and already at the door. ''We hadn't even tried to run it in a week.''

Isaac Hoperin was following in the wake of the others headed presumably for the upstairs lab. He paused at the doorway and gave Sara Jean an abstracted glance. Then he, too, disappeared up the stairs.

Somewhat sheepishly, Selve carried his gun over to the locker. Sara Jean did not look up until the door leaves rang closed.

Selve caught her eye and gave a brief, nervous smile through the chain-link fencing. ''You're all right?'' he asked as he walked out of the enclosure.

''I guess,'' Sara Jean agreed. She took in his conservative but oddly cut suit. ''You're one of them, I suppose,'' she said.

He nodded. ''My name is Selve,'' he said. ''I'm sorry. What happened to you must have been a terrible shock.

Though I'm glad the problem has been solved, at least traced.''

"I'd almost convinced myself it hadn't happened," the woman said with a glassy cheerfulness. "I was holding something in my hand—there. And it was gone when I was in the lab again, so I thought it hadn't happened." She had been brushing her hair up and back with her fingers as she spoke, lifting it away from her sweaty neck. Now she held her empty right hand out in front of her. "It was a vase. I'd never seen anything like it . . . just beautiful, very delicate." She laughed. "I'm almost glad to know the—whatever happened was real. Because that vase deserves to be real."

Selve's expression of diffident concern transfigured like a rosebud unfolding. He stepped, almost drifted, closer to Sara Jean and took her extended hand. "You saw my vases?" he said. "You liked them?"

"Why, they were yours?" Sara Jean said. Her own smile flashed as a mirror of his. "On the wall, and the bowls, too? Whatever do you make them out of? It surely can't be ordinary clay."

"Goodness, you're a potter, then," the Traveler babbled. "Look, I think there're chairs in the office—" They were already moving that way, hand in hand though with the formality of dancers in a minuet. "Everything out here would smudge your clothes. Doesn't matter to me"—he flicked at the lapel of his suit with a deprecating thumb—"because the dirt won't pass when we return to, ah, to our time."

Sara Jean perched rather self-consciously on Professor Gustafson's desk. It did feel unexpectedly good to get off her feet. The office was still in a state of organized surfeit. Selve hesitated, then sat atop the books stacked on a chair instead of moving them.

"I couldn't ever have one of your vases, then," the woman said as she thought over Selve's comment about grime. "But you . . . ?"

Selve brightened again. He was not shy when he had a listener he considered sympathetic. "Not on the rebound, no, but on the initial transport, of course. As you were transported to where we came from, as I came here." He tapped the chair on which he perched. "Not forever—there is always a rebound for matter; still in a state of matter, that is. But the duration of a transport can be very long, especially if the mass and volume in the field is kept small. Even without stabilization."

His excitement sagged away abruptly. "Ah," he said, "it's important that the public not know who we are just yet. It, well, the reasons are complex. It won't matter very long, I think, now that the problem in the equipment has been found."

Sara Jean stood up and walked over to Selve. She put a hand on his arm. " 'Time travelers kidnapped me,' says housewife," she suggested aloud. "Don't worry, I won't be calling the newspapers." Pursing her lips, she added, "But I will tell my husband, you know. I—it's the sort of thing that he wouldn't understand if I hid." The reason for her sudden bleakness was as unclear to an outsider as Selve's loss of animation a moment before when he discussed the need for secrecy.

"That shouldn't matter," said the Traveler. "One more person . . ."

"But you know," Sara Jean went on as her mind shifted gears, "I wasn't alone there—Danny Cooper was with me. And I really don't know who he might have told."

Mike Gardner whisked the tarpaulin off the tabletop unit.

"Why, this is tiny," said Keyliss as she surveyed the equipment. The odor of burned insulation had had time to become stale. It was a blue haze hanging in the air of the lab.

"Well," said Arlene Myaschensky, "we kept the resistances and impulse strengths to scale. There was nothing in the formulae that determined size."

"The one downstairs we built," added Mustafa, "was that size because you said it, not because the mathematics said it."

"So you'd try to lift a car with a string because in principle it's the same as a hawser?" Astor demanded in a caustic voice. "You were lucky you weren't killed! Smell that!" She waved an imperious finger through the stench.

"Here's the feed from below," said Gardner. He pointed out the terminal to Keyliss, but he was already fishing a screwdriver out of a desk drawer to disconnect it himself. "But nothing's live, nothing."

"Surely, Astor," said Louis Gustafson in a reasonable tone, "if the field is weaker but the signals are in balance, nothing should—"

The big Traveler set her hands on her hips and fiercely scowled the engineer to silence. "The field isn't weaker," she snarled in response. "The field is the same strength as that of our own transport unit that we harmonized yours with. It's the machinery that's ridiculously weaker but trying to maintain the same load. You could have killed us all!"

"Astor," said Keyliss as she looked around, "that of course isn't true."

"Listen," snapped Isaac Hoperin, also to the bigger Traveler, "You were swearing a moment ago that nobody here needed to know anything because you had it all under control. I think you had better fill us in. There's a great deal at risk, here, and I don't mean Louis's reputation alone.''

"Dr. Gustafson," called a voice as gray as sword blades from the hall, "I'd like to speak to you in private if you don't mind.''

Everyone in the laboratory turned. The department chairman stood in the doorway, flanked by Rice and Cooper.

"Yes, of course, Robert," said Professor Gustafson. He took off his glasses as if to polish them on his sleeve. His tone was completely devoid of affect.

"Who's that?" whispered Keyliss to Gardner, frozen where he bent over his work.

"The chairman," the grad student whispered back. "Jesus, he'll shut us down for sure if he's learned.''

"Louis," said Astor. Her arm extended itself in front of Gustafson. "Chairman—please come in and close the door. This isn't a matter for the two of you alone, because it isn't a matter for your age alone.'' Her eyes narrowed as they swept Rice and Cooper in the near background. "You, too, I suppose," she added. "What can't be helped . . .''

"Astor, if this unit was harmonized during our transport, we don't have very long," interjected Keyliss. "Selve could calculate it better, but—''

"Then be quiet and let me finish this," Astor said sharply. She stepped forward. Myaschensky and Bayar made way, the Turk with the stiffness of a soldier executing an element of drill. The Traveler extended her hand to Chairman Shroyer with the forcefulness of a climber helping a fellow over a lip of rock. "Please," she repeated. "Earth saved itself in your era by turning inward, into time and not to war. You must listen so that you at least know what it is you would threaten if you acted hastily.''

"Dr. Shroyer, I'm going back to the office now," Danny Cooper said in a small voice. It was not certain that anyone even noticed the slim man turn and walk down the hall with his spine rigid. Rice, by contrast, was braced as if to thrust the chairman forward should Shroyer decide instead to leave.

"All right," said the chairman. He stepped inside without taking Astor's hand. "Explain to me why experiments conducted in my department are"—he shrugged—"giving people seizures."

"Oh, hello, dear," called Henry Layberg from the living room. His voice was a surprise. Sara Jean had parked in the driveway, so she had not noticed whether or not the Porsche was already in the garage . . . and besides, it was always a surprise to find her husband home.

Henry strode into the entryway with a cheerful expression. "Shroyer comes over tonight, doesn't he? I just wanted to make sure everything's taken care of. We had some good times back in Michigan, he and I."

"I've got the rabbit marinated," Sara Jean said wearily. "I was just about to put it on." She turned toward the kitchen. Normally she would have changed into a housedress first, but she was going to have to change again for dinner. The additional effort did not seem worthwhile to save possible stains on a dress she rarely had a chance to wear anyway. Her husband did not appear to notice anything unusual about her appearance; or to notice her appearance at all, for that matter.

"I switched my phone," Henry said as he followed her. "Used the call forwarding so that anybody who rings tonight gets the answering machine at my office. After all, with thousands of MDs practicing at the center, they can do without me for one night."

They could have done without him for his fifteenth anniversary, Sara Jean thought as she took the pan of incipient hasenpfeffer out of the refrigerator. That had been the night she had called Mike Gardner, even though the kiln was finished.

She paused in midmotion. Plumping the rabbit down on the counter, she turned and hugged her husband. Dr. Layberg patted her shoulder, though his expression was puzzled.

"Henry," she said with her face turned so that the pens and beeper in his shirt pocket did not poke her nose, "something happened in the Engineering Department today, and I don't know if Bob'll be coming or not. I—I was talking to a man, and he disappeared. And before that . . ." She raised her eyes to his. "Let's go into the living room," she went on. "I need to tell somebody about it or I'll burst. And make sure that"—she tapped the stainless-steel carapace of the beeper—"is turned off, too. I have to tell someone."

Meekly, while his mind tried to recall the private number of a friend in psychiatry, Dr. Layberg obeyed.

"Good afternoon," said the tall woman with the attaché case and the motorcycle jacket. "My name is Schlicter, Sue Schlicter. I've been trying to find Professor Gustafson's office, B Two, but none of the rooms have that prefix."

She spoke sharply enough, thought Danny Cooper, that she had probably been waiting some time for him to lift his eyes from his hands clasped on the desk in front of him. Christ, she must be six feet tall and built more like a fencepost than a woman. The severity of her dark slacks and white blouse made her lines seem harsher and roused unwelcome memories of the Travelers in black and white. . . .

"You're too late, I'm afraid," Danny said. Natural amiability overcame the flatness of voice that his present level of energy would have justified. "There was, we had a bit of a problem here today with some equipment, and I believe Dr. Gustafson went off for a conference with the chairman." He nodded toward Shroyer's empty, darkened office.

"Ah," he continued, "the office is in the basement, if you'd care to try back another time. Down those stairs, just across the hall"—he pointed—"will get you there. But I don't think he'll be back tonight."

Gustafson and Shroyer had paused to pick up a file from the chairman's office before they went out again. The faculty members were talking about the way the two Travelers had disappeared in the middle of a sentence. That had shocked Cooper even more than the memory of what he had gone through himself. The fact that his body had winked out, had ceased to exist in the only world there really was—destroyed, expunged, made never to have existed!

Two policemen had vanished the night before, just outside the building. The search for them had caused a stir among the office staff, though few of the faculty had arrived early enough to hear about the incident directly. Had the same thing happened to those men? Danny's eyes glazed, and he shuddered again.

"Look," said the woman. She shifted to stand hipshot in front of the desk. "This is because of Professor Gustafson's project, right? What . . ." Sue paused, because she had once before seen the look on Cooper's face. She had been interviewing the mother of an accident victim. It was several minutes before she realized the woman had actually watched her six-year-old dragged down the street by the truck's undercarriage. Now the tall woman hooked a chair from the wall and pulled it around beside the secretary's desk. She sat in it so that it was to him and not toweringly at him that she said, "Sir, are you all right?"

Danny's attention had drifted again. He did not usually go to Friday-night meetings, but there was one at the hospital. Expunged. He needed AA tonight, or he needed—

"You look like you need a drink," the woman said in what seemed to be real concern. "Was someone injured in the experiment?"

"Best idea I've heard in five months and seventeen days," Danny Cooper said in a jagged counterfeit of cheerfulness. He rolled his chair back and stood. "Want to come have a drink, Miss Susan Schlicter"—his unconscious mind had retained information, and the tall woman wore no rings at all—"and hear about the things that happen to me when I'm straight?" The light tone evaporated. "Oh," he continued, "but I don't have a car. . . ." Or a license, of course, since the last conviction.

Sue cocked her head but did not rise for the moment. "This is the professor's project, isn't it?" she said.

"So it seems," Danny agreed carelessly.

"Then," the woman said as she stood, "I've got a friend with a cupboard full of Scotch who'd like to hear about it, too. And I've got an extra helmet, if you don't mind traveling by motorcycle." If there had been trouble, Mustafa was probably at Charles's house already. If he weren't, they could summon him for a stereoscopic description of the event.

"If there's a drink at the end of it"—Danny Cooper took the woman's arm with exaggerated gallantry and led her toward the door—"then I wouldn't mind traveling with a rocket shoved up my ass for thrust. Not since this afternoon."

"*Hel*-lo, m'dear," said the cheerful voice. "Something happened this afternoon and we need to talk about it."

Lexie Market looked up. She thought she had locked the office door after briefing the last of her laboratory assistants for the coming semester. Obviously, she had not remembered to; and anyway, she knew Barry Rice too well to believe that a spring lock was going to stop him if he suspected she was inside.

"Oh, for God's sake, Barry," she said as the engineering professor closed—and locked—the door behind him, "maybe another time, but not tonight, huh? I'm just not up for it. Go home to your wife."

"Not up for it?" Rice repeated as he sprawled into the armchair and crossed his legs. "Come on, that's not the Lexie I know. But to tell the truth, that's not why I'm here. I need a physicist, and you're the best one I know."

"Gallant as ever," snorted the woman, though it was true enough. Rice was six kinds of bastard, but he was always a gentleman in the eighteenth-century sense. And though his repertoire was limited—her hands were massaging the aches in their opposing wrists—he was very, very good in the sack at what he did. "What do you need a physicist for, Barry?"

The engineer had been toying with a silver-barreled pen. He pointed with it toward the sidewall. "Your next-door neighbor, Hoperin? He and one of my esteemed colleagues" —the sneer was in the voice as well as the lips—"think they've built a time machine. More precisely, think that time travelers have taught them to build a time machine. And I think they've been sold a load of bull-puckey."

"Ike Hoperin's saying that?" Market said in amazement. There were plenty of screwball things she could imagine Hoperin being involved with, but as a scientist the man's work was impeccable.

Rice nodded, his brows knitted as he recalled the events of the afternoon. "Yeah," he said, "I don't mean he's just gone off his nut. Or Gustafson, either, though he's been missing a few cards from his deck for years now, if you ask me. Thing is"—and the scowl released into an expression more of puzzlement than of anger—"there *is* something goddamn strange about these Travelers. I saw two of them just blink out in a crowd of people." He snapped his fingers. "Just like turning out a light. And when Gustafson says they appear the same way . . . well, he may be senile, but I don't think he's having hallucinations like that, no."

The engineer got up and walked around to Lexie's side of the desk. His hand rested on her shoulder. She did not turn. "I can't put my finger on just what's wrong," Rice continued. "The whole thing's crazy, but the explanation fits the facts as well as"—his free hand fluttered in an empty gesture—"anything would. But you can't bullshit an old bullshitter, eh, Lexie? And I know these folks are hiding something, I know it!"

"What do you want me to do?" Market said to her hands. "Talk to Ike?"

"Better than that," Rice replied as the fingers of both his hands worked firmly on the knotted muscles of the woman's back. "They're going to give Shroyer a demonstration tomorrow morning, but the big cheese doesn't see any reason I need to be present."

"Shroyer doesn't?" said Lexie. The last syllable rose in a little gasp which had nothing to do with the conversation.

"He never has liked me," the engineer said bitterly. "Thank God this is the last year of his appointment as chairman. Gustafson can do work for the Army Research Office, sure, but when I have a damned good chance to do a study on fission triggers for the air force, 'I think we have to be cautious about involving the university in certain kinds of programs, Dr. Rice.' "

Rice took a deep breath. His fingers continued to work with mechanical skill. "Well," he continued, "I'll miss the snow job that Shroyer and the rest get tomorrow, but in the meanwhile, you and I'll take a good long look at the whole rig tonight. I'm going to learn just what they've really got going on, these Travelers. Gustafson may get his picture on the cover of *Time*, but next week it's going to be Dr. Barry Rice who exposed the hoax of the century. And you, my dear, can have anything up to half credit, because you're going to help come up with the theory behind all those coils and transistors."

"Tonight, then," Lexie said. She was slumping forward, away from the chair, so that Rice could work farther down the taut muscles over her ribs.

"We'll wait till dark," the engineer explained. "No point in calling attention to ourselves. I've got a key that'll fit Gustafson's office, and he's got keys to his equipment hanging right on the wall on a pegboard. We're not going to hurt anything, we're just going to take the sort of neutral look at the project that somebody should have taken before it started."

Rice's earlier frustration had been wearing off as he outlined his plan. The grim edge returned for a moment as he added, "You know, I can't believe that anybody at Army Research Office really knows what's going on with their money. I'd like to see Gustafson raise a stink if he found us looking at his toys!"

Market said nothing. Rice's face relaxed again as he looked down at her. Her blouse was loose at the waist. He slipped his hands beneath it and used her firm, globular breasts to guide her torso upright. "We'll get some dinner before we come back to look around," the engineer said. "I told my wife that I'd be working late on something important, and that's the truth, after all."

Lexie felt her nerves begin to tremble in intersecting circles centered on her breasts and her groin. She stood up slowly and turned. The chair was in the way. She kicked it aside with a rattle of casters.

She would help Barry solve his problem, a part of her thought as she began to rub herself against the handsome man. And he was going to help solve hers; for the time being, for the next few hours at least. . . .

"They're going to want to know who was responsible," said Keyliss gloomily. Her fingers touched switches. They had been forced to check each circuit, first independently and then in concert. The interlopers could have disturbed foci simply by trying to open access panels on the equipment. "They haven't said anything yet, because they know there's no time for anyone else to take over. But afterward . . ."

"Afterward, we'll quite literally be the people who saved the world," Astor said, more defensively than the words themselves would imply. The three of them had changed back into their normal garments of pale blue with coppery overtones. Astor was comparing the programmed signals with the actual ones as the two blinked alternately on her screen at thirty cycles a second. "Check. Try Portal Nineteen."

"We've done Portal Nineteen," said Selve from the opposite side of the same console. "We've done them all. Everything's operating just as we left it—here. And now that we've disabled the fourth leg of the circuit that Arlene and the rest had built, there won't be any more backflows and duration anomalies."

"They could figure it all out from that one incident, you know," Keyliss said in the same doom-ridden tones. A chasm had gaped before her when she'd realized that the project was not—had not been for weeks—under their sole

control. Keyliss had handled the crisis professionally, but
now that it was over, she had fallen into a deep depression.

"They could do nothing of the sort," Selve said testily.
"For the same reason that we couldn't understand why we
were having the anomalies. Until you know that there is a
fourth leg in the circuit, none of the results make sense.
And they don't know about . . ." His voice trailed off.
Standing, he turned to look toward the display of bowls
and vases over the door to his room.

"Anyway, nothing did go wrong," Astor said. "That
we gave out only the information the project required was
proved by the fact that the additional unit wouldn't work
by itself. It merely reacted to a harmonic induced when
this"—she gestured to the console rather than the ebon
pillars behind her—"and the unit they built at our instructions were both live."

Selve walked toward the outer door and opened it. As
he had rather expected, the fragments of a vase lay there
on the Peripheral Road. Regular maintenance was not due
for another thirty hours. There was nothing in these few
crisp shards to require emergency cleanup. It went without
saying that no one outside of Maintenance would have
made it her business to pick up the pieces.

Using as a tray the largest fragment—it was the size of
his cupped palm—Selve began collecting the remains. The
edges were not sharp. The strength of the artifact had been
in its unity. Now that the wholeness had been breached,
the structure was willing to crumble away like a sweater
unraveling from an unwhipped end.

Selve remembered making the vase. He had chosen the
bud with a nonchalance which bespoke experience, not
haste: he did not need to examine a hundred further possibilities to realize that the first he had seen was perfect.

After choosing the bud, he had clipped the stem above

and below it. The lower end went into a nutrient solution. Plain water had sufficed in the distant past, but Selve was intent on creating a work of art rather than a table service. For the other cut, however, he had used the traditional smear of half-congealed sap from another plant instead of a modern, less messy, plastic cap.

Similarly, Selve had followed tradition in forming the bud without tools, without even the wooden stylus which some who called themselves purists were willing to sanction. The nail of his own right forefinger had been grown and trimmed into the point of a gouge. It was clipped short for stiffness, and it did not interfere with Selve's ordinary duties. With that fingernail he had scooped out the pulpy tip—the "brain"—of the bud and had shaped the surrounding material into a form very different from the branch into which its nature would have grown it.

With no woody core to strengthen it, the cambium had exploded into unrestrained growth. After thirteen hours, Selve had replaced the nutrient solution with a salt bath. The swelling edges of growth shrank inward like a sphincter muscle closing. They remained in perfect symmetry because Selve's original pithing stroke had been perfectly circular. At twenty-one hours all growth had stopped. The bud had swollen, then shrunk abruptly, into a vase. Over the next three days the cambium had hardened into eggshell rigidity along the lines which Selve had imposed upon nature.

Sara Jean had the eye of a connoisseur. That vase had been the most nearly perfect piece Selve had ever created.

"What happened there?" said Astor from the doorway. "One of yours?"

"Yes," Selve agreed without turning. "One of the transportees was holding it. It fell, of course, when she rebounded." He had picked up all the fragments he could find, so he rose to his feet again. It was not the sort of thing which could be repaired, but he thought he might burn the shards instead of merely leaving them for Maintenance to compact.

"It sure did fall, didn't it?" said Astor as she saw the handful of remains. "Say, that's a shame. But I guess you can make a new one as soon as the project is completed."

Astor had always appreciated the craftsmanship her colleagues displayed, thought Selve, in this as well as in matters relating to their mission. But it would be a very long time before the big female came to understand Art.

"Yes, that's right," Selve agreed as he walked back into the project room. "But you know . . ." He juggled the fragments in his palm so that they clicked together like insect mandibles. "If Sara Jean's world is blown into pieces no bigger than these, who's going to build her a new one?"

Both Astor and Keyliss watched Selve's back as he stalked toward his private quarters.

"Dave, it all came loose, I'm telling you," said Arlene Myaschensky desperately. "I don't think I'll even be going on the, on the transport tomorrow, now that Dr. Shroyer's learned about it and everything."

"Arlene," said her husband, "sit down and shut up for a minute." He did not raise his voice, but the intensity in it was as sharp as a slap; and a slap would follow, they both knew, if she did not obey at this juncture. Arlene sank back into her chair. She crossed her plump white hands on the kitchen table.

Dave Myaschensky pointed again to the camera he had set on the table. He said in a tone of textured calm, "What you do every day is a lot harder than this. I've loaded the film and set the lens for minimum focus." He would rather have used the bellows than the hard extension tubes, but the greater bulk and complexity of the flexible arrangement outweighed any benefit his wife's inexperience could draw from them.

"It's a single-lens reflex, so you don't have to worry about getting a picture of your thumb. You just slide up to an insect, make sure the needle in the viewfinder's in the notch"—he had bought fresh batteries for the light meter so that Arlene didn't have to learn about turning it on and off between shots—"and the insect looks sharp in the field, like you were just seeing it through glass. The background'll be blurry, but that doesn't matter. It doesn't even matter if all the insect is sharp. Get the head, say, and then move to get him from the side. Your depth of field with the extension tubes is going to be half an inch at the outside, but that's okay."

"D-Dave," his wife said, "the little camera is automatic and I could hide it—"

Dave Myaschensky did not move. His face settled into gray curves like a concrete casting. His right hand, with which he had been about to indicate the cocking lever, twitched; only twitched. "Arlene," he said in the deadly silence, "listen this once. I need identifiable photographs, not colored blurs. The Nikon's big and old, but we couldn't afford a new package that does the same thing."

He curled his fingers around his wife's right wrist. His swarthy skin was a contrast to the white delicacy of hers, and his tendon-ridged grip began to sink as well into her plumpness. "We could have bought a new camera if you hadn't decided you needed a master's, couldn't we, dear?"

"Dave, let go of me," Arlene said in a small voice. Then, louder and with undertones of strength rather than panic, "Dave, if you hurt me, I won't be able to go at all. There'll be no pictures." The fingers released like springs.

Into her husband's startled eyes Arlene added, "They may not let me go anyway. Really. The chairman's going to go, and I don't know what'll happen next."

"Now, doll," the entomology student said. He converted his grip of a moment before into a pat for his wife's soft shoulder. "You always say what a sweetheart Gustafson is. He won't keep you off when your heart's set on it, right?"

"He may not—" Arlene began.

Again the gentle pat, but Dave's face was congealing. "And if you have to, you'll remind the chairman that all this he's joining is a fraud on the government, isn't it?"

Dave Myaschensky put his hand back on the camera. "You've got to understand what it means," he said. For the first time that evening his voice held an emotion that was not frustrated anger. "Doll, if you bring back so much as a picture of a housefly, I'll do a paper on 'Preliminary Investigations of Cretaceous Dipterids in a Living Environment.' They'll think it's a fake at first, but when the story about this comes out on TV, well . . ."

He clutched Arlene's hands, raised them, kissed them. "Doll, wherever I send it, they'll print it—*Science, Nature*, it's my choice. If we wait till it's all public, the big names take over and I'm out in the cold forever. But if I'm the first, I'm a big name, and I'm on the ground floor of the biggest thing that ever happened to entomology."

Arlene nodded slowly. After all, no one had said anything against taking pictures . . . and according to Mike Gardner, there was no reason not to walk around, just out of sight, so that the question would not arise.

"Okay, bunny," she said aloud to her husband. "Show me again how I keep the light right on this one."

"Tomorrow's going to be a great day!" Dave Myaschensky beamed.

*   *   *

"The funny thing is," said Mike Gardner, "that yesterday I believed in it, in the time machine. But now that I've gone and it really works, it's like I was watching a movie, is all." He smiled. "A pretty boring movie. They needed Godzilla tramping down the middle of the swamp, didn't they?"

Isaac Hoperin grinned back abstractedly over his own beer. The bustle of the pizza parlor was warm insulation instead of a distraction to him. "Well," he said, "I continue to be less concerned with what we saw than I am in *how* we were able to see it. It's an awkward position for a physicist, being quite certain that the apparatus I see couldn't do anything except set up a fluctuating magnetic field—of the sort which might indicate a Dobbs phasetime basis for . . ."

Hoperin stopped and glanced up, realizing that his companion was not equipped to care about what he was being told. The physicist began again, "But to actually have been a part of the, the temporal shift these Travelers claimed was going to occur." His lips pursed, just over the rim of his mug. "I've met their type, you know. So sure they have all the necessary data. So sure there's two ways to look at a problem, their way and the wrong way. Every soldier and damn near every politician I've met was that way." The lips relaxed in a smile. "Most engineers as well, Gardner."

Mike grinned. "But it's Astor you mean," he said.

"The tall one?" clarified the physicist. "Yes, well . . . It's a mistake to think any group is monolithic, I know. Astor has the face and bearing of a colonel who told me how much he'd like to order his men to use me for bayonet practice, though that was a long time ago. I can never believe that a person like that has the right answer to anything. Even though we both were part of the proof.''

The two men had met for the first time that afternoon. They were together now because, alone of the jetsam hurled out of the day's events, they had no one else with whom to discuss matters. "What I can't understand," Gardner said, "is—the test unit the three of us built, it never worked. Never. Down in the basement, the big one made things disappear, and they came back . . . even a cage full of guinea pigs. But only when the Travelers were there. Why the hell does the little rig work when the power to the coils isn't even on?''

"I take this with a grain of salt,'' said the physicist. "With a whole handful if you like, but your Astor seemed to be claiming that the coils were energized by induction so long as the correct control signal was reaching the boards. Now even if that were true, we should be talking about field effects in an asymptotically flat spacetime, not a''—he barked a laugh at the absurdity of the thought— "not time travel, whatever that could conceivably be. I seem to be being offered the engineering benefits of Grand Unification, a form of simulated initial instant in which omega equals one, and thus symmetry—and tunneling— can take place.''

He shook his prematurely balding head. "Forced Unification? Well, perhaps if Einstein were here, he'd be able to make something of this. But I keep expecting to learn that this tunnel has an oncoming train at the end of it, too.''

Hoperin studied his companion for the first time as a person. A nice-enough fellow, whose observations of the general circumstances and of the event itself were as clear as the physicist's own. But Gardner came from a different generation—eighteen, maybe nineteen years, but a genera-

tion nonetheless; and even with the same background as
Hoperin, the younger man's personality would not react to
certain forms of authority in the same way.

The physicist said, "The truths that people like Astor
tell you, uh, Mike, are false. Partly because the truth is
never so simple that it can be grasped by a mind with only
go/no go responses. And partly because that sort of
mind always prefers a lie." He smiled because he fully
realized how absurd his absolute statement was according
to his own terms. But it was nonetheless the philosophy
which had guided Isaac Hoperin throughout his adult life.

"Not my sort of lady, either," said Gardner as he
stood. He was smiling also, but wryly and thinking more
about women for the moment than he was about the
project. He'd gotten into something without thinking much.
Not thinking about it further wouldn't make it go away—if
that was what he wanted—but it certainly felt better in the
short run. "Well," he continued, "I'm going to take a run
back to the school and look things over. Just for the hell of
it. You want to come, too? I've got keys."

Hoperin shook his head in self-amusement. "I'm going
home with the formulae," he said, tapping his briefcase.
"I'm going to see if they make any more sense to me now
than they did over the past two months. Quite frankly, I
find concrete objects confuse me more than they help."

Mike Gardner laughed as he fished in his wallet for his
half of the bill. "That's one thing we sure don't need," he
said. "More confusion."

"What confuses me," said Charles Eisley as he sipped
his drink, "is what these future visitors do with their time
machine. Besides help us build time machines of our own,
of course."

"They explained that," said Mustafa Bayar. He was the

only one of them drinking raki again this evening, and he was sipping rather than tossing glasses down the way he had the night before. None of them were drinking heavily except the newcomer, Danny Cooper. Cooper had anesthetized himself with Scotch before he had time to give a connected account of what had happened to him and was now slumped on the couch, holding a glass no one had volunteered to again refill.

"You see," Mustafa went on, "they find crises and correct them, so that their world—their time is peaceful, comfortable."

Sue Schlicter frowned. "You mean they make things like, oh, Auschwitz not have happened?" she said. "Or World War Two, period? But they did happen."

"Do you suppose the machine has to be invented, so-called invented, before they can travel to an era?" Eisley suggested. He had become interested in the situation as an event, not just because of Mustafa's involvement.

"No," said Sue, "because they did go back to whenever, long before man. Right?"

Mustafa pumped his head vigorously and said, "But to change, not just to visit—perhaps that?"

"That's all bullshit, you know," said Danny Cooper in a gloomy, muzzy voice.

The other three looked around abruptly. The secretary had not moved on the couch; in fact, he had not even opened his eyes. Toward the empty glass, he continued, "Peaceful? If they're so peaceful, why the guns?"

"Well, those were tools," said Mustafa with a frown. "They were for animals when they guided us back into time. Common sense, not . . . unpeace."

"Bullshit," Cooper repeated in a singsong. His body was struggling to lift itself upright, but his eyes were still closed. "You weren't there, boyo, you weren't there."

The Turkish student's mouth opened momentarily. He closed it again, swayed either by the fact that Cooper was drunk or remembrance that they both were guests in a friend's house. Eisley was already moving to place himself between the other two men, just in case.

"At first there wasn't a damn soul," Cooper was saying, "just the walls and the furniture that looked like somebody poured it. And the city, the mother-huge city, but they were all ants, you know?" Unexpectedly, Cooper's eyes popped open. He glared at the other three people intensely. As suddenly, the lids closed again and the voice went on, "It was a goddamn army when they came for us, though, wasn't it? I don't care they were all split-tails, they all had guns."

"Split-tails?" Mustafa whispered in puzzlement.

"Women," Sue Schlicter translated with the shadow of a smile.

"Pointing guns at us and shouting," Cooper said. "Ready to shoot, you bet your ass. Ready to rub us away like we never were. . . ." The secretary stood up with more coordination than he had shown since the second glass of whiskey. "I need a drink," he said clearly; and as he crumpled at the knees, all three of the others caught him and lowered him safely to the couch.

"You know," said Charles Eisley as he looked down at Cooper, "he's got a point. If the future really is so peaceful, what are the armed guards doing?"

Astor slung the gun on its hook again after she had taken her atmosphere suit from behind it. Keyliss had already removed her orange garment from the locker, but Selve's still hung in back of his weapon. The tall female stared at her male colleague with disapproval. As he continued fiddling with something in the center of the docking area, the disapproval hardened to outright anger. "You'd better get ready, you know," she said. "All three of us are to be present to check the programming."

"The programming at Four, yes," Selve agreed coolly. "I'll be ready. I've set our unit for a preliminary transport to Eleven, however—before we go. Tight focus, but let's both get well out of the way, shall we?" He beckoned the woman with a gesture which took account of the tiny parcel he had aligned for transport.

"What?" blurted Astor. She started directly across the docking area to Selve, but the mounting hum of the pillars warned her. The coils were already cycling at a far higher rate than they should have been if they were accumulating for the scheduled transport. "Keyliss, come here," she called as she skirted the docking area quickly.

"What's the matter?" demanded Keyliss as she flung open the door of her room. She was mostly into her atmosphere suit, but one sleeve and shoulder dangled and her left breast was bared. "The unit—is it running away?"

"This one," Astor snarled at Selve, "had the bright idea of doing a preliminary run. I suppose you realize that you've destroyed the whole schedule? You've maybe destroyed the whole world, the timing's so close?"

The three members of the team were in simultaneous but varied motion. Keyliss was running from her room with the loose sleeve flapping. Astor, closer to Selve, was scuttling around the area that might be affected by the transport. And Selve himself was walking nonchalantly back toward the instruments, which were already well into the course of guiding the unscheduled run. The trio met at the consoles with a timing which could not have been choreographed more precisely.

"But Selve," Keyliss said as she peered toward the docking area, "what are you trying to send?"

"A bud," her male colleague answered. He recognized and appreciated the fact that Keyliss spoke from concern rather than anger. "It'll grow into a bowl. Not an exceptional one, I'm afraid, but I think it will give Sara Jean some pleasure." With a challenging glance at his colleagues, he added, "I think we owe them that, don't you? Some pleasure."

Astor had taken the time to check the current settings before she spoke. "We'll go in on the damping curve of this run," she said, half in approval—and half for reassurance that she had correctly interpreted the instrument readings.

"Yes, that's right," Selve agreed calmly. "There'll be a balance surge at the other end, but it won't affect the schedule." Keyliss had surreptitiously begun recalling data from the memory of the console she ordinarily ran. Selve noticed her and added, "I've already programmed it, but of course check my values."

The coils reached drive frequency and flashed their fierce, soul-filling glare. Though the team were as experienced with transport as anyone else in the world, it was unusual for them to watch an operation of which they were not themselves a part. The flash, coupled with the continuing solidity of their surroundings, induced a sense of failure and disquiet in the three spectators. The tiny bud and its globe of nutrients were gone from the edge of the docking area. Nothing else had changed.

"I've shrunk the area of our transport slightly," said Selve. He spoke quietly. Without the raw buzz from the pillars behind it, his voice seemed preternaturally clear. "Wouldn't do to pick the bud up and shift it here before I could give it to Sara Jean, would it?"

Astor cleared her throat uncomfortably. Selve's behavior had put the project at risk to a greater degree—not, perhaps, a measurably greater degree—than it would have been without his antics. While Astor could not have verbalized that thought, it was a subconscious component of her unease. She said aloud, "You'd better get your suit out of the locker now."

Selve nodded. He walked across the docking area. It was safe, although the pillars were already beginning to sing with the next charge.

Keyliss fed her arm through the sleeve and sealed the torso of her suit. She did not bother to close her hood as yet. "What duration did you send the pot for, Selve?" she called.

Her male colleague had begun to strip off his ordinary clothing at the locker. Time was short, and the three of them lived too closely for the normal ceremonies of modesty. "About thirty-seven days," he replied as he stepped into his orange suit. "I was more concerned to get the damping curve right than I was that the initial transport be precise, of course."

"We can't be absolutely sure that we've cured the ghosts and backflows," Astor said with a partial return to her normal hectoring demeanor. "That could throw everything off."

"If we still have anomalies," Selve snapped back, "then we've got to cure them before we report the project is operational, don't we?" His hand brushed closed the seam of his suit forcefully. "The system will work or not work independently of any change I made today in the pattern of testing."

Keyliss touched her bigger colleague's elbow to silence the useless argument. "We'd better take position," she said. Then, louder, she added, "Yes, thirty-seven days should be adequate. A great deal more than adequate."

*   *   *

"I don't think you've got an adequate program, Gustafson," said Henry Layberg, "without a medical adviser." He gestured with the rabbit scapula from which he had just sucked the meat. "Think of the situations you could get into, hey, Shroyer?"

"Barring a failure of the entire system," said Louis Gustafson with a puzzled frown, "I can't see that we're any more prone to injuries than"—he shrugged—"anyone else who climbs stairs to their work place. These aren't lengthy excursions, at least at present. No one's going to become seriously dehydrated in twenty minutes, even in the midst of a desert. For instance."

Robert Shroyer laughed and thumped Layberg on the arm. "What my old roommate's trying to suggest, Louis," he said, "is that he'd like to watch things tomorrow."

"To go along, actually," the MD corrected with a grin.

"Oh, dear God," whispered Sara Jean Layberg. She lowered the tumbler she held to the table with a thump and a slosh of water onto the cloth.

Everyone stared at her in concern. She looked around with a brief smile, then patted her husband's wrist. "I'm sorry," she said to the watching men, "but it was such—such a disorienting experience—that I can't imagine anybody wanting to do it to themselves. Not you, Henry."

"Ah," said Professor Gustafson, "it was very kind for you to feed me so wonderfully, Mrs. Layberg, when I just appeared with Robert. But—"

"Well, don't worry about that," said Henry Layberg. He did not realize that the engineer's statement was an apology in advance for disagreeing with his hostess. "You tried to call, after all, and if the calls hadn't been shunted to my office, we would have told Shroyer of course to bring you. This whole business has fascinating possibilities. Haven't you ever wondered how an additional three hundred generations would affect modern man through microevolution?''

''But—'' Gustafson had noticed the interruption only to the extent of not trying to talk over it. When Layberg stopped, the engineer took up at his original point. ''I think your disorientation was caused by the circumstances rather than by the process itself. Those of us downstairs were apprehensive to begin with, but the actual event did not cause problems.''

''But you knew you were going into the past,'' said Chairman Shroyer, pointing with his finger, ''and she had no idea she was going into the future. I think it bothered Danny very greatly indeed.'' He frowned, then added, ''I should really have paid more attention to Danny, but of course I was primarily interested in what had been going on. I think I'd better look him up.''

''They must be able to totally replace internal organs,'' Dr. Layberg was saying in something close to a reverie. ''They must have a society without clumsy half measures like dialysis machines and insulin injections.''

''What they have, Henry,'' said his wife in a low voice, ''is women with guns. And they have pottery,'' she added, studying the ceramic tumbler she had made herself. ''They have that.''

''Well, I've got as much notion of what it is,'' said Barry Rice as he turned over the bud and nutrient container, ''as I do of how in blazes it got here. Which is none.''

''Maybe it was an accident,'' said Lexie Market. She shined her own flashlight down the long expanse of equipment with them in the enclosure. ''It looks to me like a rooting bulb of some kind. You know, for plant shoots. It doesn't have anything to do with the process, that's for sure. Not if these do." She jogged her field of light from one massive, nonbiologic piece of hardware to another.

The key to the enclosure was where Rice had expected it. The two of them had entered and had been shocked by the extent of the task they faced. Even though Rice had glanced at the experimental array earlier, its size magnified when he looked at it in the need of understanding each individual part so that he could synthesize the purpose of the whole.

The Layberg woman had babbled about the noise and a bright blue flash when whatever it was had happened to her. There was no noise at all tonight, and there was not enough light to warn Rice directly as he jotted notes beside a bank of instruments. Market had suddenly turned off her flashlight and called, "Barry—look by those columns."

There was a nimbus, vaguely green and very faint indeed, forming in the air between the huge vertical coils and the instruments closest to them. The light was more like the ghost of a fluorescent fixture than a real illumination. It would have been invisible by day or even with the overheads on.

There had been a stir of air too slight to be a pop. The glow was gone. On the floor beneath its memory now sat a . . . well, as Lexie said, a rooting vase, if it were anything of normal attributes.

"It may have been there when we came in, and we just didn't notice it," the physicist said. "I don't see how it could have anything to do with—"

"Turn out your light," Rice rasped in a desperate whisper. His skin had begun to tingle. With the flashlights off, both of them could see that they were bathing again in the nimbus. It was as if they had been enclosed in a fish tank whose crystalline walls were too pure to be seen.

Rice put down the clear bulb with more haste than care.

It slipped and bounced back from the concrete, unharmed and ringing like metal rather than plastic. Lexie reached over to right the object so that it stood more or less as it had when they first noticed it. Then both of the intruders darted back into the shadowed interior of the enclosure.

The three Travelers wearing orange coveralls puffed into sight. Their arrival made no more of a stir than had that of the bud. There could be no doubt that they *had* just appeared, however. Barry Rice shifted behind a rack of coupled transformers so that he could see the figures more clearly. He was cursing under his breath. If it was an illusion, it was a damned good one.

Selve and Astor both flicked on their belt lights as soon as the glare of transport had faded from their retinas. A thirty-degree wedge of light glowed in front of each in the darkened basement. The light was balanced farther into the yellow-orange portion of the spectrum than an ordinary incandescent bulb would have thrown it. Astor strode to the instrument banks beside the marked-off docking circle. Selve's sole apparent concern was the globe which had preceded him. He carried it from the floor to the top of an oscilloscope—nearby, but beyond the present focus of the transport system.

Lexie watched through a cabinet whose edge-on circuit boards shielded her like the louvers of a Venetian blind. She noticed with interest that the lights, though apparently point sources, did not glare as the Travelers moved. The lenses provided a sharp demarcation at the upper edge of the illumination, so that the user did not blind his fellows as he turned toward them. Further, that upper edge remained parallel to the floor even though the wearer's motion must surely have flashed it upward on occasion.

Keyliss latched and sealed her hood. "Ready?" she

called. Her voice through the chestplate of the suit was thickened, slurred.

Selve stepped back briskly into the docking circle. "Yes, all right," he said as he closed his own hood. The last word extended itself as his speaker, too, cut in automatically.

"I'm going to trust your calculations, Selve," grumbled Astor from the control panel. The voids in the console and the ribbons of communications wire made her uncomfortable every time she had to depend on local equipment; but the key was function, and they did function, had to function, or the world would . . . She threw the main switch. The residue of their own transport had already acted as an exciter field for the coils looming against the chain-link enclosure. As the system began to hum, the tall woman walked to her waiting colleagues.

"You've always trusted them, Astor," Keyliss said in the defense Selve would not make for himself. "At any rate, they've always been right, haven't they? Except when that other unit was affecting things. We don't need arguments now that we're so close."

Astor ignored her. Very possibly she could not even hear because of the rising amplitude of the buzz.

Barry Rice began to straighten from his crouch, although the trio of Travelers still stood in the fans of their own light. The overhead fixtures were trembling enough to snow down dust and the wings of insects dead for decades. The individual coils of chain-link fencing sang, each in a note determined by its precise length and the vibration which it harmonized. The ensemble was a suggestion not of Hell but of Chaos.

Then the blue flash sucked away all sound and the three figures in the docking circle. A trick of light made it seem as if the Travelers spun in a helix through this and other forms of reality.

"Goddamn!" muttered Rice as he ran toward the after-image of the figures. The flash had been blinding. Even though he had switched on his flashlight again, he stumbled hard against a shin-height table. The engineer was so focused that he did not even bother to curse.

The jalousie effect which had hidden Lexie from the Travelers also saved her vision from the worst of the glare. She was able to pick her way at leisure through the maze of equipment and still reach the control panel as soon as Rice did. Even as they met, there was a metallic snap from the panel's face.

"There!" said Rice excitedly. He used his flashlight beam as a pointer to probe among the switches and dials. The light steadied into an ellipse on the slanted gray surface. "That's the one they threw, isn't it? Sure, it must be—they've even painted it red."

The big three-position toggle switch Rice indicated had been sprayed with red paint after it was installed on the panel. Most of the other switches bore cryptic legends in Dymo tape, but the red one was otherwise unmarked.

"If you mean the one they threw before they left," Lexie said cautiously, "I couldn't see from where I was. I'm not even sure that it was one switch and not several." The physicist's day had begun in bondage to a partner who had acted out psychoses which he had not hinted earlier. What she had just seen was the perfect complement to that beginning. She had watched an event of patent unreality, and the man she was with was requiring her to treat the hallucination in concrete terms.

"No, I'm sure it was just the one," said Rice peevishly. "She checked some of the others, but we would have heard if she'd thrown one."

The physicist knelt and shined her light through one of the voids on the control panel. "It seems to be an ordinary thermocouple," she said. "It's a circuit breaker, for all practical purposes."

"Well, let's see what it does when our friends in orange aren't around to stage-manage it," said Barry Rice. He snapped the switch home again. Sparks paled Lexie's flashlight as the contacts arced closed.

"Barry, don't be a damned fool," the physicist snapped. She stood and slid around to the front of the panel in a motion just short of panic. The painted circle had obvious implications. Her position had put her hips far too close to that boundary for ease.

"What I'm being, my dear," said the engineer as he walked by her, "is the early bird. This is the best way to learn what they're doing, and it'll be that much simpler to decide how they're doing it. Care to come along?" Rice crooked his arm for her to take and gave an insouciant wink. He was standing well inside the circle.

"If they are lying, they're not going to let you come back, Barry," Market called over the rising hum of the machinery. Gauges on the panel before her reacted to the new inputs by quivering into upward curves. "Come on, let's think about this before something happens." She extended her own hand as a gesture, but as she did so her body pulled back instinctively from the area that would be affected.

"They don't have a choice," Rice said. "It's automatic, you see? What happened to Cooper and that Layberg woman." The engineer's hair was beginning to fluff as if from static electricity. There was no sign of a glowing cloud as those which had presaged incoming transports. "And you know just where I am. I'll tell them that. They don't have any choice but to show me the truth!"

He was shouting now, and only in part because of the

mounting background noise. Rice was poised like a wax figure as he stared at the woman safely withdrawn from him and from his choice. He had to believe that there was enough data for a decision, because he had to make that decision, he was an engineer—

But he could hear Lexie crying out in icy logic, "If they're liars, you can't trust what they say about coming back, either. You don't know what you're getting into, you don't know the rules!" In her mind were the soft pressures on her wrists and ankles, the hard angles of the pistol with which the friend with the now contorted face was fondling her, entering her . . .

The fluorescent fixtures paired along the high ceiling flickered on with a palpable impact. Someone was clinging to the wire of the enclosure and shouting, though the gate was still unlocked.

Rice turned. His vision was blurring. It was one of Gustafson's students, not the wog or the fat girl, but he still had no authority to give orders to a tenured professor. Rice drew himself up. The hauteur of his expression would have done credit to Lord Cardigan riding toward the guns at Balaklava. "I'll discuss this with—" Rice began, and the flash that was as intense as a sound seared through him, blinding him, dissociating him from himself and from his universe.

On the other end of the transport, there was solid ground and time to scream. As well as need for screaming.

Even with the overheads on, the glare had burned its memory into their eyes. Mike Gardner rubbed his face with one hand as he used the touch of his other hand to guide him to the gate of the enclosure. "Miss," he said in a voice underlain by anger, "you've got to come out of there right now. It could be very dangerous."

"I'm Dr. Alexis Market of the Department of Physics," replied Lexie stiffly to underscore her status. She picked her way carefully toward the door, however. There was a bleach-bottle sharpness in the air which made her sneeze. Not ozone, but some other result of what they had done, she and Barry.

"Oh," said the student. His tongue poised before the next word. Rather hopefully, he went on, "That was Professor Rice, wasn't it? Ah, did Professor Gustafson send you here tonight?"

"I believe you'd have to ask Barry about that," said Lexie in a neutral voice, but with a warm and transfiguring smile. She had dressed for what amounted to a break-in when they'd left her apartment, but she was always careful of her appearance. Her slacks and long-sleeved jacket were dark gray, but they were tailored to her figure. The spray of lace at the throat of her blouse was dressy without being confining. She looked the part of a physics professor . . . and that was just as well, because if this nonsense became too public, there were going to be serious interdepartmental problems.

"Barry?" the engineering student repeated. "Oh." He nodded toward the tall coils, now silent. "He . . . he did, didn't he?"

"Yes, he did," said Lexie with a wry smile. "Something, at least. You mean, it isn't Barry's project, Mr. . . . ?"

"Shit," he said without emphasis. He looked up. "I've got to report this, Miss—Doctor, I mean. Oh—my name's Gardner, Mike Gardner."

"Yes, I think a report might be a good idea," agreed the physicist as she followed Gardner toward the office. If Barry was going to disappear—literally—while taking schoolboy chances, he was just going to have to accept the consequences.

*   *   *

The phone rang. Henry Layberg froze in midsentence before he remembered that after the single ring, the call would be shunted to his office and oblivion.

The phone rang again. "Oh, my goodness," said Sara Jean in surprise. "It must be mine."

Carrying her napkin in her hand like a forgotten banner, she strode down the hall to her workroom and caught the phone on its fourth ring.

Before she could speak, Mike Gardner said in a tense voice, "Sara Jean? Something's happened, in the basement. The professor was going to your place tonight, wasn't he? They said so when they left."

Gardner was feeling more desperation than he allowed to show through. He would have been reasonably comfortable if the hardware were behaving in an unplanned way, but whatever was going on tonight put him deep in university politics. He had memorized Sara Jean's personal phone number in months past. That brought him through the barrier of call-forwarding on the listed number without even knowing there was a problem.

"Yes, he's still here," said the woman. Part of her was feeling normal social surprise at the call. Another part felt a surge of sexual longing; but that was a separate person, a remembered person, who could no longer speak. "Bob Shroyer brought him. Do you want to speak—"

"Look, Sara," Mike rushed on, "tell him that Professor Rice was fooling with the equipment and seems to have sent himself somewhere. Tell them both. I'll wait here in the basement of the engineering building. Oh—and there's a lady from the Physics Department, too. I—I think it'd be a good thing if they hurried."

"I'll take care of it, Mike," Sara Jean said in the calm voice with which she would have spoken to a preschooler in an emergency. "You don't need to speak to them yourself?"

"If they need me, I'll be at the extension in the professor's office," Gardner said. "I—I appreciate this, Sara." He hung up.

Someone to hold his hand? thought Sara Jean as she trotted back to the dining room. Was that what Mike appreciated, needed? And perhaps that was what they all really needed in one way or another.

Her return to the dining room focused attention on her as a motion. The men's interest would have as quickly flickered back to their discussion had not Sara Jean faced Chairman Shroyer and said, "Your Professor Rice has done something to the, to the equipment. He's sent himself." She turned to Louis Gustafson and added, "Mike Gardner is looking over things now, but he thinks you had better come back to the lab yourself."

All three men leaped up. "Come on, Shroyer, I'll drive," said Henry Layberg in a burst of pleased excitement.

"You'll do nothing of the sort," Shroyer retorted as he checked his pockets for the car keys. "I'm parked behind you, and anyway, I know where the building is."

Sara Jean snatched up a wrap of her own as the men shrugged into their suit coats. She was amazed to find that curiosity was leading her back to the scene of her recent terror. Perhaps it was the instinct that picked at scabs.

Aloud, but more as a note jotted in his memory than a statement to his companions, Louis Gustafson said, "We'll have to inform the Travelers of this as soon as we can. Whatever Dr. Rice has done may affect their calculations."

"Check on Twenty-three," said Keyliss as she compared the pattern of red and orange on the gauge against that on her template.

"We are competent to program our settings here, you know," said Deith, the squat Monitor who was as physically powerful as Astor and at least equally aggressive. "Even if we've been stuck at the butt end of the universe."

"Nobody doubts your competence," said Selve. His fingers worked on the main console. "You have your duties and we have ours. Twenty-three A?"

"And we," said Astor with a brooding glance at Deith, "have the ultimate responsibility, don't we?"

The quarters here at Base Four were safe enough, but they felt flimsy. Though the complex spread for miles, literally, it was of two- and three-story construction. That should not have mattered—there would have been no windows in either case, especially not here—but somehow the idea of the blanketing atmosphere penetrated the walls.

The atmosphere did so in fact as well. It clung bitterly to clothing and to the dead spaces of vehicles which had not been designed to shrug it off. Baths of nitrogen for everything entering the complex kept the concentrations well below the level of danger or even of active discomfort. The sharp reminders could not be filtered out, however. As Deith had said, Base Four was the butt end of the universe.

Astor's gibe brought Deith forward with her hands on her hips. She was simply one of the twelve Monitors at Base Four. The Monitor Group was collectively responsible for the three hundred construction personnel who had built the transport unit here, but they had no relative rank among themselves.

Unofficially, Deith had achieved total ascendancy over her companions.

"There have been no problems, here," said Deith. She spoke in a rocking singsong that would work into a scream if her target did not back down before the volume was necessary. "Stabilization's gone just fine, seven hundred thousand troops and all their equipment. Starting from scratch, from ore, here on this—"

"Is it your duty to delay the project, Deith?" Selve demanded shrilly. Only in the upper registers could he speak loudly enough to interrupt. "Do you wish us to abort this test and to announce that we have done so because of your behavior?"

"Twenty-three A, check," said Keyliss in her own attempt to defuse the confrontation. Astor had been a fool to speak the way she had, but she was not technically wrong; and besides, the Contact Team was an entity, just as was the Base Four Monitor Group.

The enclosed areas of the base were on a cramped, inhuman scale that itself did much to increase the tension. The Monitors had lined two walls of the control room as they watched the Contact Team recheck the calibrations. Two Monitors wearing their buff and gentian uniforms now stepped to Deith. One of them whispered and patted her shoulder. Deith swore and spat on the floor, but she moved back to the wall without speaking further.

The control room could be small, because it did not enclose the drive pillars in the usual fashion. That, and the dozen pairs of eyes watching with at least the hint of anger, made Keyliss feel more uncomfortable than she did when working with the unit at Portal Eleven. Base Four had been constructed in tiny, laborious stages. Men and equipment had processed local ores, interrupted at frequent intervals by their rebound. The quantity of simultaneous work needed made it impossible to extend the duration to more than a half hour, even using the heaviest practical drives. When materials from the portal region had themselves been formed into construction equipment, only the crews needed to be exchanged, and duration went up to a practical level.

Whatever is necessary becomes practical; and Portal Four Base was as necessary to survival as the simultaneous construction taking place at Portal Eleven.

Despite the fact that all the equipment at the base had been built to standard designs, there was a brutal crudity of execution to it. At every stage, the production machinery—and the machinery which produced the production machinery—had been used in haste and run to the widest-possible tolerances which would still permit functioning. Deith and her colleagues were indeed to be congratulated on their success; but the powers who decided the Portal Eleven Contact Team would be responsible for fine-tuning the entire system had evident reason for their choice.

The task at Portal Eleven had been parallel but very different in detail. It would have been impossible to move hundreds of technicians and their equipment in to begin stripping ores from the middle of an occupied area. The locals would have responded with a volume and quality of violence that would overwhelm any defense which could be conducted at long range.

The same scientific and industrial base which made open intrusion impractical permitted success through peaceful contact. Professor Gustafson could build from local components the apparatus which the ruthlessness of the Directorate could not impose. Nothing in the engineering school basement looked as it should. Everything was bulkier. That was not only because the builders were less sophisticated than Deith and her colleagues, but also because almost all of the components were off-the-shelf items adapted to their current use rather than being purpose-built for a limited task. In fact, the apparatus within Professor Gustafson's enclosure bulged and glittered with functions and load capacities greatly in excess of the transportation circuitry of which it was now a part. If the unit at Portal Four could be compared to a huge lawn, cropped to order, then what had arisen at Portal Eleven was a wild landscape no less functional for its leaps and vistas.

And it did function. That fact gave Keyliss a warm feeling toward the locals who had succeeded where rote would have failed. Their copper wire was too pure for the drive coils, for instance. Deposition-refined, the metal did not have the quarter percent of alloying silicon which set up the necessary internal resonances in a unit constructed at home. Gustafson's team had worked around the problem with banks of resistors on the output side of the signal generators and by skewing the centers of the—normally—concentric coils in each column so that they induced delays and accelerations within one another. That would have been Isaac's contribution, Keyliss now realized. They should have known that some such help would be necessary, that technicians—as they on the Contact Team were themselves—would not be adequate to solve all the problems which local circumstances involved.

Of course, Keyliss knew that her feeling toward the locals was really that of a person whose pet has learned a particularly involved trick. She was a decent enough person herself that self-knowledge of her attitude bothered her.

"Starting Column B," said Astor. She rolled the shunt, a sphere with dimpled alternative settings, held by magnetic repulsion.

"Check," said her colleagues together, not so much bored as thinking about matters of greater tension. The Portals were like beads on a wire. They were perfectly linear, although their array was of course non-Euclidean. Because any two points could define a line—even in trans-

port physics—it was possible to interconnect columns of
Portals. That required transfer points, however, and it was
by no means a simple matter of a linear shift, as was
transport within a column. The Contact Team had just
traced and calibrated the Portals between Base Four and
home. It remained to repeat the process on the intersecting
column.

Large-scale displays glowed on the consoles when Astor
transferred the scan. Normally, all the general display
would have done was to indicate which Portals were
uploaded for use or examination. In this case, the problem
was of so gross a nature that it was obvious even at a
glance.

"Eleven's off scale," said Selve. Astor, with her judgment added to the facts, was saying, "You forgot to factor
in our own transport!"

"I did not forget—" retorted Selve furiously.

Keyliss spoke loudly to end a squabble that was bringing wolfish grins from the assembled Monitors. "That
input was loaded correctly. We may have a fault in the test
program."

Several of the group from Base Four stepped away from
the wall with expressions of shock and anger. Astor ignored them. Her own irritation had returned to an earlier
cause. "Well," she asked, "was it the scheduled transport
or the one that really brought us here? That's probably
the—"

"The test circuit's fine," said Selve without emphasis.
"Don't worry about the program, look at the operational
record. There's a second peak, one just after our own
transport."

"But there wouldn't have been—" Keyliss started to
object. Then she remembered and added aloud, "Oh, of
course. . . . Because we transported to Eleven in a figure-

eight instead of direct, there would have been a charge in the coils a few minutes after they drove us."

"That pot you sent, Selve," Astor muttered, but the emergency was too real for even her to use it to win an argument. She was sealing her suit even as she strode for the door to the passageway.

With the consoles still live and the test program unfinished, Selve and Keyliss trotted after their colleague. The Monitor Group burst into excited babbling. None of the Monitors understood the nature of the problem, nor were they wearing atmosphere suits. Presumably, the Contact Team was headed for the docking area.

And nobody without an atmosphere suit could visit the Portal Four docking area. And live.

"Good God, Louis, what are you doing down here?" Chairman Shroyer demanded as he followed Gustafson in through the basement-level door.

"It's bleach," said Sara Jean Layberg.

"Well, it's chlorine at any rate," her husband said. Though when he thought about it instead of simply reacting to a judgment couched in the form of fact, he realized that the chlorine probably had been liberated by bleach. Somebody trying to clean, to disinfect, a scene of—

A scene certainly not of bloody tragedy, after all, now that Layberg had a chance to look around. The open basement gave more nearly the impression of a furnace room than of electronics research and time travel. The scale was at fault. The pillars he had been told about stood near the door, just inside the fenced enclosure. To look at, the pillars were as featureless as a pair of water tanks. The precision with which they had been built from layers of fine wire, like huge vessels of lacquerwork, was hidden by its very delicacy.

Mike Gardner and a woman Louis Gustafson did not know stepped from the office when they heard the outside door. Mike's expression combined relief with a level of new apprehension. "He hasn't come back, Professor," the student called. He thumbed toward the plastic-cased drive coils.

The young woman with Mike—well, she must be thirty; Gustafson had only two categories of women, under forty and over forty—stepped forward with a greater formality. Her gaze and a brief smile touched all four of the newcomers. It was to Gustafson specifically, however, that she extended her hand and said, "Mr. Gardner here tells me that this is actually your project, Professor. I'm Dr. Market from across the way, physics." She gestured. "I seem to owe you an apology. I know Barry Rice and his wife socially, so when he said he had hardware he wanted a physicist to look at, I didn't make sure it was his hardware, as I probably should have."

"Just what did you and Rice—" the chairman began. He paused when Lexie turned her friendly smile on him. "Pardon, I'm Robert Shroyer, I—"

Lexie took the hand which was only tentatively extended. "Of course I know you, Chairman Shroyer. We met at one of the chancellor's teas, didn't we?"

Thoroughly disarmed by now, Shroyer said, "Ah, I'm sure I would have remembered that. Ah, this is Doctor and Mrs. Layberg, they're concerned in this affair themselves. Can you tell us just what did happen here tonight?"

"Well, I met Barry here as arranged," Lexie lied. "He had a set of keys to the gate—" She pointed.

Mike and Professor Gustafson had wandered back within the enclosure, talking in low voices. Mike now turned and called to Shroyer, "The keys are missing from the professor's office, sir."

"He said something about people in orange suits using it," Market continued very carefully, "but I didn't catch just what. And then he turned a switch."

Mike Gardner pressed back against the fencing in order to better hear what the physicist was saying. He half beckoned, half tugged Professor Gustafson along with an extended arm. "She means the Travelers," the student whispered. "They had suits in the locker along with their guns."

"I really can't explain what happened then," Lexie said, able to be completely honest for the first time since she began her explanation. "Even though I saw it. Because it seemed to me that Barry just disappeared. There wasn't anywhere for him to go. And"—she turned, but because she did not raise her voice, the impact of what she was saying took a moment to register—"I think that sound was part of it."

"Okay," said Mike Gardner, "this'll be the rebound." He walked quickly to the bank of instruments reflecting the performance of the pillar on the left. It was the position he had expected to watch during the scheduled run the next morning. The day's chaos—Sara Jean, Chairman Shroyer, and the test rig which had threatened the whole project— had just resolved itself into an engineering problem.

Louis Gustafson also walked toward the control panels, but he stood a pace behind his assistant. Gustafson could watch the other instrument array, but he was more interested at this point in the general performance of the apparatus. Specific data was being recorded. From what the Travelers had said, there was absolutely nothing which could affect the rebound once an object had been initially transported in time. "I think the question is what will be rebounding," he said aloud. "Astor didn't tell me that they'd be running tests here without our presence, though I suppose there was no need to explain. . . .''

Shroyer and Dr. Layberg walked quickly to the enclosure gate, then back toward the controls. The hard click and raps of their soles were masked by the buzz of the apparatus, like rice grains being poured over a cache of arms. The two men were fascinated by the chance to watch an event which had seemed wildly unlikely in the telling.

Both Lexie and Sara Jean had reason to be more wary than curious about the details of transport. They eyed each other, both of them straightening and raising their brows unconsciously. Then they broke into simultaneous wry smiles. "I suppose we ought to watch," said Sara Jean, "but I think I'm just as glad of having the wire between it and me this time."

Lexie connected the woman in the tan silk dress with the woman Barry had mentioned in passing, supposedly transported to some monster city that afternoon. She touched Sara Jean's hand. Still touching, the two women turned toward the docking circle on the other side of the fencing. "Close your eyes now, I think," Lexie suggested. Then the tingling flash swept them so intensely that they could perceive the woven-wire patterning through the skin of their eyelids.

Gustafson and Mike Gardner had known to duck their heads at the requisite moment also. The basement had seemed warm compared to the cool evening outside. It was warmer now with the fresh burst of energy liberated within it, but the chlorine was gone from the air as well.

Professor Rice sprawled on the concrete. His upturned face was twisted in a rictus of terror. There was more life in the fluorescents above than there was in his eyes.

Gardner was the first of the four men to reach Rice. The student had not been temporarily blinded, nor did he have

Professor Gustafson's diffidence in dealing with a colleague under awkward circumstances. He touched Rice's cheek and looked up in disbelief. Dr. Layberg was kneeling beside him now, careless of grime on his suit as he reached for Rice's carotid pulse. Aloud, Mike Gardner said, "Christ, he's cold." He was staring at Sara Jean over her husband's hunched back. "Christ, I think he must be dead."

And then the coils began to purr as they readied themselves to act again.

The docking area at Portal Four was on the same huge scale as the rest of the base, but there was a translucent dome in the center of it. The dome was collapsible. It neither was nor was meant to be airtight. It could, however, be pressurized with neutral components of the local atmosphere. That gave the docking area a safe matrix of exchange with other portals.

The contents of the dome were never breathable. In any case, the Contact Team had just left when the second transport of the evening occurred. The influx of the chlorine-rich external environment had not been swept from the interior.

The man on the floor of the dome was as surely dead as the stone on which he lay. Selve nonetheless covered the blanched face with the emergency mask and feed from his own suit.

Keyliss touched her colleague's hand gently. "We need to see who it was," she said. "Perhaps one of their maintenance division. . . ." She lifted the mask and hand.

The sun was bright enough, but the atmosphere filtered its light into the yellow green and changed the lines of even the most familiar objects. Astor muttered something brief and bitter, then asked, "Is he one we know? I swear they all look the same to me."

"We've seen him," said Selve as he folded his emergency gear. "One of those this afternoon; the chairman, I think. This is going to mean trouble."

"Guns!" said Keyliss. "We need a gun."

"What?" Selve said.

"We don't have time to stabilize him," Keyliss explained with animation, "but if he goes back as vapor—you see? What's the communications level for Assault Command?"

"There won't be time," said Astor. She knelt and lifted the body of Barry Rice over one powerful shoulder, acting before she had time to explain. "We'll carry him to a gun. We can worry about getting clearance later."

Like smoke in a whirlwind, the weight was gone from her shoulder and the body was recovering itself to the point from which it had been launched to its death.

Three Monitors burst into the dome. There was a fresh gush of the atmosphere whose stain the pumps had begun to thin from the interior. Their leader was Deith, unmistakable despite the atmosphere suit into which she had scrambled. "You've aborted the check!" she cried, voice deepened by the speaker. "Do you realize that you're delaying the schedule? Astor?"

"It was on residual," Selve said. "Nothing to modulate the setting, but the duration would be much lower, even for the lesser mass involved."

"What are you talking about?" Deith demanded. She did not speak as loudly as she had a moment before. It was evident that something had gone very wrong. Deith was increasingly aware that it might be best if she and her colleagues were not involved in the problem. It had to be the fault of the Contact Team, whatever the trouble was. . . .

"I'm going to reverse us into Eleven," Keyliss said. "There may still be time to clean things up." She slid the atmosphere suit off her left hand and forearm, baring the iridescent control plate on her wrist.

"We can't be sure Eleven will take the strain," Selve warned with a frown.

"Well, we'd been getting the backflows before we found that fourth leg in the system," Astor retorted. "It took that, didn't it? Besides, it's no good for the project unless it can take redirected power."

"You'd better get back from here," said Keyliss to the gaping trio of Monitors. Others of the group, also suited, could be seen as blurs milling beyond the dome's translucent panels. "We're not going back on rebound. *We'll* wind up at Portal Eleven, but I don't have time to figure where people with your"—she gestured with a finger— "energy background would be shunted."

"Or whatever's in the wrong location at Eleven," Selve added somberly. "But we'll have to deal with that when we get there." Keyliss had made the decision. Selve had serious doubts about it, and even Astor seemed less than enthusiastic. In an emergency like this, however, they would act as a team. Keyliss had preempted the situation by her strong, sudden action—which was the intended result of their training.

"Look at them run," said Astor with bitter satisfaction. The Monitors were scampering away from the dome and the incipient transport. Their fear was not of being shifted briefly to some other portal. Rather, they were driven away lest they become involved in a situation which they could not fathom. The project was too desperately necessary for it to be wrecked by inexplicable events. What loomed now before the Monitor Group was such an event.

"Yes," said Keyliss brusquely. She felt—all three of

them felt—the same aura of catastrophe. Unlike the Monitors, they knew perfectly well what the problem was or might be.

Keyliss looked down at her control plate. Her exposed skin was tingling, but there would be no long-term effect beyond a slight bleaching. Selve had his plate open also, itching to make side-effect calculations which were wholly beyond the unit's capacity. The emergency controls had full use of the memory of their base unit, but there was no way to display that memory. Preset commands as complex as this—powered reversion through a remote unit—could be carried out. Not even Selve's prodigious calculating ability could use the data on hand to determine tertiary effects, however.

"There . . ." Astor whispered as she felt a twist in the realm of the currently possible.

They could only pray that what they were doing would not make the situation at Portal Eleven even worse.

"We got to get out of this circle," said Mike Gardner. His lack of affect made the words seem less desperate than they really were. He tried to pick up Rice's body by the arms. The face lolled hard against the concrete and the young man swore.

"But where is the power coming from?" muttered Louis Gustafson as he squinted at the instruments over his glasses. "The modulation, yes, but the power . . . ?"

"You mean it's going to—" said Chairman Shroyer. He was reacting as much to the buzz of the coils as in reply to anything Gardner had said. He skipped toward the edge of the circle but hesitated, looking back at his companions.

Lexie Market was watching with an analytical blankness as events unfolded. Sara Jean pressed herself against the fencing, gripping it with both hands. She shouted, "Get

back! For God's sake, get back before it takes you!''
Neither she herself nor a neutral observer could have been
sure to which of the men particularly she cried.

Dr. Layberg brushed Gardner's efforts aside and rolled
the body into his own arms. Layberg's softness was roped
together with muscle, and he had years of experience in
moving patients the best way available in an emergency.
When a heart-bypass patient pauses halfway over a sixth-
floor banister, there is no time to worry about whether
wrestling him back from his death will cause internal
injuries. With Rice a limp weight in his arms and the
engineering student beside him, Layberg bolted toward
safety. The flash threw their joined shadows against the
instrument cabinets and the closed eyes of Professor
Gustafson.

"There they are," called a female voice even as the
Contact Team caught its collective balance in the short
cross hall on the eastern side of the enclosure. The blue
glare was only a memory. The enclosure wall doubled its
diamond pattern in its reflection from the Lucite-covered
pillars. A group of men—one of them carrying the body of
the interloper—turned beside the enclosure with puzzled
expressions. It was one of the pair of women in the basement's long main hall who had first noticed the transported Travelers, however.

"We've got to get that body and get it back home,"
Astor muttered as the trio stripped back their protective
hoods. "Thirty seconds is all we really need."

"It's Sara Jean," said Selve in pleased surprise. Keyliss
stared at her colleague in angry disbelief at his frivolity.

The Contact Team had been transported on a reciprocal
of the relationship of the pillars to the normal docking
circle. That was a necessary result of controlling one set

of drive coils through another. The danger was that the transport would be in exchange with whatever happened to be in an area which was not specifically cleared. That seemed by good luck to have been bare concrete also. At any rate, the locals were not shouting that some*one* or some*thing* had been snatched to another Portal.

The fact that they were holding the dead body was bad enough.

"Keyliss," Astor said, "program it to send me and that one." Her nod might have meant anything, but was Barry Rice now being lowered again to the ground. The Travelers strode in a rank up the main hallway toward the door. They were wearing their orange suits and fixed smiles. The blond woman turned to watch them curiously, but Sara Jean Layberg cocked only her head and one frightened eye. "Medical assistance at home."

Selve touched Sara Jean's hand as he passed her. "I'll do that," he said. "Three-minute duration for the volume."

"The rebounds are going to twist us like corkscrews," Astor said bleakly, "and we shouldn't be treating the apparatus like this, the loads . . ."

"We have to get that man to medical help immediately," said Keyliss loudly as she entered the enclosure. "He injured himself on the apparatus."

"He didn't injure himself, he's dead," said Henry Layberg as he straightened behind the body. "And from all indications he died of chlorine poisoning."

"What's going on?" Chairman Shroyer added in a stark voice. He was rubbing his hands together unconsciously. He was forty-three years old and he had never touched a corpse before.

"That's why we have to get him home while we're still able to revive him," Astor said. She was taken aback by the detailed awareness of this local. She had feared at worst the certainty that the interloper was dead. Astor knelt by the body.

"I'm going to set this to transport them home," Selve murmured to Professor Gustafson. The Traveler's slim hands quickly adjusted settings on the cabinet in front of him, then moved to the parallel unit. The ungloved hand winked like an entity separate from the orange-suited man.

"We were checking the dielectric anchor," Keyliss improvised authoritatively. Dr. Layberg had spread a hand, palm down, above Rice, and the departmental chairman's fists were now clenched. "It's a huge chamber, and of course the atmosphere was charged with chlorine. This man must have followed us—did you send him?" She pointed like a dagger at Shroyer. Keyliss had no need of acting ability to sound angry and concerned at this juncture. "If we don't get him to treatment in our own age, he'll die. Is that what you want?"

"I'll help carry," said Mike Gardner. He bent to take the dead professor's legs.

"No need," Astor muttered in reply. With the easy strength her size and manner suggested, she stood and walked toward the center of the docking circle.

Dr. Layberg lifted his hand away but kept his fingers spread. "I can't help him," he said, aloud but to no one in particular. Robert Shroyer, embarrassed when he realized his fists were clenched, stepped even farther out of the way of Astor and her burden.

"Keyliss?" called Selve as his hand poised on a dial. He was ready to choose whichever of a pair of constants better reflected the mass of the present transport.

"You'll be all right?" she replied. She had moved not so much within the docking area as to a point where she stood between Astor and the chairman, just in case.

"You'll have to act quickly," said Selve sharply.

His colleague nodded and backed closer to Astor in the center of the circle. The room vibrated as Selve's mismatched hands touched controls as if he were molding a work of art from wet clay.

Sara Jean Layberg walked slowly into the enclosure. This time the building power did not carry with it the déjà vu and messages of fear, as the transport minutes before had done. It was nothing to do with her or hers. It was an event, a subway roaring down echoing, immaterial tunnels. Her husband watched at the edge of the painted circle. His big shoulders were hunched. Mike Gardner stood beside him, straighter and firmer but almost frail by contrast to Henry. Mike glanced toward the control panels. He caught Sara Jane's movement in the corner of his eye. Startled, stung both by fear and concern, he jerked his head straight.

Sara Jean was not walking toward those men, her men. Professor Gustafson flanked and overlooked Selve as he earlier had done with his student assistant. He watched the Traveler change settings in ways that had been unsuggested or even prohibited in discussions of the apparatus and its use. Sara Jane moved toward Selve's other side, the third point of the figure described by the Traveler's knowledge and the professor's observation.

"Ready," said Selve in a voice that cracked over the white noise. Now all those in the basement knew to cover their eyes and await the shock of coming silence.

The flash brought them back to awareness of the hot room and the stink of overloaded electronics.

"I've walked into a circus," the chairman muttered to Mike Gardner because Gardner was the nearest human being at the moment. Shroyer pulled from the pocket of his coat the necktie which he had stuffed there earlier in the evening. He used it now to mop sweat from his face. "Maybe a sideshow, a carnival sideshow."

"There's no reason for this to be overheating," said Professor Gustafson in wonder. He patted the silicon-steel core of one of the big transformers under the windows. The others had only noticed the odor of hot insulation. Gustafson's nose and carefulness had led him to the source, unlikely as that source appeared. "These aren't even in the circuit at the time of discharge," he went on. He touched the pads of his fingers to his cheek to confirm the heat they had picked up from the transformer. "And they're far larger than we needed, from anything I could understand. . . ."

Selve turned to look at him. The Traveler was wrung out by events and by reaction to the successful cap he seemed to have put on them. "No, Louis, that's correct," he said. He touched the frame of the instrument cabinet as if for support or for at least the awareness of solidity. "They act as moderators, and with the series of transports we've just run, they must be closer to design limits than Keyliss would care for." That portion of the project had been Keyliss's responsibility. "Or me," he added in wry awareness of what system failure would have meant to him physically. "There won't be any problem on rebound, though—the very complexity will serve to balance out the worst peaks."

"But they aren't connected," said the professor. He was not objecting to Selve's statement. He was simply reiterating the salient facts so that he might someday fit them all together into a coherent whole. "A timer disconnects the bank of tranformers nine point six seconds after the start-up command is entered."

"In three minutes, less elapsed, Barry will be—rebounding?" Lexie Market said. Rice had used the term, and

Selve's repetition of it had aided its retrieval from the physicist's memory. She strode alone outside the enclosure. The wire threw rhomboidal patterns across her face and hands but merged with the black of her clothing. "You'll be able to—cure him in that time?" Lexie had not approached the body. She could very well imagine chlorine corroding lung tissue like a fire devouring dry leaves . . . membranes shrinking, shriveling, rupturing to drain fluids that could not quench the hunger of their destroyer.

"They'll use the unit at home to stabilize him there until he's ready to return," Selve lied as he turned to face the woman whom he did not know. "It will be—some weeks, I suppose." He stifled the impulse to say "thirty-seven days," unnecessary and inappropriate, except as humor . . . and humor so black was always unnecessary and inappropriate. He was too tired, too wrung out, to exercise the conscious control that was now even more needful than before.

"What do you mean by stabilize?" Mike Gardner asked without hostility. "You mean everything doesn't rebound the way you told us?"

"You can keep a spring taut by continuing to press against it, Michael," Selve said wearily. He did not bother to look around at his immediate questioner. The locals pressed about him like predators and their prey, not physically, but neither was the danger they posed physical, not directly. "In transport, either a single massive stressing at the receiving portal, or a constant low input to balance the tendency to rebound. There wasn't time to explain that, and there still isn't. Perhaps someday . . ."

Sara Jean Layberg touched Selve's hand.

The Traveler turned toward her. There was no agenda hidden behind Sara Jean's smile, only fellow feeling for

one as exhausted as herself . . . and one much like herself,
perhaps, though they had spoken only briefly.

"I brought you something, Sara," said Selve. Instead of
squeezing her hand in response and releasing it, the Traveler kept a light grip and led the woman to one of the
cabinets along the south wall. The men parted to pass
them, then trailed after in muttering curiosity.

Louis Gustafson alone remained where he was. His eyes
were tracing current paths through the apparatus he had
built to others' plans. His hand rested now on the hot
casing of a transformer. The touch proved even subconsciously that there was a connection, whether or not it was
a material connection in the present universe.

Lexie Market still stood in the long hallway. Though
she was more distant from Selve than was anyone else in
the basement, she recognized the object the Traveler took
from the cabinet top to present to Mrs. Layberg. It was the
globe and bud which had preceded the orange-suited figures. Lexie had meant to look at it more closely, but Barry
Rice's reckless stupidity had driven the thought from her
mind.

Ruptured membranes, soft tissue returning to organic
soup in the body cavity. . . .

"You were admiring my craft, my hobby," Selve said.
He handed the globe to Sara Jean. Dr. Layberg craned his
neck past Robert Shroyer for a better look at the object.
"This won't be a vase like the one you touched, but it
should grow into a bowl of pleasant shape." Selve was
diffident, but he knew very well the quality of his art. He
would not disparage that, even at the risk of seeming
arrogant to himself. "I thought it might remind you of
me."

"May I see that?" said the chairman. He reached out in
prejudgment of the answer.

Sara Jean cradled the globe against her breasts, enfolding it with both hands. "Thank you, Selve," she said. "Just watch it, you say?"

"For Christ sake, woman," her husband muttered, "let the rest of us see it."

"That's right," Selve agreed. "And a few hours—or more, after the nutrient has been absorbed, cut the bowl away from the stem with a sharp knife. We"—his smile and voice stumbled—"owe you a great deal for the trouble we cause, I'm afraid."

The woman reached out to squeeze his hand again, the gloved one this time. "I hope you'll be able to come to my pottery soon."

"I think there's a—" Mike Gardner said. "Ah, I hear the coils."

The hum was indeed building again from a feeling to a sound. Instead of scurrying to the control panels as before, Professor Gustafson picked up an induction ammeter and snapped its loop over the nearest transformer's output leads.

"This should balance everything," said the Traveler. His lips quirked into a grin, "In one swell foop. Whatever the initial duration settings were." He closed and sealed his hood. His lowered voice added, "It should be an interesting microsecond."

Dr. Layberg had taken the globe from his wife without protest. He was turning it to the light, trying to get some idea of its character. Feathery petals had already begun to expand from a cylindrical section. Some sort of crystal-growing arrangement, he decided. A great deal more sophisticated than the packets of multicolored salts from his childhood, however.

"Is it dangerous for you, then?" Sara Jean asked. She remembered the terrifying vertigo of her own transport.

"Tomorrow morning," said Chairman Shroyer over the buzz and his growing frustration. "You'll be back with a real explanation and a chance for me to see what's going on?"

"There's no danger now," said Selve. "Maybe a little when we carried on as we did initially, but there wasn't any choice."

"Tomorrow," Shroyer repeated, clutching at the Traveler's arm.

"Yes," Selve agreed, turning. "We will be back as scheduled. Everything will resume as sched—"

Selve's voice and the memory of his touch hung as the glare dissolved him from Sara Jean's eyes and fingers. The globe in her husband's hands blazed in a symphony of reflection and refraction, but Henry continued to hold it in the stillness following the multiple transports.

As usual in the aftermath, the great room felt warmer. There was no odor of hot insulation this time; Selve had been correct in saying that there was no chance of an overload.

The air seemed, however, to have a tinge of burned flesh.

Astor clutched her face shield open and began to vomit. Selve had understated the effect of simultaneously unraveling multiple consecutive transports. Even Selve was in three places at once—or as near to once as made no difference to the synapses of his brain. The females of the Contact Team had made an additional transport home. That was one more vertiginous twist, though the pair began and ended the series of rebounds in practically the same place.

Keyliss grunted. She took a step in the antiseptic docking area and stumbled, pressing her hands to her temples.

Selve reached out, either to steady her or to steady himself. "It'll pass in a moment," he said in what sounded like a voice of prayer.

The equipment locker just outside the docking area was open. Near it lay the guns which Astor and Keyliss dropped when the transport system sucked them back. The guns had not been transported initially, so they fell to the floor instead of rebounding through the catalog of Portals. The air was hot. A splotch of the cast flooring, ten feet by twenty raggedly, still bubbled and smoked.

The guns had no low-power setting, so Astor and Keyliss had flared the muzzles to their widest apertures as they enveloped the body in fire. Narrower beams would have scored too deeply into the building's heart, eviscerating other chambers and their contents. Even the energy scattered with a broad brush had darkened half the chamber by cutting a cable. The door of Astor's room had crumpled as one gun or the other jiggled.

Local atoms had combined with those ripped from the corpse under the cascade of energy. The rebound left those atoms nascent. The bitter tinge of ozone began to join the less identifiable products sublimed from the building's structure. Black feathers the size of thumbnails floated in heat-spawned convection currents and the desperate attempts of the ventilation system to deal with the circumstances. Still nauseous, Astor began to stumble toward the outer door. The feathers which brushed her made sooty, indelible stains on her orange suit.

The door opened as she reached for the latch plate.

For a moment, the big woman thought she saw in the doorway a hallucination born of disorientation and combustion products. She bowed anyway and said, "Pray enter," because even a mirage of the Directorate deserved honor.

The two women and the man in their suits of coronal white entered the room. Outside the door, the air crackled and flashed with a temporary force screen and the silver-shot vehicles of the guards.

Keyliss had begun to step out of her atmosphere suit. She was too logy and wretched to have bothered to seek the privacy of her room. Now she gaped and whimpered at the Directorate. The conscious part of her brain reasserted itself. She straightened and stood with quiet dignity, drap-ing the tangled suit over her arm. The situation tran-scended normal modesty. All she could do at this point by trying to scramble back into the garment was to make herself absurd. Selve, for his part, smoothed the glove portion of his suit down over his left hand. The fabric slipped back over his fingers and sealed seamlessly.

"A confusing situation has been reported by Portal Four Base," said the male Director mildly. They had names, the Directors, but probably no one was intimate enough with them to use those names.

"We don't want you to think that we are concerned about your abilities or dedication," said one of the female Directors as she tactfully lifted her eyes from the blasted patch of the floor and the guns beside it, still hot from firing.

"We came ourselves," said the other female; she had started to close the outside door, but the fiery reek within caused her to swing the panel open again, "rather than send to you or call, to make it clear that we are not interfering. We are offering you whatever of the world's resources you think you may need."

"Because," the male concluded, "the world's survival depends on you."

As soon as there was a target, the Directorate had put any number of parallel projects—perhaps a thousand of them—into development. Most of the groups had not found a suitable host Portal. Even those which found such a portal were beset with problems—perhaps greater than the problems of the Contact Team, perhaps just less adequately surmounted.

The three of them had been certain for a week that no other group was close to coming on line. They had been chosen from the scores, from the thousands of their recent peers, to be the group which programmed Portal Four for use. But what that fully meant had not been clear until this moment and the personal appearance of the Directorate.

"There have been problems," Keyliss agreed. She nodded toward the floor, which had provided a burning ghat for Barry Rice. The nod was the wrong motion to have made. Surprise had overcome memory of nausea, but that nausea was ready to reassert itself. Swallowing back the lurch of her stomach, Keyliss continued, "One of them was there, yes. We think we've taken care of it."

Astor cleared her throat and said, "There'll be more trouble, Your Worships. The project is attracting more local attention, involving more people. We didn't want that, but it's happened and it was going to happen. Your Worships." She had drawn herself up very stiffly. Feelings of respect made Astor almost more willing to fail the world than to fail its Directorate. The same respect forced her to be candid about the difficulties. It would have been irrational to try to gloss over the blast-scarred flooring; but the whole situation was irrational, and another personality would have tried to hide the obvious.

"We are on schedule, Your Worships," said Selve. Keyliss, having asserted her personal honor and dignity, was now deliberately donning her atmosphere suit. Selve reached out a hand to steady his colleague and proclaim their joint identity. Astor was sidling closer as well, though

her eyes remained turned deferentially toward the Directorate. "The locals have minds of their own," Selve continued. He pointed toward the gouge in the floor. "That
means there are problems for us, for them. Somebody died
because he had a mind of his own. But it also means that
the project goes forward, as it couldn't if we had to
make all the decisions."

"Your Worships," Astor resumed, "there is no help
you could give us now except time and troops. And there
is no way to be certain of holding Portal Eleven by force;
not undamaged, not even for the brief time we need to
make the final calibration. Not even if you transferred the
whole of Base Four there."

"So you all agree?" said one of the Directors. A tiny
smile modified the smooth contours of her face. "The
freedom you have given your locals—or they have taken—
that is necessary for success?"

"Yes, Your Worships," said the members of the Contact Team in unison. They spoke without haste, but they
spoke in mutual certainty despite the fact that they did not
bother to look at one another before speaking.

A Director coughed. "As you say," he said, "there are
only two things that might help. You don't need troops."

"And unfortunately," said another Director, "we can't
offer time, either."

"But we are on schedule," Keyliss blurted in surprise.

"We fear that others are, too," said a Director.

"Anomalies in the magnetic envelope are recorded as a
matter of course."

"But it takes time to check them. Sunspots, Portal
activity all over the planet."

"Sometimes even a meteor can be responsible. Everything is recorded. It can be checked, can be eliminated,
but it takes time."

"Except that this time, there is an anomaly that couldn't be explained. Except as a small-scale transport, a probe too tiny to call immediate attention to itself."

The Directorate paused. Through dry lips, Astor said, "Your Worships, the locals at Portal Eleven built an ungoverned unit of their own. Perhaps . . ."

The male Director gestured negation with one finger. "The anomaly occurred almost six months ago," he said. "Five months and twenty-seven days."

"One day," said Selve, who needed no one to help him with calculations, "before our project was put into effect. You think they discovered us simultaneously."

The Director who had smiled now smiled again. "We did not wait a day to act," she said. "We doubt that the Vrage waited, either, once they had the information. The day they lead us may mean nothing. There are so many variables, so many things to go wrong. . . ."

"Your Worships," said Astor. Tears began to well from her eyes. She knelt, not only in reverence but because her knees suddenly quavered too much to surely support her. "We can't make Portals Four and Eleven come in phase more often than they do, so we can't speed up the schedule. But we won't fail you. Whatever it takes."

The sun was setting past the open door. Its rays, diffracted by the force screen, bathed the Directorate in auroral splendor.

" 'Rise, shine, give God glory,' " sang Charles Eisley, very much under his breath. The Foreign Servive officer lay on his back, covered by the sheet in which his toes made two tented mounts. It was particularly easy to suck in his belly from this position. For the first time in Eisley's life, morning was becoming something halfway to look forward to.

Not that gravity's effect on his paunch had much to do with his relative cheerfulness.

Eisley slid a hand between the upper sheet and lower to pat Sue Schlicter's haunch. The woman wore a pair of nylon briefs, but the flesh of her thigh below them was firm and dry and warm. " 'Rise, shine, give God glory,' " he repeated somewhat louder, with his lips caressing his mistress's earlobe. His mind was on the last verse of the stanza, but no one could have determined the words, much less the tune, from his cracked mumble. " 'Soldiers of the cross.' " He licked the inner surface of her ear.

"Umm," said Sue, turning so that she could slide both her arms around his neck. Her eyes were still closed, but her lips smiled as they kissed his. "It's Saturday, silly." Her right nipple began to harden as it brushed his hairless chest. "Or did I convince you that we ought to go watch this next experiment ourselves?" Her eyes were still closed.

"Can't you see?" murmured Eisley. "I'm bursting with enthusiasm. You've wrapped me around your little finger, shameless wench, bent me to your will." It was often easier to tell the truth when he made a joke of it. His whole working life had trained him for deceit.

Sue's arm maneuvered under the sheet itself. "Dunno," she said, "it doesn't feel very bent to me." She giggled, then opened her eyes and leaned back so that they could actually look at each other. "You really do want to go, Charles?" the black-haired woman said. "You were right last night, there's nothing we could do there . . . like you can for Mustafa behind the scenes, I mean. I just thought it would be exciting."

Eisley bent and gave the woman beside him a brief peck, as chaste a kiss as could have been bestowed on a nipple. "I thought it would be exciting, too," he said, "and that was why I was against it. I've gotten used to never doing the interesting thing, because it might not be dignified. . . . And last night it struck me that in all the years I've spent in the Foreign Service, the two days I remember most—I don't know, warmly, I suppose—are the day we destroyed the consulate records in Nha Trang, and the day I was ambushed west of Malatya."

"You never told me about that," the woman said. All her muscles had briefly tensed.

Schlicter's hand was still on the man's groin. She felt his penis shrink with the shock of what he had just admitted. "Didn't I?" he said aloud. "Well, I don't talk about it very much, I suppose." He started to sit up.

Sue held Eisley's shoulders down, gently but firmly, with her left hand. Her right swept the sheet down till her feet could kick it fully clear of their bodies. Her briefs were a bright crimson. "Right, we're going to go off and do exciting things in a little bit," she said. "But right for now, we're going to stay here and do exciting things instead." She bent over.

Eisley's hand stroked the woman's back, as bony and supple as a snake's. Was this the heart of the allegory of the Garden of Eden? Aloud he said, "Well, I'll just never forgive you—oh, God—if we're late and I don't get in. Never."

The woman ran her tongue around the tip of his member, which had stiffened again instantly as her lips enfolded it. "First things first," she said. She chuckled. "First this. Then you get in. And then we go off and watch time machines." And her lips went back to what they had been doing a moment before.

The globe on the kitchen table was larger than it had been the night before. That was initially more of a surprise than what the bud within was doing. Buds were intended to grow, after all. Inanimate objects should retain their rigidity as well as their glassy perfection.

Sara Jean poked the—bubble. It had flattened and was no longer globular. There was noticeably less fluid within than there had been; the remainder rolled sluggishly. She carried the container over to the stove and turned on the light in the exhaust hood for a powerful, close-up illumination of what had been merely a bud.

"A bowl," Selve had said, and it was clearly going to be one. The feathery petals of the night before had flattened and expanded into a surface six inches in diameter. The leading edges were still translucently thin, but the center of the hollow had taken on an amber solidity. There were coffee-colored veins swirling from that center toward the edges.

If the container had kept its original shape, the crystalline walls would have cramped the growing bud into their own upward curve. Sara Jean had in fact supposed that was the intent, that the external shape molded the growth like a living form of plaster of Paris. Instead, the edges drove the container at least a millimeter ahead of themselves, squeezing the crystal lower as it became wider.

"Oh, there you are, dear," said Henry as he walked through the door. He was pulling on his tie from habit, although there was no need to be concerned with patient acceptance this morning. "I wonder if they'll bring that fellow back today, Rice. I'll believe they can deal with brain death and trauma that extensive when I see it, I must admit."

"I won't—I don't intend to go anywhere," the woman said. She turned out the light and turned to her husband with a wan smile. "Not that I did the first time. But I'd like to see Selve again, to take him this."

On the kitchen table was the goblet Sara Jean had set

out even before she went to bed. It was not her largest work, nor were its walls necessarily thinner than those of any of her other efforts. It was, however, as nearly a perfect rendering of her intent as she worked on it as anything she had ever created.

"Well, all right," said Henry, a verbal nod of dismissal to the subject. "We'd better get moving, then." He brought his car keys out of the side pocket of his coat.

"I'll drive," Sara Jean said as she set the goblet into a paper-lined box and covered it. "I'm parked behind you, remember. And I know the way to the school of engineering." Her lips smiled in a hard face.

As they walked out the door together, Sara Jean asked, "Henry, do you ever notice me? As a person?"

"For God's sake," her husband said, "of course I do. If you want to drive, then drive. I just don't want to miss this business."

"It's the doctor from last night and his lady," called Mustafa Bayar. The Turk had opened it at the knock in the hope that Charles Eisley would be there. Instead of stepping aside, Mustafa now stood in the doorway opening and called for instructions.

"Well, of course let them in!" Chairman Shroyer retorted, breaking a sentence of his discussion with Louis Gustafson and two Travelers to do so. "Hank, over here! You're still determined you want to go in on this?"

"Couldn't be more so," Layberg responded as he walked in without even the notice of Bayar that one gives a servant.

There had been no air circulation overnight. The air had cooled, but it still had an unpleasant undertone, as if a rat had died somewhere in the maze of equipment. Sara Jean's nose wrinkled, though she had been subconsciously prepared for the bite of chlorine which had struck them the night before. There was no sign of that, and no one had explained enough about the—machine—to her for her to know whether either reek had anything to do with what was going on.

Isaac Hoperin was inside the fencing, but he had no task and no particular interest in the preparations going on. He strolled through the docking area, oblivious to the possible danger. He said through the wire to Lexie Market, "I hadn't realized that Louis had gotten you into this, too. Do you have any sort of a handle on what really is going on? I certainly don't, and I've—well, been a part of it. Gone back."

"Barry Rice got me in on this last night," the woman said. She rubbed her hands together as if they were cold. Lexie had been very doubtful about coming this morning. When she finally decided to do so, she had dressed with particular severity: her blond hair in a bun; a dark brown dress with sleeves and a high neckline; no jewelry whatever. "I gather this project was none of his business, really, but . . . since I got involved, I thought I'd better see if there was any word about him. About Barry." She didn't owe that bastard anything, and she knew that . . . but human interactions are not on the basis of deserts, but rather on either side of the personality of the individuals. Lexie could not ignore her memory of Rice's sprawled figure, even though the man had gone out of his way to bring himself to that pass.

"Rice?" Hoperin repeated. "I don't think I know him. What went on last night?"

"One of the engineering faculty made an unsupervised transport," Market explained. Scientific detachment made it possible to answer all the relevant questions in a very few words. "He landed in what those—others—say was a chlorine chamber that's part of all this.'' She gestured with two fingers toward the pillars behind Hoperin. ''They also say that they can cure, can repair the damage to him. I—don't know that I believe them, but it was the only choice. They took Barry off with them when they left last night.''

''Chlorine chamber?'' the other physicist said. ''And in the circuit. . . . But what on earth would that . . . ?'' Hoperin was turning to survey the apparatus while his mind struggled to convert what he saw into balancing forces instead of physical objects. A vessel of chlorine not on any of the circuit diagrams or hinted in the formulae. His eyes lit on Astor. He stepped toward the Traveler, leaving Lexie Market wrapped in her own thoughts behind him and almost equally oblivious.

Astor opened the locker which she and two grad students, as before, had slid out of the docking area. It was an invariable rule that the Contact Team not transport to Portal Eleven holding their weapons. The locals were civilized, but—as Astor herself had reminded the Directorate—they were by no means so peaceful that a perceived threat might not be met by force. The guns could be issued only when it was clear that no one in the basement would take them amiss. For the previous demonstration, the weapons had been superfluous. That was by no means the case on this coming transport to Portal Thirty-one.

''Then the party,'' said Keyliss without quite shouting but making sure that all those affected could hear her, ''will consist of Louis, Isaac, Robert, and Henry.''

Sara Jean stood just at the edge of the group, waiting for a moment to talk to Selve. She found herself grinning. The Traveler's use of given names made the catalog sound like a preschool function of some sort.

Arlene Myaschensky said shrilly, ''And me. Arlene.''

The plump student had been helping shove against the locker transported with the Travelers. Now she wiped the sweat and dust from her palms onto the sides of her corduroy slacks. She picked up the purse she had set down for the task. "I'm to go on this, too. We agreed."

Professor Gustafson looked at the woman in some surprise. Her face appeared more flushed than her physical efforts required, and she was clearly upset about something. It wasn't like Arlene to act that way. "Well, yes, we did, earlier," Gustafson said in a doubtful voice. "Ah, I don't think it's really necessary that I—"

"No, no, Louis," said Isaac Hoperin from beside the open locker. "I don't even want to go again. This time, I mean. I want to watch the process occurring instead of being a part of it, this time."

"The numbers really don't matter," said Selve with a touch of frustration of his own. "We simply have to know what they are to set the controls." He walked toward the instrument panels as he spoke.

"What's this about a chlorine chamber?" Isaac Hoperin demanded with his head thrust forward. He did not touch Astor's sleeve, but his voice plucked the big Traveler's ear as she lifted out the shoulder weapons.

"This isn't the time—" Astor began. She was more irritated at the interruption than she was concerned by its subject.

"No, it's a good time," Hoperin broke in. His voice rose. The guns dangling before him by the tops of their slings would have subdued another man. They put the spark to the fuse of the physicist's temper. "Why are there parts of this—apparatus"—he waved in a controlled, chopping fashion—"that you haven't told us about? That aren't even here or when or whatever? Why have you been lying, and what are you covering up?"

"There are—scores of ways to achieve the same desired end; that is, time travel," said Keyliss. Astor was gaping, searching for a pattern of response. The most likely response to such an attack at home would have been violence, inappropriate here, but never buried very deeply in Astor's personality. Keyliss's interruption was as much on behalf of the mission as it was for her startled colleague.

Now she stepped a little apart from the group of transportees so that her motion would help to draw all attention toward her. "Like a car, Isaac," she continued. "Once the principle is determined, the details of, say, power source or suspension are fluid. This is a self-standing unit. There are other units of different design for other uses. That makes random testing very dangerous—but it's not something anyone is hiding from you." She reached out her hand to the physicist.

The graduate students traded glances about the twenty-foot triangle their locations described. All the tests of the great coils here in the basement had been successful—under the direction of the Travelers themselves. The same tests applied without the Travelers' knowledge to the table-top unit upstairs had no effect whatever on the objects the students had attempted to project temporally.

And yet the small unit worked, the previous day had proved that. There was a connection. It might be as innocent as a safety device, to save people like Professor Rice from their own ignorance . . . but there was a connection somewhere that only the Travelers themselves knew to make.

Mustafa Bayar stood with military stiffness, chin raised; certain in his assumptions but very doubtful about where his duty lay at this juncture. Mike Gardner opened his mouth to speak, to show what he knew rather than from any feeling that the truth needed to be published. Astor's lowering countenance and the guns she now seemed to grip with more than a bearer's affection chastened Gardner as it had inflamed Hoperin only moments before.

Paramount in Arlene Myaschensky's mind was the heavy purse she clutched to her side and the task her husband demanded she perform. Well, he did need the pictures, she could see that. And they would do no harm. And—though this was not even visualized, much less verbalized mentally—Arlene had always been fat, had always been raised as an unattractive child, though bright. Dave Myaschensky had been the first man to take notice of her. At a very deep level she doubted her ability to get through life without him. If the choice were losing Dave or losing her career through some scandal connected with this project, then she would take the photographs for her husband and she would not raise any objections which might delay the test.

Hoperin looked at Keyliss's hand in puzzlement, as if he were trying to fit it somehow into a puzzle: the inexplicable hardware around him, and beyond that, a world where napalm incinerated infants. He took the hand in a combination of ordinary courtesy and scientific wonder at an offered datum. Keyliss was shorter and far slighter than the balding physicist. His anger was at authoritarian lies. It would have been absurd to direct that feeling against Keyliss's gentle reasonableness. And yet . . .

Selve had made the last entry at the terminal fed by the mainframe computer on the first floor. He studiously refused to look at his colleagues, either Astor's honest anger or the false, pellucid believability of Keyliss at this moment. He turned his head to take himself out of the tableau of which he was a part.

Sara Jean Layberg shyly held out to him the small box she carried. Their eyes met and he was at once grinning, in relief at the change of mental subject as well as in pleasure.

"It's not—" the woman began, but she stopped herself. It *was* much of a gift; she knew it, and Selve was artist enough to see that himself. "The bowl you gave me is already beautiful," she said, "and it's fascinating to see it happening that way, too. I wanted you to have this."

It took Selve a moment to realize that the box was a top friction-fitted to a bottom, each portion being five sides of the six-sided prism they formed together. The goblet was incredibly delicate for its material and manner of construction. How fingers could know the thickness just the safe side of cracking in a high-fire kiln was beyond him, utterly beyond. "This is beautiful," said Selve. "I will treasure it."

He would. He would use the focused power of the unit at home to stabilize the goblet, even if they executed him as a result for misuse of the equipment. . . . But that would be afterwards, after the project was complete and its effects were completely irreversible.

"Take this, Selve," Astor demanded in a low, angry voice. She was holding out a gun to the male Traveler. She glowered equally at him and the local woman with whom he chose to talk at this time. "Are we ready? We have a very narrow entry window on this one, you know."

"I've done my work, yes," Selve replied with a sullen harshness. He gripped the weapon at its balance but deliberately refused to pull it out of Astor's hand. "Sara," he said, "I'll have to ask you to hold your vase until we return. It's—very important to me. Thank you."

Astor started to say something further. Either she thought better of it, or she was interrupted by Keyliss calling, "Will all those who are being transported please join me in the docking area? Selve, you may start the timing sequence now."

From that announcement on, the preparations were a

matter of mechanics for Gustafson and the three Travelers. The professor walked to the center of the docking area with the bemusement of a man entering an elevator while thinking about other things. The Travelers checked their weapons in more than cursory fashion and positioned themselves equidistantly, just within the circle on the floor.

The locals on their first transport reacted with far more variety. Henry Layberg rubbed his hands and patted Chairman Shroyer solidly in the middle of the back. "By God, Bob," he said aloud. "By God."

Shroyer was stepping toward the marked circle with the hesitation he would have shown approaching an unfenced excavation. Layberg's arms and enthusiasm were both of them offensive to the chairman's hesitance. He twisted his head back toward the propelling arm, trying to smile good-naturedly but achieving something between a scowl and a fearful rictus. His friend did not notice, though Sara Jean, watching through the wires, did.

Arlene Myaschensky walked with a careful stiffness suggesting fear of another kind: that of a child still erect and awaiting the final round of a spelling bee. Mike Gardner nudged Mustafa Bayar as they took their places at the control panel. Both of them watched their fellow student with narrow-eyed concern. Arlene's rigidity had a drugged look to it, very unlike the woman's normal personality even when an endeavor was going wrong. She stopped, facing in the direction she had been walking to enter the docking area. There was no reason to turn toward the control panel, but the rest of them had done so naturally enough. Myaschensky stood close to the three men, but her mind was in another level of existence.

The reflectors of the overhead fluorescents, then the wires of the enclosure, blurred as the coils rose through their harmonies. Henry Layberg's look of wondrous excitement faded. His arm on the chairman's back tensed in something more than camaraderie. Professor Gustafson leaned toward Shroyer from the other side and shouted, "I've been a little worried about mechanical damage to the coils. We gave each layer a coat of epoxy paint before we wound the next one, but that may have been too brittle to st—"

It was not too brittle to stand up to at least this further use. The flash, invisible to those it served, intervened to thrust Gustafson and his companions out of their present world while in midsentence.

"Oh!" said Robert Shroyer. He placed his feet and hands as if to take up the shock of a long fall.

"Uh!" echoed Henry Layberg beside him. The MD stared around in renewed wonderment.

"It is a strange feeling," Professor Gustafson said, "but it seems to pass away as quickly as it occurs." He paused, remembering what Selve had said the previous night. "I suppose multiple, ah, twistings of the same sensation could be more than disorienting, however," he added.

"We've drifted!" Astor snarled to her companions and the world about them. They should have been in a clear, rocky area. Instead they were in a forest of huge spikes like nothing so much as bamboo with stems ten feet in diameter. That in itself was not of great concern, but there was also a great deal of undergrowth. Mostly it was of soft-stemmed bushes with blackish, multilobed leaves. The leaves were as effective as so many bead curtains in hiding the members of the party from one another—and hiding also any of the extremely dangerous life forms which might be lurking nearby.

The test had been necessary for final calibration of the system. The Contact Team had intended it also to be final proof to the locals—particularly the chairman—that the time machine was real and was safe, so long as it was operated under the team's supervision. The result of this transport was by no means safe. It was to be hoped that the locals would not have reason to learn just how great the potential danger was.

"Please, nobody wander," said Selve in a nervously high voice. The dark suits that the Travelers wore made them invisible to one another and almost so to the locals, who were virtually within arm's length of their guides. Selve's face bobbed like a white blur behind a curtain. He spread the focusing muzzle of his gun for the broadest-possible coverage, then narrowed it again when he realized that the range was so short that only a beam of the highest intensity could ensure safety.

The humidity was high in comparison to that in the basement from which they had just been transported. It was the healthy, cool atmosphere of vegetation transpiring rather than the peat-laden acidity of Professor Gustafson's previous experience with the equipment he had built. Now the professor plucked one of the leaflets waving in his face and rubbed it between one thumb and forefinger. The leaf surface was too slick and firm to gall beneath his skin's pressure.

The Travelers were backing and sidling toward one another. They needed to talk in reasonable privacy, but they needed all the more to keep a lookout in every direction. "How long did you set this transport for?" Keyliss rasped over her shoulder to Selve as she neared him.

"Please, stay close," her male colleague called to the locals.

* * *

Arlene Myaschensky did not need to sneak away as she had expected. She walked through one spray of dark vegetation, then another, and around a bole of waxy smoothness. It was the size of a water tower. She relaxed as completely as if the wires holding her up had been clipped. She pressed her right palm and cheek against the tree trunk and drew long, silent breaths with her eyes closed.

The tree was cool to Myaschensky's touch, but the quivering it transmitted from the upper air made it seem animate and even friendly to her need. When she opened her eyes, she was an adult again—and an engineer with a task to perform. Nothing in her fellows' chatter, muted by the foliage, suggested that Arlene's absence had been noticed.

There were plenty of insects, at least; she had been afraid she would have to search for them desperately over a barren landscape. Creatures ranging in size from dust motes to dragonflies glittered through the vegetation. Occasionally, one of them would land on the tree, generally where sunlight dappled the creamy bark.

In order to give herself working space, Myaschensky trampled down several stems from a clump of the dark-fronded vegetation. In gross outline the plants reminded her of mimosa, though the color and texture of the leaves were quite different. With part of the spray crushed beneath her jogging shoes, she had ten square feet of the trunk clear as a background for her photographs. She opened her purse and lifted out the bulky unfamiliarity of the old camera which her husband had fitted with extension tubes. She could now concentrate on the task before her. That permitted her to forget about Dave on the one hand, and on the other about Professor Gustafson and the project—all the people she might shortly fail or betray.

An insect as long as her forefinger landed on the bark in

front of the woman. It had four wings and a pair of eyes like cabochon-cut sapphires. Arlene put her eye to the camera's viewfinder and began to lean in to focus, the way her husband had instructed her.

"Well, what's the problem, then?" Henry Layberg said. He spoke with the determined authority of a high official confronting an unruly group of his subordinates; but it was to the preoccupied Travelers that he spoke. Layberg stood with his hands on hips and his chin raised, just short of belligerence.

・ "What?" demanded Astor as she glanced around abruptly. She made a pitchforking gesture toward the surrounding foliage with the muzzle of her weapon. "This is your Mesozoic, remember. There are animals here that can be quite dangerous, and we aren't quite—"

"Here," said Keyliss an instant before her bigger colleague backed into her.

"Right," Astor muttered. The three Travelers were tightly together again. To Dr. Layberg, Astor completed her previous comment: "We seem to have transported a short distance from the clear area we had intended."

"It isn't necessarily a fault in the hardware," said Keyliss, now that she had taken time to think. She muttered to exclude the locals from her conversation, but she continued to speak in English. Her training was not to be overruled for such reasons as had appeared thus far.

"The programming wasn't at fault," Selve said. He spoke crisply, to hide the suspicion that the fault was indeed in the programming—and in himself. "This is the third test, after all. It should be just the final cue-in."

Astor was glaring ferociously at the centrifugal locator built into her belt pack. She had dialed it to the absolutes for Portal Thirty-one. If that was correct—if they had not somehow exited through the wrong Portal entirely—then they really were within a few miles of their intended point of entry. It was inconceivable that two Portals would have such nearly identical intersections of rotational moment and magnetic field that the location readings would correspond to that degree. On the other hand, the location of a Portal, once fixed, should be no more subject to change than would the wavelength of a beam of light. Something had to be wrong, either with Selve's programming—which Astor did not believe—or with the hardware back at Portal Eleven. Either way, the situation meant delay and perhaps disaster.

"No, we're forgetting the extra unit, the one they'd built upstairs," Keyliss was saying calmly. She was holding back her own fear of failure with a sheet of icy reason. So long as she did not have to dip beneath that surface for data stored deeper in her mind, she could perform with mechanical precision even now. "It's out of the system now, but it wouldn't have been during the previous tests. Mightn't have been. That could throw us off."

"A little over two miles," Astor said to the locator. She grimaced around a quarter circle of their surroundings. "I can't believe that short a distance could—go from mostly bare rock to mostly this." She snatched at a dangling frond. After considering it, she stripped the leaflets between her thumb and palm, more in frustration than for any reason.

From far away, but from no particular direction because of the foliage, came a sound that could have been thunder or a rock slide. At the end of its tremble, the sound rose into a fluting warble—bird or animal, surely distant . . . and surely huge.

Keyliss swallowed. "A watered valley, a valley that isn't . . . It doesn't matter now, surely?"

Louis Gustafson had knelt down. He was peering at a stem some feet from the point to which he had been initially transported. "Robert, come look at this," he called. "You, too, Dr. Layberg. I think you'll be interested."

The other two men were looking about them with pursed lips and a feeling of growing concern. The sound—the bellow, distance-weakened though it was, had given point to the Travelers' nonspecific warnings. A cow would have sounded much the same, of course. In fact, the bellower was probably just that—a very large, very harmless equivalent of a cow. But the surroundings whose close sameness had been as boring as the interior of a rhododendron thicket now regained a degree of interest unconnected with their immediate physical presence.

Layberg and Shroyer did move closer to Gustafson, however. The engineer bent at the waist after throwing an openly nervous glance toward the Travelers, who were still arguing among themselves. Dr. Layberg squatted instead— bobbed up to tug his trousers higher over his knees—and squatted again. He had to put one hand on the loamy soil to keep from overbalancing, and the extensor muscles in his thighs began to burn immediately.

"You see?" said Gustafson. There were tiny yellow flowers hanging from the underside of the stem. Gustafson jiggled one from beneath, then drew his forefinger away. On the pad of the finger were orange specks. The others assumed the color was pollen until they saw the specks were beginning to move: mites or larvae of some sort, living in the cup of the flower.

Layberg squinted and leaned forward against his balancing hand to see if there was anything of particular note about the specks. That was not Gustafson's point, however. The engineering professor had already wiped his fingertip on the opposite cuff. He then tapped another flower, one farther along the stem and thus closer to the area into which the group had been transported. "Now, see this," Gustafson said as he displayed his fingertip again.

"There are no insects in that flower," Chairman Shroyer said, limiting himself to facts and not the interpretations of which he had not a clue at the moment.

"From here on up, nothing," Gustafson agreed. He nicked the stem about a yard from the base with his square-cut thumbnail. "Farther back, they all do. Our transportation field took the little bugs out of all the flowers within it, but it left the flowers themselves and the plants—even the ones right in the middle." He waved, but the other men did not bother to glance at what they knew was behind them. "Quite a sharp line, really. And you see, Robert—just as they said it was."

Beaming, Gustafson gestured again. This time all three of them turned to stare toward the fiercely arguing Travelers.

"No," said Selve, hunched over the answer he had just drawn from the calculator and control unit on his wrist. "Modulation by the small unit at that point couldn't have thrown us off by this amount, not twice and so precisely. The period of the coils is too different whatever point you start at. Once, perhaps, though I doubt it. Not—"

"Do we know it was twice?" Astor demanded as the tip of an explanation intrigued her. "We don't know exactly when the small unit came on line, do we? Or if they made modifications to it between our first test and our second?"

"Right," said Keyliss, not because it was the answer but because it might be the answer. She straightened from the huddle into which the three of them had merged. "Arlene!" she called. "Arlene! Would you please come over here for a moment?"

There was no sound but the susurrus of air across the tips of the high, spiky flora.

"Arlene!" Astor bellowed. She slipped her hands back onto the stock of her gun in ready position. "Where are you?"

"Oh, dear goodness," whispered Louis Gustafson as he scrambled to his feet. "I'll never forgive myself if something's happened to Arlene. . . ."

The camera was ill-balanced, but that made it easier to hold steady after a few trial shots. By supporting the weight wholly with the neck strap and her left hand on the lens, Myaschensky was able to trip the shutter with her right index finger. With luck, the images did not bobble at all in the viewfinder. The whick-clock sound of mirror and shutter shifting within the camera body startled the photographer every time it occurred, but it did not appear to concern her subjects.

It was still a frustrating business. Arlene was not trained to see insects. Dave had not encouraged her to—had savagely discouraged her from an interest in his chosen field. The shimmering wings that called attention to potential photographs also carried themselves blithely off into the foliage or the upper air again. Worse, as the woman bent cautiously to within the lens's ten-inch focal length, the blurred image would repeatedly flutter away before the shutter could be tripped. The insects flew either because of the looming bulk of a human; or because of the subject's own reflection in the objective lens . . . or from whim, their need to rest of shorter duration than Myaschensky's need to prepare to photograph them.

The task, though unfamiliar, was of no greater difficulty than, say, soldering cables to a ninety-six-post bus. The problem was that her time was limited: ultimately by the duration the Travelers had set for this test; and practically, because the others would surely notice before long that she had disappeared.

Partly with the idea of being searched for, Myaschensky tramped a further twenty feet into the glade. An unexpected splash of color turned out to be a thicket of vegetation whose every tendril seemed tipped with a red flower. They were the first flowers she had noticed. The tiny bells beneath the dark fronds had not caught her eye, and the insects they attracted were too small for her present equipment in any case. The clumped red flowers vibrated with the life feeding on them. In the air danced what might be the first butterflies Myaschensky had seen in these woods. She pushed her way toward them with more enthusiasm than she had felt in days.

There was a crash. A huge gap opened in the middle of the thicket. The gap, the tunnel through the flowers and the stems that waved them, was black and blotched gray green. It shifted. A clawed forepaw rotated to stuff more of the thicket, stems, flowers and all, into the great mouth. Only at that moment did it become a living thing rather than a fragment of an unfamiliar landscape.

It was too big to be alive. If it was no larger than an elephant, then Arlene had never seen an elephant only six feet away from her. The beast was darkly scaled, but large patches of fungus—the gray green—overlaid the facets as well as the color of the scales. The snout was beaked, but the head itself was almost houndlike in its hollows and overridged eyes. Though they could both face forward, the eyes were swiveling independently when Arlene accepted the reality of the creature. Her left hand had been holding the Nikon against her ample breast while she pressed her way through the foliage. Now she started to raise the camera while the rest of her body remained frozen.

The creature twitched, ramming within its mouth most of the rest of what it had bitten off. Some scraps fell to the ground. One chip of bark flew off as if to join the cloud of dismayed insects. The broad, whitish throat spasmed in a belch. An odor as sweet as that of crushed wisteria rolled over Myaschensky. Then the creature's eyes both locked on her.

The great herbivore had been eating its way through the thicket on its belly like a hog in slops. It whuffed with a vehemence that blasted scraps of the latest mouthful back through its nostrils. The beast scrambled to its feet, adding another yard to a ground-to-spine height that already over-topped Arlene.

The woman let her camera fall onto the neck strap and began backing away. There had been only a blur in the viewfinder. With the extension tubes behind the lens, the camera would no longer focus beyond arm's length. And what the metallic sounds of the shutter would bring was—

The creature squealed and stamped both forefeet. Myaschensky screamed with the abruptness of it. She did not panic, although she ran. Instead of trying to flounder back the way she had come, she dodged around the bole of the nearest of the giant trees. The oddly shaped tree was too big for even an elephantine creature to power through, and Arlene was confident that she could circle the trunk as fast as the monster could follow her. The foliage here did not include the vines and brambles of normal undergrowth at home, but it would have delayed her and not the lumbering beast which might pursue. She was terrified—too frightened to keep the camera from slamming her breast, too frightened even to shout for help and the Travelers' strangely shaped guns. Arlene's mind still worked in fine alliance with instincts honed in ages when such confrontations were the order of the day.

Toward the side of the tree on which she sheltered blundered another of the scaly monsters. This one was of significantly lighter body coloration than the first. From the pair of calves squealing at its flanks, it was probably a female. The adult saw Myaschensky and drew up with a steam-whistle screech. The very ground was quivering like a pond in a rainstorm. In the immediate area there must have been hundreds of clawed feet trampling with tons of weight above them.

The female slewed sideways to miss the tree and Myaschensky. The mother's shoulders turned the calf to her right. The pair of them angled off at a tangent from their previous, lethal course. The remaining calf danced in a bleating, half-ton circle of its own. The calf's tail, fully as long as its body, flicked at the waist of Arlene's corduroy trousers. She barely felt the contact, but the ridged scales were sharp enough to snatch parallel lines across the fabric.

For thirty seconds which seemed a lifetime, Arlene had not made a sound. She was not given to screaming, and the surrounding cacophony mocked any human attempt at sound. Now, as the calf bolted after its mother, the woman dodged back around the tree. The bark was smooth as a drumhead, the bole too broad for a dozen humans to clasp hands around it. Climbing was impossible. If scampering around the circumference was pointless, then at least it was something a body could do. Myaschensky ran now as a fish flops in a net. She was half-certain that she was running under the claws of the beast which had first startled her; that one, or a pair just as large.

There was no animal charging to trample her down like a squirrel which dithers in the roadway. The tangled thicket had sprung up again in surprisingly good condition, though most of the flowers that had led her to it initially were now stripped away. The general undergrowth still heaved as if in the aftermath of a windstorm, but the living thunder was settling away. The panic began to settle out of Myaschensky's mind, also. She let out her breath. Only then she realized how long she had been holding it. An insect with orange-and-purple wings fluttered by. Arlene's hands remembered the camera, still slung.

With no more sound than the whisper of leaves brushing it, something the size of the herbivore calves slid its way through the dark vegetation. The thing was magenta below and black above. Its skin was as smooth as a teardrop, with no projections to snag the foliage.

Arlene had consciously intended to look for the others of her group. She did not realize she had actually moved, however, until she backed away from the oncoming thing and it was a full step before the tree trunk slammed against her. She could hear human voices, not far away, but the blood in her ears was louder than the words.

The thing halted. It was in plain sight, though a spray of leaves and their shadows still blurred the back end. Arlene's tongue lifted to cover the tip of her upper lip. It was an unconscious gesture, meant as much as anything to silence her as she absorbed data. The thing did not touch the ground. Not at any point.

It was not hugely large, a side-lying cylinder six feet long and perhaps four in diameter. The front end had been bulged out into a half sphere. It was the top of this which was black instead of the incongruous hot pink of the rest; and it was the black portion which lifted up from the back like a clamshell. The creature inside stepped out of its conveyance.

Arlene began to sneeze so ferociously that she stumbled to one knee.

"Don't you move!" the creature demanded in excellent

English. Sunlight pumped through wisps of the yellow-green atmosphere released from the conveyance when it opened. "You will be cared for properly, but if you try to run, I'll blow you away."

The thing stepped toward Arlene. It was wearing what had to be a suit, a fabric of ceramic luster with the same magenta color as the body of the vehicle. The suit, even the black panel like an eyeslit across the bulbous helmet, was opaque. There could be no question but that the creature was inhuman, however.

One of its hands held vertically the axle of a translucent wheel the size of a pie plate. The device looked like nothing Arlene had ever seen, but its function could be guessed easily enough from the warning. The creature's other three hands were empty, and it was walking toward the woman on four spindly legs.

When the fit of sneezing left her, Arlene screamed again.

"Well, she's a sensible girl," said Chairman Shroyer in what was for him a compliment. "I'm sure she won't have wandered far. Miss Myaschensky?"

Something blatted like an air horn, then crashed through the nearby undergrowth like an eight-inch shell.

"Back to shelter!" roared Astor, very much within her element. She pointed with her left hand, not her weapon, toward the nearest of the tall trees. "Quick! We can't watch all ways if there's a herd!" She caught Louis Gustafson's coat by the shoulder and half tugged, half pushed the professor in the direction of safety.

"Don't shoot!" cried Selve. "We don't know where Arlene is!" His lips spread in a grin of terror.

With his own gun advanced at waist height, held at the grip and forestock, Selve was obviously the closest of the three Travelers to blasting away either by accident or intent. Keyliss was grimacing also, but she had jumped to interpose herself between the initial commotion and the three local males. Astor held her gun by the grip and the butt seated in the crook of her right elbow. Its muzzle slanted over the heads of her companions, a danger only to trees unless she chose to dip and fire it. Her free hand continued to scurry the locals to the tree that would block at least half the approaches of danger.

Twenty or thirty huge animals charged past the group. The creatures were divided into clots—a trio, a handful, handfuls more—rather than smashing across the landscape in a line abreast. Robert Shroyer, who had hunted ducks in his youth, was wonderstruck by the present similarity to flights of waterfowl coming in at evening. Only these beasts weighed tons, and it would require not a shotgun but a howitzer to bring one down. . . . The chairman looked from the thundering creatures to the Travelers.

Astor had shouldered her gun, but she was using her left hand to grip Selve's upper arm. Every time more of the black-and-mottled creatures made the nearby brush thrash, Selve raised his gun with a convulsed expression on his face. Astor's hand kept him from firing. Though the creatures repeatedly passed in view, despite the close cover, they invariably split to either side of the tree against which the party had backed. The huge spike of that trunk was visible at a distance, and the stampeding animals were prepared even in their panic to avoid it.

Keyliss also had her weapon raised. She held its butt an inch away from her shoulder, however, as if to disassociate herself from the gun's capabilities. The Contact Team was made up of persons with special abilities. Though they were all cross-trained, and though each of them was exceptional in his or her own right, only Astor responded to violent danger with a warrior's enthusiasm.

Twenty silent seconds that felt like an hour passed. No further monster forms could be heard stamping closer. "All right, let's find her," said Astor. The big female ported her weapon and let out a breath which showed how tense she, too, had been only moments before.

"Good God," said Dr. Layberg. He had been leaning back against the tree. The trunk flared at the base, more as if it were supported by a bulb than by normal roots. He levered himself fully upright. "What sort of dinosaurs do you suppose those were, Shroyer?" he asked.

"Yeah, we need to keep together," Selve said in tones as normal as his panting permitted. "All of us, please don't stray this time."

"How on earth would I know, Henry?" the chairman said curtly. Shroyer wiped the sweat from his palms onto his trousers. There was a rip under the right side pocket. He could not remember getting the tear, nor could he now at leisure see anything in their surroundings which might have snagged the cloth in that fashion.

The forest floor looked as if someone had been laying out paths with a spade. The nearest of the tracks forked some ten feet from the tree against which the party had huddled. During the stampede, the beasts had looked as huge as locomotives. Louis Gustafson knelt to touch one of the footprints. The claws had been driven down through the topsoil and had overturned a wedge of the dense yellow clay beneath. It was quite obvious that the beasts had been as dangerous as so many runaway locomotives.

By contrast, the dark foliage had come through almost unscathed. Trampled stems were springing up again from their common centers. Occasionally a spray would hang askew because the twig supporting it had been crushed, but even that was noticeable mostly because the plant's inner bark was a dull red. Leaves that the claws had torn were scarcely more ragged than undamaged fronds. For that matter, the toughness and slick finish which had kept a leaf from fraying in the chairman's hand had preserved others from the greater stresses of the stampede.

"Arlene!" called Selve again.

"Please don't stop like this, Louis," said Keyliss as she tapped Professor Gustafson on the back. She offered her hand to help the apologetic engineer rise.

The party had formed itself without formal discussion into a spearhead. Selve was at the point, using his gun as a staff with which to brush foliage out of the way. Selve treated the weapon with a nonchalance unusual for him, perhaps in reaction to his fixity on it during the stampede. There was a soapy odor in the air, an effluvium of the great beasts in panic. There were different sorts of insects as well. One with an iridescent orange body landed on Gustafson's wrist and stabbed him before the professor's other hand could slap it reflexively.

Astor and Keyliss walked behind and to either flank of Selve. The three locals were framed within the triangle of Travelers. The group's overall tension was much less now than in the instants after arrival. Before, the Travelers' concern had been with what had gone mechanically wrong with the transport and with what unknown dangers were lurking nearby. Now, the immediate dangers seemed to have exposed themselves, and the need to find the missing local overshadowed the long-term seriousness of the calibration discrepancy.

"We don't even know she went this way," Astor grumbled. Vegetation trampled down by the herbivores was springing back in the faces of the party as they moved against the direction of the stampede.

"Arlene!" Selve shouted again. The local men did not call out themselves. The chaos of the stampede had thrown them psychically under the guidance of the Travelers, who at least might understand what was going on in an alien universe. The huge animals had appeared as suddenly as a jack-in-the-box. That shock constrained the locals as no previous warnings could have done. It would not occur to them at this moment to shout into the forest unless they were literally directed to do so.

"This is the direction the herd was spooked from, Astor," Keyliss said from the other flank. "I'm sure she can't have gone—" She looked down. Her foot was tangled in a creeper lifted in coils from the ground when the animals stamped across it. Keyliss raised her foot out of the loose snare and continued, "Gone very far."

Beside Keyliss, a Vrage soldier stepped out of the foliage. The Vrage wore the usual magenta garment which acted both as atmosphere suit and body armor. In one of his hands was a raised weapon. Almost as shocking as the fact of a Vrage here was the way it acted. Instead of shooting from ambush and killing most or all of the party, the alien's vocalizer said in English, "Halt where you are. If you move, I'll blow you away."

Keyliss shot the Vrage in the middle of the chest. Her weapon was still turned up to maximum aperture from being used to cremate Barry Rice. It threw a cone which glanced from the magenta armor and shriveled foliage which the stampede had scarcely bruised.

The Vrage fired back. The horizontal disk of its weapon spun. The thin, rusty beam from the handgrip was merely an aiming plane. Though Keyliss's blast could not be lethal at its present dispersion, the shock and glare of it made the Vrage twitch his own weapon upward instead of sawing it carefully across his target.

The wand of reddish light flowed up the right side of Keyliss's chest, her shoulder, the gun she held, and her ear. The tough material of her gun resisted, but even it shrank toward the line of the invisible discharge like polystyrene touched by a flame. Where the beam crossed only flesh and fabric, the target divided on glass-smooth margins. Bone ends gleamed as coat and flesh fell away like bark from a veneer log. The right arm and the silenced gun it had held flopped to one side while the body itself collapsed the other way. Keyliss's ear, thrown off by muscle fibers spasming as they parted, fluttered away in a distant arc.

The air was full of blood and the sound of the Vrage weapon screaming like a saw on nails.

"They've got to be able to hear us," Sue Schlicter said angrily. She banged the door again with the heel of her hand and shouted, "Mustafa!"

"I think we best shouldn't emphasize our interest in Mustafa," Charles Eisley said. He touched Sue's waist and leaned past her to look through the door's small, wire-reinforced window. "For his sake, you know, with his superiors." Though Gustafson and his companions would certainly demand an explanation for why a pair of strangers wanted to barge in.

"Can you see anyone?" Sue asked in a subdued voice. She chewed carefully at the heel of her right hand to work out some of the bruised feeling from pounding.

The window gave a perfect view down the long aisle to the stairwell at the other end of the basement. Because of the angle, however, the closer meshes of the enclosure's cyclone fencing were a solid wall to anyone who wanted to see through them. By craning his head to the side, Eisley got a marginally better view into the end of the enclosure. No one was in sight behind the vertical coils, either.

"Maybe," he said aloud, "we can get in through the front of the building and find the stairs there." He nodded to indicate the far doorway, though Schlicter was not looking through the window anymore. She stood hipshot toward Eisley. Her waist beneath his hand was as soft and supple as his mood an hour before. The touch recalled that earlier touching. The diplomat squeezed Schlicter close in amazed delight.

Schlicter gave Charles a broad smile and a cheerful pat on the rump as she disengaged herself. "I've got a better idea," she said. The smile glowed wickedly across her face again. "Well, I've got a lot of better ideas, but right for now let's try the far door."

Twenty feet down the loading dock on which they stood was another metal door. This one bore the legend BOILER ROOM stenciled in red paint. There were no windows set into it. With Charles in tow by one hand, the tall woman strode toward that door.

"If they lock this one, the other surely's going to be locked," Eisley grumbled without heat or conviction. He did not really care about the business they were about. For the first time in his life, the veteran diplomat was feeling purely euphoric. The most marvelous part of the whole feeling was that it was not primarily physical. Not now, at least.

Schlicter worked the latch with her free hand and tugged the door open. "Voilà!" she said, waving Charles inward. He obeyed, wincing despite himself at what his mistress thought was French pronunciation.

The boiler room was large. It felt hollow, though it was nowhere near as big as the adjacent portion of the basement devoted to storage and experimental use. The heating plant was shut down at this tag end of summer, though stacked ladders and tools indicated that crews were working on the equipment during the regular work week.

While the boiler room was cool, it was not silent. As soon as the door opened, Charles and Sue could hear the hum and the resonances it wakened from the pipes and plates of the heating plant. For the moment, they did not connect the sound, the ambiance, with that which Bayar and Cooper had described as part of the operation of the time machine.

"Well, if this one opens," said Eisley as he took the lead, "then we'll see if the inside one opens, too." Still holding Schlicter's hand, he walked toward the door in the interior wall to their right. He was surprised to find that he had to raise his voice to be heard. The vibration was so all-encompassing that it did not seem loud.

"I wonder what they're doing in here?" the diplomat added as the inner door also swung open to his pressure. The metal of it trembled like a sparrow's heart in his grasp.

Selve spun toward the Vrage even before Keyliss fired at it. He cuddled his weapon down against his hip from instinct and against training. It was instinct again which froze his finger on the trigger: the locals beside him were bleating in amazement. Though they were not in the direct line of fire, they might . . .

Part of Selve's mind functioned with its usual clockwork precision. That part was correlating the appearance of the Vrage here with the wandering zero of the equipment that had transported their own party. The facts interlocked perfectly in one terrifying set of circumstances.

The air was aflame with Keyliss's shot, then tortured by the responding bolt that lopped Keyliss apart.

Unlike Selve, Astor was a dozen feet from the Vrage and could glimpse only a portion of its head through the vegetation and the bobbing locals. She made up for that deficiency with greater skill and a ruthlessness which was, in the circumstances, necessary. The spray of Keyliss's blast hid the Vrage for the fraction of a second before the alien's own weapon slashed through the fire.

Astor nudged her trigger. A bolt, not a cone or stream, curled and yellowed the wisps of Professor Gustafson's white hair. The alien's helmet gouted chlorine and gases vaporized from the body within. The Vrage's weapon continued to shriek and slant its marking beam up into the forest at a thirty-degree angle. The alien's limbs locked in position so that it stood like an abstract sculpture painted magenta.

"Get away, there'll be more!" Astor shouted. "They'll run to here!"

Henry Layberg threw himself down, not for cover but because Keyliss had fallen. Professor Gustafson touched his left hand to the side of his head. His ear felt sunburned, and some of his white hair crumbled brittlely beneath his fingers. He and Chairman Shroyer gaped at one another, then ran together into the undergrowth as they had been ordered to do.

Now with a clear field, Astor snapped a shot at the Vrage's weapon to silence it. There was a pop and a green flash like that of an arc across tungsten—nothing very impressive, certainly nothing to suggest that the limb holding the weapon and most of that side of the alien would disappear. A sphere a yard in diameter had been directly ionized by the uncontrolled release of energy.

"They've got a transport unit here!" Selve screamed as

if the Vrage weapon still keened ravenously across all normal sounds. Selve's face was distorted by indecision and fear.

"You've got to recall us," Astor said forcefully but with no undertones save those of command. "Nobody could do that but you. Get a few yards away, lie low, and—"

The snout of a Vrage antigravity vehicle brushed around the tree which had briefly sheltered the party. It was a light transporter closed against the hostile environment, not a weapons platform. For all that, the vehicle was heavily armored against just such chance as this.

Astor turned while her lips were still forming words. She notched a two-second burst across the center of the vehicle's frontal slope. The black portion was not a matter of aesthetics. Though the driver received all sensory impressions indirectly, a large portion of the frontal surface was made porous for such reception and transfer of data. This was, after all, a utility vehicle with armor, not a fighting vehicle per se. The black sheathing was resistant, but Astor's point-blank, full intensity burst carved the material like the skin of a sausage.

The red streak from the Traveler's weapon left spluttering fibers curling away from either side of the cut. There was a dazzling flash from within the vehicle. It was so intense that the car's body panels glowed like the flesh of fingers held over a powerful light. The car staggered a few centimeters to the ground over which it had been floating.

"Get going!" Astor shouted to complete her thought. "I'll keep them busy!"

Chlorine was drifting from the wrecked vehicle like smoke from a fire.

Selve plunged out of sight and out of the area targeted for the Vrages by the fighting. As his colleague had said,

Selve and the chance of recall were the only chance they had of survival. They: the transport party, and the world.

There was nothing Henry Layberg could do for Keyliss, but he was a doctor and he was going to try. The Traveler had fallen on her right side, hiding the extent of the injuries there. The severed portion lay beside the body. The cut surface rose from the point of Keyliss's hip to the middle of her shoulder joint. Blood and cellular fluids slimed the flesh now. Where the bone was dense, however, its ends gleamed in the light. The damage had been done without physical contact. The weapon cut like a microtome and polished objects smoother than jeweler's rouge could have done.

The damage to blood vessels was surely fatal, even though the beam had not sliced the internal organs. The greatest shock of Layberg's first human dissection had been the amount of the body's mass given over simply to transportation and support: bone and muscle, nothing more. The body cavity seemed absurdly small when emptied. Most of even that volume held intestines and the later stages of food processing. The brain had been yellow gray with death and embalming. It was a double handful, a liter and a half of the total body, but all that was required for the portion of life which was wholly human.

The brain and the life it embodied were dependent on the support system, and Layberg knew as he rolled Keyliss off her glistening wound that her support system was damaged beyond any but the most sophisticated repair—and that if the help were received at once.

Among the things that made Layberg gape with surprise was the way Keyliss's clothing—the severely professional charcoal-gray suit coat—was growing across the bloody wound. Tendrils were extending swiftly enough to be seen as moving. . . . The cut edge of the fabric was still as razor sharp as the Vrage weapon had left it, but the margin was now hemmed by a band of what looked like the silk of a spider's egg case. It was gauzy and cream-colored with a hint of yellow in it. Blood oozed across the new material from thousands of minor vessels severed when the Traveler's side was planed away. There was a vivid spurt from the brachial artery, although the attached tags of shoulder muscle were fully retracted as if to squeeze shut the tube through which life gouted. The gore soaked and darkened the coat itself, but none of it clung to the gauzy extension. Drops sparkled and beaded and slid away like mercury from a drumhead.

Layberg reached out to clamp the end of the brachial artery between his left thumb and forefinger. His other hand was thrusting frantically into his pocket to find something, anything with which to tie off the vessel. Something twitched beneath his clamping fingers. He squeezed harder, very hard indeed, and the cut end squirmed away from him anyway.

Layberg looked from his pocket to the wound. The center of the area—the original raw surface had totaled more than a square foot—was still slimy and dripping. The edges were being swept clear by the gauze, however, and that insubstantial fabric had just crawled fluidly between fingers pressed together with all Layberg's considerable power. The doctor more or less expected to see the surface beneath the transparent gauze distending with blood which Keyliss's heart continued to ram out the severed artery. Instead, the sheathing which had slipped over the artery like a liquid itself was sealing the vessel as completely as could a haemostat.

And the result was achieved without pressure on the wound. The artery was still clearly visible. Layberg probed it in a spirit of scientific fascination which he knew was better suited to nonhuman subjects. The surface gave at his touch like meat, like muscle prodded through a layer of skin. The fabric that now was sealing itself along the center of the plane of the injury was not acting as a pressure bandage and compressing the injury to rigid impermeability.

The ribs were quite evident. Their stub ends were sectioned as cleanly as slides waiting for the microscope. The extrusion from the cloth was no longer visible now that it formed a sheet without the raw wound for contrast. The gauze was a texture rather than a color, a matte finish which had stripped twigs and loam from the flesh as effortlessly as it had mooted Layberg's well-meant efforts.

Henry Layberg swore in wonder, and swore again even more softly. His index finger moved again. This time it did not quite touch the diaphanous layer holding in what remained of Keyliss's life.

Vrage weapons howled nearby. There were shouts in muffled and distorted English, always the same, "Halt! If you move, I'll blow you away. . . ." A brief hiss that might have been Astor's gun and a racking discharge which recapitulated the sound of the first alien vehicle being smashed.

And then there was something subliminal, too faint to be a sound and yet perceived by the doctor hunched over what should by now have been a corpse. Layberg cocked his head back over his right shoulder. A second Vrage car was floating past the wreckage of the first. The vehicle stopped gently as a thought the moment Layberg moved. The black viewscreen lifted silently.

The alien behind it was already pointing his weapon through the opening.

*   *   *

Even if the forest were as thick with Vrages as with its native herbivores, Astor knew that by freezing in concealment she could be almost certain of avoiding them. Any Vrage who stumbled over her would have made the worst of luck for himself. The Traveler's formal clothing was ideal camouflage in the current environment, while the atmosphere suits and enclosed vehicles which the Vrages required were a serious impediment to their own perceptions.

The problem with that tactic was that it would work for Astor, but for no other member of the party. The big female was too goal-directed to hesitate about sacrificing even Selve; and as for the locals, that decision had been made. Selve was necessary to the project's success. Selve would be struggling with the emergency controls, making calculations with apparatus which would be as useless to Astor as to any of the locals. If a Vrage found him concentrated on his task, Selve was dead despite the weapon beside him. It was therefore Astor's duty to focus Vrage attention away from the area in which Selve hid.

And that was just fine, because Astor had chosen to call attention to herself very simply: smash her way noisily through the undergrowth and depend on reflexes to blast anything colored magenta. That would be some slight recompense for Keyliss.

The Vrages could not have been more cooperative. Three of their utility vehicles in line ahead met her squarely as they raced toward the initial gunfire. The cars were moving at almost twenty miles an hour, too fast for conditions and their mechanically flimsy construction. Astor shot and dodged, a black shadow in a world of black shadows. The lead vehicle sprayed sparks and chlorine out its punctured windscreen. It lost speed, touched the ground, and exploded as the second car rearended the wreckage before Astor could snap her next burst into that planned target.

Foliage curled and yellowed along the track of her first shot and where the Vrage vehicles were scattering molten remnants of themselves.

The driver of the third car was very good. If he was as handicapped as his fellows by the conditions which the environment forced upon him, then he at least knew how to buy himself some time. His vehicle spun on its axis, short of the joined wreck of his leaders. Astor fired, but she had only the brilliantly armored flank for a target. Her stream of focused energy was an orange-white line till it struck the vehicle. Then the line diffracted into a garnet spray. It wilted vegetation for a hundred feet and stung the shooter's own eyes, but it did not scar the surface at which it was aimed.

Either the Vrage knew he had a single opponent, or he was operating as if that fact were true because he had no chance at all in a crossfire. By reversing he protected himself against that opponent and sent the vehicle back toward cover until more weight could be brought to bear.

The car dodged behind one of the giant trees. Astor rose and sawed through the bole.

It required a four-second burst, which meant the woman had to override all her training to accomplish what was necessary. She was no trembling neophyte to freeze on the trigger and chance cooking her gun when she needed it most.

But right now she needed the tree. Its rigid cells were blasted away a handsbreadth to either side of the beam. The trunk was hollow, though here near the base something close to a third of the diameter was wood rather than weight-reducing void. Astor's gun could slice steel armor, given the time. It tore sideways through the wood at a walking pace.

Smoke and sparks spewed from the line of impact. They

were virtually smothered by the steam into which thirty gallons of cellular fluid were flash-heated. Astor was aiming down at a slant. The earth spattered beyond the tree and blazed where it was mixed with enough organic material.

There was no certainty as to how the tree would fall. A light breeze with the spike's hundred feet of leverage could have toppled the whole mass back toward Astor. Worse, if it slipped sideways, the top could threaten Selve more imminently than did the Vrage soldiers who were searching for all of them. War is not a business which can be conducted without risk; and, in the event, the tree crashed down onto the low side of the cut, away from the Traveler.

The Vrage had equated "unseen" with "unthreatened." He was broadcasting a call for support. This was not the magnetic anomaly the Vrage troop had been sent to investigate. The location signal from his car was the beacon to which his fellows were being summoned. The Vrage popped up his viewscreen and began to clamber out of the grounded vehicle with his weapon in his hand. The destruction of the two leading cars had shocked him. He knew that his opponent could even now be shifting for a clear field and the end of what the crackling ruin had started. At least on foot there was some chance to get off the first shot if he glimpsed a target through the curtains of foliage, through the play of wrong-colored light over and around his viewslit—

The speed at which the tree was falling was understated because of the object's size. The Vrage crouched in his vehicle's shelter and scanned the undergrowth for lurking gunmen. When the tree became a motion rather than a barrier in the Vrage's restricted vision, it was already far too late for him.

If the bole's speed had been in doubt, then its inertia

was not. The ground hollowed, then rose as the tree bounced upward. Nervous ripples in the soil succeeded one another half a step ahead of the sky-filling crash. The undergrowth did not affect the giant as it seesawed back and forth on its ends to find equilibrium. The car did not affect it, either, except that chlorine from the flattened vehicle bleached a broad swatch of the outer bark.

The Vrage's death had even less effect on his environment: his suit lost all semblance of shape, like a squashed foil wrapper. The fluid which leaked through every flattened joint was a saturated copper-sulphate blue that pooled and darkened on the magenta armor.

Astor sprinted twenty feet. Then she flopped on her belly, half curled around the multiple stems of a clump of the prevalent undergrowth. She found she had fair visibility through the curtains of compound leaves brushing the forest floor. Good enough to see and respond to a flash of purple-red suit, at any rate.

By staying low, Astor could avoid the wild blasts with which Vrage soldiers were even now slicing the vegetation— and likely one another, as the only sentients erect in the forest. They would come to seek her and seek an answer at this place where their fellow had summoned them and died.

Astor hoped that Selve would not finish his business before she herself had the opportunity to greet the Vrages again.

The alien who confronted Arlene Myaschensky paused a yard from her. It looked uncannily like a huge spider in a posture of defense: four legs planted firmly on the ground, the other four lifted with the thorax toward a perceived threat.

But Arlene was not the threat, was not *a* threat, as she knew and the alien must know.

Its head was a flattened bubble on the human-sized torso. The only facial feature was the band which looked like six inches of electrician's tape across the smooth magenta. That twisted a full 180 degrees away from the kneeling woman and back toward the vehicle from which the alien had stepped.

Arlene coughed sharply, rendingly. The head's arc of movement was that of a machine, not a living thing; but a machine's internal workings would not require a chlorine atmosphere. She started to rise.

The head spun back to a 0-degree, not 360-degree, attitude. Two hands with opposable thumbs but mittened fingers grasped her shoulders. The translucent disk now nodded very close to her. Although it was cold and no more outwardly threatening than a piece of shower stall, Myaschensky felt the object's presence deep in the reptilian valleys of her mind.

"If you move," insisted the alien's voice as he tugged her upright, "I'll blow you away." The incongruous words came from somewhere in or on the creature's chest. Myaschensky recalled what Mike had said about the Travelers speaking the night before through apparatus seemingly woven into their orange suits. But this could not be Selve, could not be Astor or Keyliss, this spider-limbed thing which tried to pull her toward it.

"If you move, I'll blow you away!" the voice repeated. Context put a tone of anger and frustration into the words which were in reality mechanical. The alien could not really speak to her. It could only parrot that single phrase like a desperate tourist who needs a restroom but can only ask for directions to a hotel. Myaschensky realized that the distorted hands that clung to her were no stronger than a child's. She tensed to slap the creature away in loathing as if it were a pawing wino.

The alien gestured toward its vehicle—with its weapon.

Arlene's heart jumped. Her feet shuffled of their own accord, hindered rather than guided by the sprawl of limbs beneath the reddish-purple suit.

A forest giant crashed lingeringly to the ground, somewhere close but hidden by the undergrowth through which burst Doctors Shroyer and Gustafson, close together and both looking over their shoulders toward the sound of the falling tree.

The alien's head rotated, and the weapon in his hand swept toward the newcomers. This time, the alien did not bother to voice a warning.

The falling tree had beaten Shroyer and Gustafson from cover like quail, straight into the sights of the gunner.

Henry Layberg had seen death and persons brought back from it often enough to feel a certain scientific detachment even now. He reached for Keyliss's crumpled gun as the only hard object in the landscape. The Vrage extended its own weapon with a quick assurance.

A thumb-thick beam of fire hosed from the undergrowth and splashed on the sides of the floating vehicle.

Astor was the only one of the Travelers who could be expected to do the right thing with a gun. Selve had been lucky enough to remember to focus his beam tight, however. He was less fortunate in his target. He had a fragmented but surprisingly good view at ankle level from the bower in which he furiously tried different parameters. When the fourth trial setting failed to get any more response than the three before it, Selve had grimaced and stared sidelong at nothing in particular. He could see

Layberg and Keyliss sprawled. The swatches of magenta a few yards away made a fully understandable tableau.

Astor—in Selve's position—would have ignored what was about to happen. Selve could not ignore it. He snatched up his gun and ripped a long burst into the egg-shaped vehicle.

The lance of fire became a cascade where it hit the armor. The edge of the lifted windscreen crazed and went milky where redirected energy washed it. Layberg's outstretched arm flashed hot. Fine hairs curled on the back of his neck. The car continued to float without structural damage. The Vrage driver was untouched because of the angle of the shot. He leaped out of his vehicle, keeping its armored side between him and the Traveler's gun.

Selve could not have marked his own location better with a series of billboards. Foliage within a yard of his beam had shriveled and turned yellow. Because Selve had swept his burst down the length of the car, the yellow scar was an arrow with him at the apex. He had been trained to always shift position after firing. In the stress of an unexpected firefight, he instead hunched lower to the ground like a newborn fawn. His hands were mottled with their grip on his gun. His conscious mind prayed that he had done lethal damage to the Vrage. His subconscious screamed with the irrational certainty that he had not.

The Vrage was a soldier, not a technician with a gun. He sidled to the back of his vehicle, looking more than ever like a crab. His own weapon was poised and his four legs flexed, ready to bounce him up for a shot.

Henry Layberg rushed the Vrage from behind. He wasn't sure why. He had once seen a street mugging without feeling an urge to intervene. This was a dream world, a never-never land where ordinary conduct did not apply. He gripped Keyliss's ruined gun by the muzzle end as if it were a golf club.

The Vrage soldier's peripheral vision was as bad as that of a man wearing a mask. His sense of touch was still inhumanly good through his protective suit, however. He felt the impact of Layberg's first stride. He was turning back and dodging even before the doctor's foot hit the ground the second time.

Layberg swung in desperation. His gunstock missed the alien and even the weapon the alien was whirling to train on him. The clubbed gun smashed into and through the side of the car. Parts shorted explosively.

The magenta armor was atmosphere tight and could have turned the fire of the three Travelers' shoulder weapons in unison. Its mechanical strength was more on the order of plate glass, however. Layberg's follow-through carried him sprawling into the car because it shattered so easily under his blow. The Vrage gun screamed a line of dissolution over the doctor.

Something within the car burped. A section of sheathing ruptured from the inside and splashed itself across the alien's suit. The Vrage leaped backward like a cat from a hotplate.

Selve had steadied his nerves and his breathing. His first blast had cleared a field of fire even as it marked him. Now he squeezed off a half-second burst that would have made Astor feel proud. Chlorine and chlorine compounds puffed as the Vrage shrank around the hole in its torso.

Henry Layberg pushed himself upright. The side of the vehicle felt warm. When he tugged at Keyliss's weapon he found that it was already fused immovably into whatever was going on in the guts of the car. The Vrage curled up like a spider touched by a candle flame.

Layberg turned and looked down the yellow wedge

through the undergrowth. Selve stared back at him over his gunsights. The muzzle was cherry red and made the air dance above it.

"Get the hell out of here!" the doctor yelled in fury. The pointing arrow was as obvious as a retractor in an abdominal X-ray. "Get out of here, and for God's sake get us out!"

Shroyer and Gustafson gaped at the Vrage swinging its beam weapon to cut them apart. Arlene Myaschensky reacted as if the weapon lifting away from her head were a key turning to unlock her own personality. She lunged. The alien's hands on her shoulders were pressures, not restraints. She caught the Vrage's gun arm before it bore and jerked it down just as the weapon fired.

The scream of the Vrage weapon was geometrically worse than anything else the woman had heard in her life. The purple beam zigzagged its line of destruction across the ground and undergrowth. Stems and leaves flopped away with no sign of burning or violence.

Arlene ignored the swath of destruction because the noise was driving her literally insane. She flailed with the arm she held as if it were a club to kill a snake. Instead of shouting to the men for help, she was crying, "Shut up, shut up, shut up!" to nothing in particular.

Shroyer and Gustafson could not hear her, but they stumbled to her aid anyway as soon as their minds cataloged the situation.

The Vrage was not as strong as Myaschensky alone and not nearly as strong as it was frightening. Its legs were as flexible as its arms, however, and the permutations of all eight limbs in a brawl were startling.

Two of the Vrage's hands were locked in Arlene's long hair, attempting to twist her head back. As Louis Gustafson awkwardly tried to pry one of those hands loose, a magenta leg kicked him off-balance and Myaschensky's struggles slammed the Vrage weapon down on the old professor's forehead. Gustafson sat down on the forest floor, his mouth opening and closing.

The spinning, shrieking weapon bounced from the hand from which no amount of simple shaking had been able to fling it. The relative hush was so sudden that the woman's shouts cut off in midsyllable also. Collops had been lopped from the trees while the weapon waved in wild figures. Chunks still falling from high up sounded like whispers in a cathedral.

Robert Shroyer flung himself onto the Vrage a moment after the weapon ceased to be a factor. The chairman's hesitation had not been cowardice so much as an unwillingness to alter the situation before he was clear as to the factors involved. He grasped two handsful of the suit and used his weight against those fulcrums. The Vrage had managed to stay upright against Myaschensky's tugging. Now all three went down, the alien more or less beneath the two humans.

Professor Gustafson blinked and touched his forehead. He lowered his hand and blinked again at the blood on his fingertips. There seemed to be no room for him in the thrashing brawl, but he started to get up to rejoin it anyway. The forest rotated. Gustafson blinked and sat down again hard. Beneath his right hand was the Vrage weapon. The professor began to examine the artifact with the care he would have offered to any other unfamiliar tool.

Arlene Myaschensky had moved in something approaching a trance from the moment the first of the herbivores had lurched into her awareness. The cessation of the gun's chalk-grating scream had brought back her intellectual control. The earlier hysteria had been useful, just as were the rages of tenth-century berserkers. Full awareness meant that Arlene's hands ached with their death-grip on the Vrage. Her scalp felt as if square inches of it were being tugged loose as Chairman Shroyer made the mistake of trying to pull free one of the alien's hands. It was a well-meant action, but it only added to the agony which was already scarcely bearable. Arlene shrieked.

Shroyer jerked instead with his other hand, the one which gripped the flexible surface of the alien's hood. The viewslit was stiffer than the armor proper and provided something of a handhold. The black slit came away and peeled the hood back as well. The suit lost its buoyant flexibility and molded itself to the Vrage like skin over a mummy's bones. There was a puff of gas from the sudden opening. Shroyer sneezed and coughed. In a tinny voice he blurted, "Watch it! Watch it!" and tried to pull Myaschensky away from the danger.

The Vrage's mittened hands opened when his suit did. All eight of his limbs flailed like those of a drowning man. Arlene was already rolling free, eyes shut and hands clutching her scalp as if to squeeze it back in place. There had been no real damage, but the whole right side of her head felt as if it were soaked in molten lead. Pain, not the chairman's warning, kept the woman from inhaling the poison that dissipated around her.

Robert Shroyer backed a step before he caught his balance. He was still holding the swatch of hood in his hand. The material had a metallic slickness when gripped on the outer surface. The inner side of the fabric was a drab brown. Hanging free as it was, the whole piece waggled like so much linen.

Gustafson, barely aware of what had gone on a few feet away from him, was immersed in his study of the Vrage weapon. His physical equilibrium had returned sufficiently that he could have moved if he had to do so; but there was no need for it so long as Robert and Mrs. Myaschensky were all right.

The Vrage had hands, so the weapon had a handgrip scarcely distinguishable from that of a human pistol or electric drill. The grip was a trifle small, even though Gustafson's own hand was by no means large. The professor did not actually wrap his hand around the slanting grip but used two fingers of his left hand to position the grip close to his right palm. The translucent disk which seemed to provide the driving force was connected to the grip by a wand fifty—Gustafson used his index finger as a ruler; long experience made each wrinkle, even blurred by bad vision, a known distance—two millimeters long. The whole unit seemed to be one piece, so perhaps the disk only appeared to rotate.

There was no trigger or button of comparable function, either. Gustafson touched the cool, porous-feeling surface gingerly.

"What *are* these?" Arlene Myaschensky asked in a weak voice. She stood up, continuing to rub the top of her head with one hand. She gestured toward but not quite to the Vrage with a foot.

"Good God," muttered Robert Shroyer. He knelt again beside the creature he had been fighting. The sharpness of chlorine was all about them, though it had been diluted into an odor no more dangerous than an overtreated swimming pool. Shroyer took a handkerchief from his pocket to cover his mouth and nose. It gave him the appearance of a man about to vomit. In fact, he did feel a little queasy, what with the exertion, the gas, and . . .

The vision slit had been deceptive. The alien had separate eyes, not the single broad organ Arlene's nervous imagination had placed beneath the black bar. There were six eyes, blazing iridescently in death, set in point-down triads on the Vrage's yellow face.

"It was going to carry me off!" Myaschensky said. The two men glanced up at her in concern, but there was no need to worry. Arlene found real humor in the thoughts that danced through her mind, the fat ugly duckling and the eight-legged monster. She had years of practice in laughing at the first, so it did not require madness to make the other a joke as well. She smoothed her corduroys over her hips with both palms. The cloth had come through the struggle unaffected. Her sweater's right sleeve had separated on the underarm, however, and the heavy camera had been twisted around to hang against her back.

Louis Gustafson went back to his assessment of the weapon. He knew that it would disappear—rather, that he would—sometime in the near future. He hoped to have gained at least some notion of the principle on which the thing operated by that time. Since there was nothing better for him—for any of them—to do until then, the professor concentrated on his Vrage artifact.

That way he could ignore for a little longer what were at best the half-truths the Travelers had told him.

Chairman Shroyer used two fingers to peel the suit farther down the alien's head, as if he were a surgeon removing a rubber glove. The magenta covering seemed to be losing some of its initial resilience now that the inner face was being exposed to oxygen.

The Vrage was covered in smooth skin which showed no hint of hair, feathers, or scales. There were not even patterns of pigmentation. The chairman used his pen to touch the scalp. The skin wriggled across a surface of bone beneath, an internal skeleton rather than the chitinous exoskeleton which the number of limbs had suggested. Set between and beneath the groups of eyes was a nose—

really only a hole the size of a silver dollar—divided internally by more than a score of radial septa. The Vrage had no mouth in its head and no certain ears, though a series of holes near the juncture with the neck could have had something to do with hearing.

"It turned all the way around," said Arlene Myaschensky, pointing to the creature's head. She alone did not know for certain that there were other Vrages combing the forest. Still, she had enough grasp of reality now to look around after she spoke. The car toward which she had been pulled gaped empty a dozen feet away. The undergrowth was continuing to lift from the ground so that even the nearby vehicle was almost hidden. Reassured that they were all concealed, Myaschensky squatted down beside the Vrage.

It had not occurred to any of them that the car gave off a locating signal.

The first Vrage support team had met Astor and destruction as it raced toward the beacon. Screaming bolts occasionally danced above Myaschensky's group even now. Astor's lethal magnetism continued to draw the majority of Vrage interest toward her gunsight. A separate team had been vectored toward the initial contact, however. Orders which could not be denied had forced the new Vrage trio to dismount a hundred feet away and blunder through the undergrowth on foot.

All of them were terrified. Vision through the broad screen of a utility vehicle was as good as the forest itself allowed—but closed in the hoods of their atmosphere suits, the Vrage vision was as restricted as that of humans wearing gas masks. Further, the heavy armor of the team's cars, now forsaken, was a psychological benefit, even if the soldiers suspected—as their leader knew—that the armor had failed to save at least a dozen of their comrades thus far.

They scuttled through the vegetation. Their team leader in the center was homing on the beacon. His flankers, six feet to either side, were trying to look in all directions for the gunman who would blast them if he saw them first. Stems swished and flopped fans of leaves across their faces, each touch bringing a flash of panic.

The Vrage on the left side of the line stepped on Professor Gustafson's foot.

It was not really surprising that the Vrage soldiers missed seeing Gustafson when they passed to either side of him. The professor was hunched, tweedy, and physically motionless while his mind analyzed the alien weapon. One of the Vrage's leading feet rocked on the professor's ankle as if that ankle were a fallen branch—and with no more interest than the branch would have aroused.

The back foot of the inside pair brushed Gustafson's leg again. The professor was startled into the complete paralysis which alone could have preserved his life under the circumstances. Like many people who concentrate on a task to a degree which others find absurd, he had no real awareness of how focused he became. The magenta forms he saw when one stepped on him seemed figures of a mirage. Gustafson had time only to think that the brilliantly clad Vrages had been transported directly atop him by a time machine before they stalked on and all hell broke loose.

When Robert Shroyer stood up to stretch, the midmost alien was six feet away and equally startled. The chairman screamed and hurled the pen with which he had been probing the dead Vrage. The pen's stainless-steel barrel might have done some useful harm if it had struck its target. Instead it slapped away through the compound leaves which had concealed the parties from one another until they were close enough to touch. Bellowing in fright,

Shroyer bolted in the direction opposite the newcomers. He collided with Arlene Myaschensky as the woman jumped up to see what was the matter. The two of them went down in a heap as the Vrages' guide beams raved through the forest around them.

The abandoned Vrage vehicle had gone unnoticed in the shock of contact, though it was not really hidden. Because its windscreen was lifted, there was not even that limited protection. When a Vrage scythed the area waist high, his beam slashed across the car's gaping interior. Instead of melting down, as had those which Astor destroyed, the power source of this vehicle flashed into white plasma.

Because the Vrage communication was psychic, not oral, the shout that saved the humans' lives was not one that they heard.

The explosion of the dead alien's car was deafeningly evident, even over the shrieking hand weapons.

Foliage touched by the flat cone of radiance folded in on itself. A wedge of the nearest tree shrank away as abruptly as if from a giant axe stroke. The tree slumped and twisted above the injury, the weight of the upper trunk pulling and breaking undamaged fibers like a platoon of machine guns.

Because the blast had been directed upward, none of those in the vicinity was injured by it. The Vrage soldiers realized they were firing on their fellows: all three simultaneously stopped shooting and shouted mentally to their comrades to stop also. Leaves fluttered down.

Chairman Shroyer stared incredulously at the big toe of his right foot. His flesh was unharmed, but there was an oval gap in the leather, a smaller hole in his sock, and a tiny crescent missing from the toenail.

Louis Gustafson had not moved even after his moment of surprise had passed. He had watched with the delight of discovery as the Vrage soldiers picked their way forward, noting that their reddish-purple suits were mittened, but their thumbs were free and cocked out at an angle from the grips of their weapons. The professor had arranged his captured weapon in his right palm, reasoning that the Vrage physiognomy had to be significantly different. The muscles at the base of Gustafson's own thumb did not give him a grip firm enough to carry—

Then Vrage guns had screamed and slashed as Vrage thumbs clamped against grips, and Gustafson, beside and slightly behind the rank of aliens, did the same. When the utility vehicle exploded, the professor's thumb lifted by instinct as if it were responsible for the blast.

But *his* weapon had not fired at all, perhaps—he shifted his grip slightly—the pad of his thumb touched the cool, glassy weapon a little too far up onto the receiver.

The reddish guide beam lanced from the professor's gun to the alien who had stepped on Gustafson a moment before. The professor found it quite natural to sweep that beam across the backs of all three Vrage soldiers.

The effect was as much a surprise to Louis Gustafson as the attack itself—briefly—surprised the aliens. Instead of a line across which the target separated, a high-voltage arc leaped back from the Vrage armor to the spinning disk on Gustafson's weapon. The disk slowed, and the shimmering line across its surface drifted slightly out of synchrony with the guide beam. That did not help the alien. His eight limbs shot out stiffly like the spines of a sea urchin, as the high-frequency howl of the weapon competed momentarily with the roar of the arc.

The weapon bucked in Gustafson's hand, resisting his intent to sweep it across the backs of all three Vrage soldiers. That was a tendency rather than a demand, however, a sluggishness like that of one magnet a few inches

away from another. Arc, bucking, and resistance continued as the guide beam slipped from one alien to the next
and then the last. The third Vrage was turning his head and
weapon toward his attacker when the professor's beam
linked him as well.

The creatures in magenta armor went down like soaked
sponges when the beam no longer gripped them. Gustafson
held the weapon for several seconds on the third because
there were no further targets. The weapon began to heat up
like a resistor on the verge of failure. The professor flicked
his thumb up. His final opponent collapsed. Gustafson
thrust the weapon away in a sudden fit of revulsion.

Robert Shroyer stood up cautiously, eyeing the professor and his weapon. He held out his hand to Myaschensky.
The woman got up by herself without noticing the offered
help. "Ah, Louis," the chairman said to Professor
Gustafson. "Ah—thank you."

"Robert, I don't know what I've done," Gustafson said
simply, rubbing his palms against one another as if washing them. "This . . . I'm very much afraid I was wrong in
deciding to build the machine, the *system* that I did."

"I think we'd better get out of here," said Arlene
Myaschensky. She made shooing motions with both hands
toward the men. "They may be able to find us again
anyway, but I don't think we ought to stay around."

Shroyer nodded. He put his hand on Gustafson's arm
and kept it there in comradeship as the two of them began
to walk away obediently. "Though I'm sure," Shroyer
said to reassure himself, "that, that Selve will have us
back where we belong very shortly."

Arlene did not reply as she stepped over the trio of aliens
the professor had shot. There was no sign of damage to their
suits save a slight grayish discoloration along the approxi-
mate track of the beam. The bodies were utterly flaccid.

The woman paused. Then she picked up one of the alien weapons before she drifted into the undergrowth behind the faculty members.

"Are you doing something to them?" Isaac Hoperin asked the pair of grad students at the instrument panel in the basement.

"Nothing, nothing," insisted Mustafa Bayar angrily.

"No, but somebody sure as hell is," said Mike Gardner. "Look, Mustafa, it's building in a normal drive curve." He gestured toward the figures chasing themselves across the screen of the computer terminal.

"I think someone was at the outside door," said Sara Jean Layberg. She stood now at the open door in the screened enclosure. Ever since the transport, her thumbs had been rubbing the sides of her index fingers firmly enough to cause occasional crackling sounds.

"It's not normal," Bayar objected. He used both his first and middle fingers to point at the screen. "Look, the right-hand coils are leading." The level of noise was making it difficult for the two men to understand one another, even though they stood side by side and both understood the context.

Hoperin moved closer and said loudly, "Last night. Is this what happened last night? You said that the— Who's that?"

Two figures, both of them tall, stepped out of the doorway from the boiler room. Distance and the pattern of the fencing distorted their features. Bayar recognized Schlicter from her height and motorcycle jacket.

"Christ, if that's it—" Mike Gardner blurted. He stepped away from the racks of instruments and began waving both arms like a berserk semaphore. "Go away!" he screamed. *"Go away!* It's not safe where you're standing."

The roaring coils between Gardner and the pair of newcomers created a barrier which his words could not penetrate. The woman in black leather waved back. She and her companion were framed by the two pillars, directly opposite the docking area painted on the floor of the enclosure. The woven wire vibrated fiercely, throwing the couple into soft focus.

The flash took Mike Gardner's breath away. He was blinded. The silence following the palpable vibration made it seem for the instant that he was deaf as well. He pressed his palms savagely over his eyes and cheeks. The pressure brought the world back to him and muted the whimper in his throat.

"Good heavens, where have they gone? And who are—" Dr. Hoperin cried. His shoes slapped and skidded on the concrete. The fencing clashed when the physicist grabbed it to steady himself as he ran out of the enclosure.

Someone touched the back of Gardner's neck reassuringly. "You shouldn't have kept your eyes open, Mike," said Sara Jean Layberg. "But they'll be all right soon. Mine were."

The woman moved her fingers from Gardner's neck to his left hand. She gently urged the hand down. Gardner blinked. He could see, though there were violet blotches in the center of anything he looked at. There was a clot of figures, Hoperin and Bayar among them, beyond the cross wall of the enclosure now.

"I knew I shouldn't be looking," Gardner said hoarsely. "I— Christ. If I pretended it wasn't going to happen, maybe it wouldn't happen before those two got clear. Any idea who they were?"

Sara Jean shook her head. "Something must have happened," she said, "to, to Henry and the others. We'd better go see." She took her hand from Gardner's and moved toward the enclosure gate. The returned party and the men greeting them were now a gabbling crowd moving down the aisle toward the gate as well. Henry and Astor were carrying another of the black-suited Travelers. The burden, the victim, was not Selve. Selve was talking quickly to Gustafson and Isaac Hoperin, one to either side as they walked.

"Damn, I wish I could've stopped them," muttered Mike Gardner. He had secured the doors before the test was run. The boiler room door could not be locked, and he had not tried to wedge or jam it instead. "If they wind up like Dr. Rice, well . . . Who knows what's happened to them?"

Sue Schlicter caught at her companion's wrist and jacket. Without Charles's weight to anchor her, she would have fallen. Not only had the moment of transport been vertiginous, but the ground on which she now found herself sloped sharply.

The concrete basement was gone. There was no building at all. There was no hint anywhere in the wild landscape that buildings would ever exist. The pair of them stood in dun grass nodding at waist height. That background was broken every few yards either by brush with dark foliage or by outcrops of weathered stone. The sky was brilliantly blue.

Eisley wrapped his arm around Schlicter as he stared at the landscape. She felt him shiver. It was not because of the temperature: the air was still and the sun seemed extraordinarily hot. Sue squeezed her lover in response, then disengaged herself to take off the black leather jacket.

"I suppose," said Charles in a very distinct voice, "that you know how we got here. But do you have any faint idea of where here is?"

"Mustafa said that the, that the test would be to the Mesozoic this time," Schlicter replied. "Of course, that doesn't mean it's where we are now."

The fold of earth in which they stood sloped more steeply on their side than it seemed to across from them. Presumably there was a watercourse down the heart of the valley, but it was hidden by a broad belt of coarser vegetation. Like the scrub nearby on the hillside, the green of the foliage covering the valley floor was dark enough to appear black in the punishingly direct sunlight.

"I wonder," said Charles Eisley, "whether that means we're going to see dinosaurs? Though I don't sup—"

"Jesus Christ," Sue agreed breathlessly. They clutched each other's hands.

There was a great deal of what looked to Sue like gray stone exposed on either side of the valley. One such mass, fifty feet away, stumped a few yards closer. It lowered its head again and resumed cropping the grass in jaws that ground forward and back. When she recognized that outcropping as something huge and alive, it was stunningly evident that other rocks—not all of them, but hundreds, dear God a thousand perhaps in the miles of visibility—were also alive.

Sue reached for the flat, lock-blade folding knife she carried unobtrusively in one hip pocket. The absurdity of drawing it brought her hand away empty. These things were every one of them the weight of a car—and the size of a tank.

"I wonder," Eisley said as if the question were of no great importance, "whether any of the trees down there would be sturdy enough to hold us if we wanted to climb?" He motioned with his free index finger. It was a tiny gesture which would not call the attention of the grazers near them.

"Worth checking out," Sue said. She had much less experience in hiding a quaver in the midst of disaster, but she did a creditable job nonetheless.

They began to walk down the hillside at a slow, jerky pace. Charles took off his tie and thrust it into his pocket. Only by constant control could he avoid spinning around at every step or two to see whether one of the browsers was stalking them. He remembered that when he had been serving in Rangoon, someone had told about being chased by elephants. You were supposed to run uphill—or downhill—because the animal was as much slower than a man in the one direction as it was faster in the other.

Eisley could not remember which direction was which, nor did a direct correlation with dinosaurs seem likely, but the line of thought provided a ledge to hold him short of a sea of panic.

Sue Schlicter was holding her jacket collar with both hands. She had a half-conscious plan of using it like a matador's cape if they were charged by one of the dinosaurs. None of those gray brutes showed hostile intentions or much in the way of intellect at all. Every minute or two, each of them would lurch a pace forward and resume cropping grass. The loudest sounds the animals made were the rumblings of their intestines. The final result of digestion was proclaimed by passages of enormous flatulence.

"Will they come back to get us, do you suppose?" Sue asked lightly. She was feeling a trifle looser now that they had stepped between two dinosaurs, neither of them twenty feet away. The beasts had ignored them. "The, Mustafa and his friends, I mean. They must have seen us just before everything changed."

"As I understood Bayar . . ." said Eisley. He flicked his head sideways as an eye blinked back at him above half a bale of dun grass which was ratcheting into the broad jaws. The scale of things here was that of a parking lot, not a pasture. "As I understood Mustafa," the diplomat resumed, "the recovery is automatic. We just have to stay alive till then. I presume." And, Eisley thought, we have to hope that I did understand; that Mustafa was correctly informed; and that the fact the two of us are here at all doesn't mean that something catastrophic had happened to the apparatus.

Sue touched a miniature tree with a trunk like a pot. Its leaves were broad and patterned like those of a croton bush, though the veins were a deep cyan and the edges almost black. The ground was less steep, and the ribbon of dark vegetation had separated into discrete trees. They grew taller and were more densely sited farther toward the center of the valley. The water table seemed to be a crucial factor in the type of vegetation, suggesting that the brilliance and heat of the sun might not be simply subjective phenomena.

"Well," the tall woman said, "I didn't really expect to have company here." She was swinging her jacket loosely, now that they were beyond the area in which the dinosaurs grazed. From higher on the hill there were signs of paths beaten through the broad-leaved trees, probably by beasts seeking water. Sue hugged the man. "Anyway, I can't think of anybody I'd rather be trapped in a time machine with."

"Halt. . . ." called a very distant, very loud voice.

The two accidental transportees stared at one another in amazement. Back up the slope, one of the grazers lifted its head and snorted. That ordinary, bestial sound disposed of any possibility that what they had heard before was not a voice speaking English.

Sue squinted and looked up the hillside. The valley's echoing walls made it impossible to really determine the source of the sound. The trees where the couple now stood were short and spaced generally yards apart, so the foliage did not interfere with Schlicter's view uphill. For the moment, it did not seem important to her that the trees provided camouflage though not concealment.

"Halt," the voice called again. This time it repeated itself with the antiphony of competing echoes, "halt-halt-halt," the single syllable stepping over itself, out of synchronization and from several locations.

Over the rise surged a dozen vehicles of two unfamiliar types. Ten of the vehicles were magenta-and-black egg shapes that reminded Eisley powerfully of the three-wheeled German bubble-cars of the 1950s. Though the high grass made certainty difficult, these did not appear to have any wheels at all. The two other vehicles were the size and general layout of flatbed trucks. They seemed to be circular rather than rectangular in ground plan, each with an identifiable cab sticking up in front.

What was far more shocking than the vehicles was the cargo which the pair of open trucks carried. At first sight they resembled mechanical contrivances contorted with their antenna arrays, six to the back of each of the larger vehicles. But they moved nervously, independently, acting not like machines but rather like the one thing their limbs made it certain they were not: human beings.

"Halt! Halt!" the trucks shouted. They were half a mile away, but their voices boomed with the distant authority of public address systems in sports arenas.

Eisley and Schlicter tensed. One of the grazing dinosaurs whirled with unexpected speed toward a truck. A corona of spikes which the two humans had not noticed before sprang erect on the beast's neck. It coughed a thunderous challenge toward the vehicle, a creature worth its notice.

Beings on the back of both trucks bathed the dinosaur in beams of intense, rusty light. The sound of giant fingernails on slate filled the valley. Pieces of the beast scaled away like rind clipped from a hard cheese. Grass and brush flattened and did not spring up again. A face of rock, touched by a stray beam, popped and scattered pebbles of itself down the hill.

The beast leaped onto its hind legs and flailed the air. Half a dozen beams converged. The vehicles' own forward motion sawed the beams forward. Claws, toes, and then the huge flat skull itself fell away. The torso strode onward, spouting blood from the neck and the half of the forelimb still linked to the heart. Another dazzle of beams cut at the hind legs. The animal crashed to the ground. Its blood continued to hose the grass, turning it black instead of dun.

"Halt!" resumed the speakers as the vehicles swept past the squirming corpse. "If you move, I'll blow you away!" The nearly synchronized words created harmonics which alone might have been enough to make Eisley's skin crawl.

"Let's get out of here," he muttered as he turned. Sue patted his rump, not in affection so much as a signal to urge him to run beside her as she bolted.

Behind them, the voices followed, "Halt . . . !"

"Wait," shouted Selve, and the word bounced off the ceiling of the cavernous basement lab. Isaac Hoperin tugged a sleeve for attention, but the male Traveler shrugged him off. Selve touched Astor, who, stepping backward, was cradling Keyliss's head and torso. The maimed Traveler's hand trailed on the ground. "Wait, Astor," Selve continued, even though his bigger colleague showed every sign of intending to walk through him. "Take her back to that side. I'll program the reversal."

"You can't!" Astor snapped. The weight of the body she held did not affect her, but the delay was driving her wild. Keyliss's chest was rising and falling with breaths as swift as those of a panting dog. The mutilated plane of her right side was gray with the gauze of film that protected it. Though the film was wholly beneficial, it had the look of gangrene. "We don't have the time for you to fool around. Get out of the way and get to work on the program!"

"Any of you, who *were* those creatures?" demanded Robert Shroyer. It was the third time he had asked the question since Selve had found the parameters he needed and plucked them all vertiginously back into the engineering building.

"We've got the time, it's faster," Selve insisted. "If I wait for the field to dissipate, it'll be ten extra minutes. We'll ride back on the first reversal. We'll have Keyliss fully dissociated before the reversal shock hits her."

"Mr. Eisley was just there," said Mustafa Bayar. "In the docking area. Where are they now? Are they all right?"

Astor nodded abruptly to Selve. "Go," she said. Selve broke from the group, running toward the control panel.

The female Traveler turned back to Dr. Layberg. He was breathing heavily, more from the events on the other side of the transition than because he carried the lower half of Keyliss's body. "Back where we were," Astor said curtly. No one else in the room existed for her at this moment but Keyliss and the local helping to carry her. She began shuffling around with her share of the burden. "Keep out of the way, then, or you'll . . . Keep well back."

The excited group halved, then fragmented. Isaac Hoperin started to follow Astor with his questions because Selve had rushed past as if he were not there. Professor Gustafson caught the physicist's arm. "I don't think now, Isaac," the older man said. He had not understood Astor's previous warning against being transported from the unmarked docking area. First Dr. Rice, now whatever it was that had happened to Keyliss, to all of them. "We'll have to talk about many things, but for the moment I don't want anything worse to happen."

Robert Shroyer had started to follow Astor in red-faced determination to get an answer. Professor Gustafson's words made the chairman pause, then recoil. His anger had been a reaction to the fear he had felt so recently. The possibility of a further nightmare trip if he were not careful stopped him. He was trembling.

Arlene Myaschensky walked down the long aisle toward the stairs at the other end. The plump woman did not seem a part of the group around her. She had rather the aspect of an atheist in a crowd of Christmas shoppers, affected by common stimuli but separate nonetheless.

Selve's haste had drawn Mike Gardner back into the enclosure. There was nothing for the graduate student to do, though. The Traveler's fingers danced over the terminal keyboard, using his left hand for the alphanumeric pad and his right for the function keys. At intervals, Selve reached down and changed a setting on one or another of the control panels.

Rather than interfere with what he could not help, Gardner said, "Are you okay, Arlene? Did—well, what went wrong, I mean?"

Myaschensky looked at her fellow, then down at herself. Her flesh was white and puffy through the gaping seams of her sweater; the camera still flopped against her back. She reached around carefully and lifted the strap away from her neck where the skin had been badly chafed during the fight. "I guess I'm all right," she said. "I'm going to soak in the tub for a couple of hours." She took a deep breath.

Gardner was frowning at her in concern. Beyond him Selve was snapping his fingers while the computer ran an involved series of procedures. Selve never cursed—none of the Travelers did—but his nervous frustration was obvious in his stance and gestures. The Traveler's suit was stained by plant juice and the blood which had spurted when Keyliss toppled.

Arlene said calmly, "There was something back there that was purple and had eight legs. Like a joke. But it wasn't a joke. I think I need to get home."

Mike Gardner rubbed his palms against his trousers as he watched Myaschensky walk stiffly away. Behind him, Selve shouted in triumph. The knife switch on the control panel clunked home. The male Traveler brushed past Gardner and ran back down the aisle toward Astor. Gardner watched the two healthy Travelers clasp arms briefly above the sprawled and drooling Keyliss. Mustafa Bayar was speaking animatedly to the three faculty members. The Turk gestured frequently toward the Travelers—or toward the patch of aisle from which the two interlopers had disappeared minutes before.

Sara Jean Layberg was holding her husband's hand. Gardner noticed neither of them were speaking. They were close enough to the pillared windings that it would have been difficult for either to be heard over the summoning vibration. Mike looked at the couple and licked his lips. He began to walk toward Mustafa and the faculty members.

It was more comfortable to think about the people who had been snatched away.

Deeper into the forested belt, the trees grew taller. Their barrellike trunks splitting into two, four, even a dozen slimmer stalks from a common base, each individual stalk the thickness of Eisley's thighs. Where they crisscrossed from adjacent clumps, the boles not only spread dense curtains of foliage but also barricaded routes of escape.

Sue and Charles had started out running; now they ducked and clambered their way through an obstacle course. The screech of weapons behind them was a reminder of why they fled. It was impossible to tell what the beams' target was meant to be this time.

A score of hand-sized creatures flushed so suddenly that Eisley could not tell whether they had leaped or flown from the ground cover. They chittered glassily. Sue cried out and flung the jacket she carried toward the leaves which flapped behind the covey.

Charles Eisley, shifting direction to snatch up her heavy jacket again, staggered and banged into one of the trees instead of making a smooth maneuver of it as he had intended. He was almost blown already, though they had run less than two hundred yards. "Dear God," he whispered.

Schlicter was gone through another stand of trunks growing like fingers from a palm. She paused and swung herself back to where she could see her gasping lover with the jacket in his hand. "Leave it, Charles, Jesus!" she cried. "It's too heavy to fuck with now."

The diplomat swallowed and began to stumble onward again, the jacket of studded black leather swinging from his hand. "Can't, they'll find it," he said in a voice intelligible mostly from context. "Don't let 'em know we're here."

"Oh, Charles, they wouldn't *be* here if they didn't know, would they?" the woman said, but she reached out to help Eisley through the immediate tangle. He continued to grip her jacket.

The watercourse Eisley had expected was a stream twenty feet wide and shallow enough to show bottom all the way across. At its gravelly margin, the short-trunked trees made space for plants like giant dandelions whose stems oozed amber sap when Schlicter trod them down. She paused and threw a glance at Eisley.

"We've got to," the diplomat said. The open water gleamed like a killing ground in the brilliant sunlight. The current cast dazzling highlights where larger stones broke the surface. Touching his mistress's wrist with his free hand, Eisley splashed into the stream. Sue ran with him. From the hollow in which it laired during the daytime leaped a carnivore the size of a pickup truck.

The beast was four-footed, like the grazers on the hill-side above. There could be no doubt regarding its own diet, however. Its forepaws crossed its hind legs in midstride. As the forelegs extended, claws the length of Schlicter's fingers sprang out of their sheaths in all twelve front toes. The jaws were as long as a crocodile's. They were raggedly armed with curving black teeth. The withers bulged with a muscular hump. Tensed, the muscles would rip the foreclaws through bones orders of magnitude heavier than those of the two humans.

Eisley slung the jacket as an instinctive follow-through of the motion by which he had turned toward the attack. Though the predator did not give tongue, the crash of its tons leaping to slaughter was as obtrusive as a safe hitting the pavement. "Go!" Eisley shouted as Sue seemed to pause in the gout of spray.

The couple's brief hesitation short of the creek edge gave them the reserve of strength they needed to dash across the water. The current was strong enough to have swept its channel silt free. It was not, however, the sort of torrent that rolled all the pebbles away from the polished domes of quarter-ton boulders. The stream-bed footing was good. The drag of the few inches of water on the fugitives' feet was lost in the panic of the moment.

Now in direct sunlight, the predator's rufous scales glared like iron from the forge; while the creature lay in wait, shadows had made its hide resemble dull patterns of earth and leaf mold. The eyes were set close beneath a brow ridge. Their view to the sides was limited, but they provided a sharp, range-determining view for a predator which killed in a quick lunge from cover—good enough to permit the clawed forelegs to scissor together on the flying jacket.

The motion was preternaturally swift. The beast rocked back on its haunches in the water. Its hind legs were relatively short, like those of a bear. Only as a carnival act could they alone have supported a creature weighing several tons. The foreclaws rent the jacket with a jerk to either side. Fluff from the quilted lining twisted in the air. The odors of cowhide and human body oils were unfamiliar but piquant to the predator. It stuffed both halves of the shredded garment into a mouth whose black-toothed jaws could have held either human as easily.

Sue and Charles had gained the far bank in the interval. As Eisley tried to duck out of sight around a slanting tree bole the way his mistress had done a step before, his foot slipped. He rang his head on the solid trunk, then flopped to the ground, stunned and visible. The predator's eyes focused as if its ridged snout were a gunsight turned toward Eisley.

The creature gathered its haunches beneath it, just as three of the egg-shaped Vrage utility vehicles squirmed out of the dense forest. The heavy vegetation was an obstacle to the humans and a maze for the Vrage cars. To the trucks with their loads of ready infantry, the belt of forest was an impassable barrier. The gunners had dismounted where the trees began to flare with multiple trunks. The Vrage weapons carved easily through the wood, but that alone was not enough to form a path. Armor-suited soldiers were now struggling to drag clear the fallen trees. Inattention had already fried one Vrage with the beam of a fellow who had meant only to section a tree trunk.

The lighter vehicles had penetrated the forest with varying degrees of success. The initial trio had been successful enough to burst straight in on an active carnivore.

One car slewed and stopped in midstream. Schlicter, staring in shock from the far edge, noted that the current rippled normally beneath the vehicle. The black windscreen hinged up. An alien like those on the truck beds aimed his weapon point-blank.

The magenta blur registered on the carnivore's peripheral vision. The beast did not leap. Instead, it slashed one foreleg sideways, the bite of its claws creating six instant jets of chlorine. The carnivore jerked the Vrage from its car as neatly as a thumb could lift an eyeball.

"Come on, get going," Charles Eisley gasped. He slithered on his belly past the trunk on which he had laid open his scalp. Sue, transfixed by the battle on the water, was not sure whether the man was speaking to her or to himself.

Twenty feet from the carnivore, another Vrage lifted his viewscreen to shoot. He clamshelled the cover back as fragments of the first victim rained from the angry creature's mouth. The motion was a flag to call the beast whose jaws frothed in irritation from the halogen spray to which they had been subjected. The carnivore sprang in a flat arc, its clawed forelegs extended as they would have during an attack on one of the young grazers on its way to water. The Vrage might have had a chance if he had scuttled clear instead of clamping closed his vehicle. The car shattered like eggshell before a bullet when the predator struck it.

"Sue! Quick!" Eisley said.

"Jesus!" the woman gasped as she whirled back into the business of survival.

The two humans scrambled away from the creek, hidden again by the foliage. Eisley's shoes squelched angrily, but he had recovered his composure and much of his strength.

Behind them, the stream was a raving battleground for the great predator and the increasing number of aliens who slashed for its life. Unlike the herbivore on the hither slope, which itself had been a long time dying under the concentrated fire of a dozen guns, this brute combined the tenacity of its normal prey with bloodlust and agility. The beams that carved across it in microns-thin lines served only to madden it.

Dismounted soldiers stabbed and ran and cried for support from their fellows. The carnivore rushed like a dog tormented by gadflies from one splotch of armor to another. Sometimes a victim dodged; sometimes the beams of a victim and his fellows drove the beast in some less painful direction; and sometimes the jaws crunched on a tormenter. The claws and black teeth dripped with ichor as blood bubbled from the animal's own mortal wounds.

The interlacing tree trunks were an effective baffle for the high-frequency sound of the Vrage weapons. By the time the humans had run a hundred yards or so, the shrieks had muted to hissing; but that hissing had the emotional overlay of whips cutting toward flesh. The sound goaded Schlicter and Eisley onward. The carnivore they had flushed was a phantom from nightmare. The eight-limbed aliens were by contrast a part of continuing reality despite their strangeness.

The forested core of the valley was as flat as the bowl of a spoon. The slight rise in the ground did not increase the difficulty of escape. In fact, when the slope sharpened abruptly, the wider spacing of the trees made it easier to move. The sunlight had not been a problem to the humans under the canopy of black leaves. Where the tree trunks became short, individual pots instead of starbursts of respectable height, it was possible to see the sky again. The sun was lower than its brilliance suggested. Twenty minutes should find it behind the hills from which the valley debouched.

Beneath a stubby tree of the last fringe, the two fugitives caught their breath and took stock. Both of them were panting. Eisley was surprised to see that Sue's face was as red as it got during particularly strenuous bouts of lovemaking. The incongruity made it possible for him to smile.

"We wait half an hour and it'll be dark," Schlicter said, nodding up the grassy slope.

"I think we better keep moving," Charles replied after he had cleared the phlegm from his throat. "They must have some way of tracking us besides sight. I think we ought to keep moving, hope they lose us in all the other stuff."

Massive herbivores were grazing placidly on this side of the valley, just as they had been on the other. Perhaps at nightfall they would troop down to water; the predator there had been built for victims that big. The fear that the grazers had engendered when Eisley first saw them now seemed to him to have been ridiculous. The beasts were potentially dangerous, just as urban traffic was dangerous. That was innocent in comparison to what had happened down at the creek.

Charles turned to face back the way they had come, his shoulder braced against the tree's horny bark and his legs splayed out like those of a corpse. It was impossible to see anything but the immediate treetops. He had thought that they could perhaps spot a surveillance post on the crest over which the vehicles had come. They would have to climb higher to do that . . . which meant being exposed against the grassy slope for at least some distance. Eisley could not tell whether there was still fighting going on at the watercourse, or if instead he was just hearing the breeze.

"Right," he said. He rolled to his belly again, then levered himself to a kneeling posture. "I'll slip out a little ways to check the lay of the—"

Schlicter started to get up also.

Eisley laid his hand firmly across the woman's buttocks and pinned her to the ground again. "Goddamn it, Sue," he said. "If there's one of us, there's half the chance of being spotted. Right?"

"Well, why don't I—" Schlicter began.

"Dammit!" the man repeated. "It's my idea to go on, yours to stay. Will you for God's sake let me go look things over without a stupid argument?"

Sue dropped her eyes and nodded. "Be careful," she said, looking away from her lover.

Eisley began to crawl toward one of the patches of brush. At this level, the grass tickled his cheeks. The blades could cut, in fact. Sweat which the sun drew from his face stung fiercely. When the diplomat dragged himself behind the clump, he mopped his face with his handkerchief before he even bothered to scan the farther hillside.

The brush grew in waist-high knots. The stems squirmed together like those of an ancient wisteria vine. It made a comfortable screen through which Eisley peered intently. The grassy slope was almost a mile away, but the magenta color of the aliens and their vehicles should have been obvious against a dun background. There did not seem to be an outpost. The group which had penetrated the valley's forested bottom was blindfolded by the vegetation that screened it from Eisley. It seemed to him that the best course for the two of them was to make a break for the next ridge.

He stood up. "I think—" he called to Sue, lost in a shadow fifty feet away.

A rank of vehicles swept over the crest toward which Eisley had intended to flee.

The ten vehicles in the middle of the line were stretched over a half-mile front. They were light cars like those which had originally pursued the fugitives into the forest. If the diplomat had not been erect and fully exposed to the view of this new party, he might have thought it worthwhile to try hiding from them in the grass.

At either end of the search chain was a tank that dwarfed the trucks of the earlier party as thoroughly as those trucks dwarfed the individual vehicles they accompanied. There were no eight-limbed soldiers on the back of these tanks with hand weapons. Charles Eisley had done enough reporting of military vehicles in his career to recognize tanks, even reddish-purple tanks with yard-diameter disks instead of proper turrets on their flat decks.

Eisley's mouth was open to shout as he turned from his mistress. He was not sure what the words would have been. The aliens forestalled him with a sound like plates of the planetary crust rubbing.

The tank weapons were not optically aimed, so no guide beams quivered from them across the landscape. Instead, the grass planed off in a downward slant and the swath drew in from either side toward a point between Eisley and Schlicter. The low sun wavered from the whirling disks of the tank armament in a dazzle that had nothing to do with the actual process of destruction. A grazer forty yards from the diplomat suddenly lurched and slumped soundlessly to the ground as grass fell beyond it: the huge beast had been sectioned through the torso with no more ado than its own teeth cropped vegetation.

"Halt!" boomed the tanks in unison, the only noise in the valley but the rush of the vehicles' passage now that the guns had ceased firing. Earth had rippled beyond the lines on which the beams intersected it. Where the beams themselves crossed between the two humans, the surface was humped and tumbled with displaced sod. Atoms had repelled one another violently along a plane of activity. The effect was geologically trivial, but it would take a century of rain, frost, and microshocks to undo it.

Nothing could undo the liquidly raw portions of the grazer which chanced to have been in the way of the warning fired by the tanks now looping toward Charles Eisley at eighty miles an hour, their speed belied by their enormous bulk. A minuscule twitch in the line their weapons drew to separate Eisley from the forest would instead have split Sue like an axed melon.

The diplomat, hands raised over his head, began to walk uphill toward the alien vehicles. "I surrender!" he shouted. He did not look behind him or suggest in any way that there might be anyone behind him. The aliens had shown that they wanted a living captive. There was no evidence that they wanted two.

"I surrender until that damned machine brings me back!"

"Well, Jesus God, Arlene, where's the camera?" Dave Myaschensky demanded as he looked up from the kitchen table.

"Oh, I—" the woman said. She hefted uncertainly the purse she had just set on one of the chairs. "I must have left it in the car. I'll get it."

Her husband pushed past her at a run. "For Chrissake, can't you be a little careful?"

Dave did not close the front door when he ran outside, but he achieved a satisfying slam with it when he returned moments later with the Nikon in his hands. He began to rewind the film even as he stamped toward the kitchen.

Arlene had pulled off her torn sweater. The Myaschen-skys' apartment was one of four divided awkwardly from a 1920s-vintage frame house. The bathroom was off the kitchen, the location determined by the drains and water pipes. Arlene studied her injuries in the medicine chest mirror. The camera strap's abrasions on her neck still hurt like fire, but they could not be serious. Bruises were already forming against her white skin, places where she had hit the ground or been groped by the struggling alien. Those, and the muscles pulled by unfamiliar strain, would be with her for at least a week. She loosed the shoulder straps of her bra to see if the ache in her left breast was from some evident cause.

"Arlene, will you get out of the way?" Dave said. He made shooing motions with his hands and the camera. "There's not room to process film in here even without you wallowing around. This is important."

The woman looked away from the yellowing mirror in surprise. Dave's photographic chemicals were set out on the board with which he turned the bathtub into a work-bench. There were not only the canisters for film process-ing, but the trays and enlarger for making prints. The apparatus struck Arlene's awareness a blow that made her gasp.

"I wanted to take a hot bath, Dave," she said. "A long bath. It was—"

"Later, dammit!" Myaschensky shouted. The tendons in his throat stood out like wires. "Will you get out of here!'' The words were not a question except in grammatical formation.

Arlene did not speak as she walked out of the bathroom, out of the kitchen. The bathroom door banged behind her, opened, then banged again. Her husband noticed the sweater. He flung it into the kitchen and out of his way.

When Schlicter lay with her head on the ground, she could feel the soil tremble as the grazers strolled into the forest. Twilight had been as brief as a kiss, the way Charles had described evenings in Nha Trang when he was there as political officer. Sue held her hand an inch above the ground. When she could no longer distinguish its shadow from the general darkness, she stood up.

The last of the grazing dinosaurs were funneling toward a trail to water a few hundred yards from the woman. None of the herd—if that was not too collective a word for the loose agglomeration—paid any attention to the one of their number which the tank had halved. Smaller creatures had crept out with darkness, however. That part of the night now smacked and snarled in a dozen rasping voices. Schlicter carried her knife open in her right hand as she strode up the hillside.

She had thought that at least the tanks would have left deep furrows in the sod, easy to follow even in the darkness. There were no signs at all of the aliens' passage. The tank to whose deck Charles had been tied with black cord had disappeared with its consort and its convoy of utility vehicles. Sue's mouth was dry. She gripped her knife hilt as if to make its brass and Micarta scream.

The haze overhead had turned the sky unexpectedly pink at the moment of sunset. After only minutes of that luster, it had become an opaque barrier to any light the moon or stars might have offered. As she neared the hilltop, how-

ever, it became increasingly obvious that the night was not
as black as it should have been. The other side of the ridge
was not a valley like the one she was leaving. Instead it
was a meteor scar, age-softened but huge, many miles
across. From it glared enough artificial light to stain the
sky.

Sheltered in the crater was a bustling encampment of
flat-roofed, circular buildings. The whole area was illuminated in pale yellow green by hedges of light standards. In
the very center of the scar was a broad cleared area around
a double structure, each portion of which was spherical—
globes some eighty feet in diameter. Sue Schlicter lay flat
to stare. There was no doubt in her mind that those huge
units performed the function of the cylindrical drive coils
Professor Gustafson had built.

The scale of the encampment took Sue's breath away. It
robbed her of the hope she had not expressed even to
herself: the hope that she, not the time machine, would
snatch Charles from the things which had captured him.
She could not even locate the diplomat in a maze more
populous than any city in North Carolina.

There was still traffic in and out of the crater. Though
there were scores of vehicles, fans of light, moving at any
moment, the area involved was so great that no aliens
seemed to be anywhere near the human fugitive. Lights
became cars and trucks as they entered the nucleus of
general illumination. Perhaps some vehicles were the remains of the patrol which had initially flushed her and
Charles. There must be outposts ringing this massive base
. . . though how bleak would outpost duty be to creatures
who found Earth as inhospitable as these did. That was
obvious from the sealed suits, the closed vehicles, and the
way all the buildings Sue could see clearly seemed to
interconnect.

God in heaven. There was a chance after all.

On a distant fringe of the encampment was a tank park. Acres of tanks like the pair which had snared Charles rested silently. Light gleamed on the edges of their weapon disks. Those halos gave an angelic aura to vehicles whose lethality could not have been less in question. But though the absolute number of the tanks must be in the thousands, only two of them were currently in motion. As huge as any of the structures fixed to the ground, they slid together into the area cleared around the drive coils.

The dark blotch against the magenta reflection of one of the tanks could be Charles Eisley. Logically, it could *only* be Charles Eisley.

There was activity between the spherical coils even before the tanks reached them. Schlicter could not see the individual aliens, but an anthill can be viewed even when distance hides its builders. Sue found herself watching the hasty erection of a cylindrical building smaller than the thousands of similar ones which comprised the encampment. Twice the reddish guide beams of Vrage weapons slanted up from the pool of ambient light. The distance long delayed but could not wholly absorb their distinctive screech.

The tall woman bleakly considered the lighted concourses which she must traverse to reach Charles. There were vehicles moving intermittently, but no pedestrians. Certainly no two-legged, two-armed pedestrians.

It struck her that the risk was pointless. They had already been stranded in this time for an hour and a half. They would surely snap back to the present at any moment. What she was considering meant danger from the aliens and danger from the dinosaurs, which would not notice crushing her beyond the momentary greasiness of one broad foot. For that matter, there was no certainty that the physical situation was what she suspected it might be.

Screw them all. Sue Schlicter wasn't going to give up the best chance life had handed her to become a hero. She began to whistle the "March of the Toreadors" under her breath as she strode back toward the forest and the watercourse. Her little knife winked like the sword of a vigilant Crusader.

The door of the workroom was open. Henry Layberg knocked on the jamb diffidently before he stepped inside. His wife looked up from her work table and the bud-formed bowl which Selve had given her, surprised. She was not sure how often Henry had bothered to enter the workroom. It was no more than a dozen times in as many years as she had been potting; it could have been as few as two or three.

"I've been watching this, this pot from Selve," Sara Jean said. There was a chair for guests in one corner, but its cushion was stacked with dusty volumes on kiln construction. Before she could stand up to clear the seat, her husband settled himself on an arm of the chair instead. He looked uneasy.

Disquieted herself, Sara Jean babbled on, "It's almost stopped now. Stopped growing. For a while I could see the, the edges expanding. Like a feather of clay on the wheel, only so much faster."

Dr. Layberg nodded. "That's nice," he said. His mouth made a grimace which was absentmindedly meant to be a smile. "Jeanie," he asked as his eyes roved along the ranks of finished mugs and vases, "why didn't we go to Bermuda?"

"Well, we couldn't really afford it after my dad died," Sara Jean said. She could not have been more surprised if the world had fallen away from her again as it had the morning before in the engineering laboratory.

"No, no, not our honeymoon," Layberg said. The sharpness in his voice was more familiar than the musing wonder had been. The wonder and gentleness were back as the doctor continued, "I know, we had to cancel the honeymoon plans for then. But we were going to go later, as soon as we could afford it, weren't we? And I swear to God I even remember we'd booked the tickets, hell, years ago. But we didn't go?" His brow was contracted with frustration at his lack of memory about something which was suddenly important to him.

"We did book tickets, yes," his wife said. She was frowning herself—not for memory, but from continuing doubt as to what was going on. If Henry had— But it didn't matter, any more than the house mattered to her now, or the Mercedes. "The first time we were going to go by boat. Then we thought we'd fly. After the third time, I pretty well gave up, Henry. That must have been, well, ten years ago at least. After I'd begun potting seriously." She reached out toward the clay-smeared wheel beside her.

"Something came up," Dr. Layberg said heavily. "For me, I guess. Each time." The only flaw in his memory had been a deep unwillingness to retrieve the data. "Damn it all, Jeanie, I'm sorry."

"I don't see that that matters now," Sara Jean said. Her coolness was a preemptive defense rather than hostility, though the distinction was not apparent to anyone outside her mind. As she spoke, the shroud which had covered the bowl pinged and disappeared. The transparent material was briefly a rainbow of dust-mote prisms in suspension over the table. They drifted down and were lost without even a suggestion of themselves.

"The Travelers aren't our descendents," said Henry Layberg. "They aren't human at all, Jeanie. Too many ribs. I don't know where they come from, but it isn't Earth a few thousand years in the future."

The doctor had linked his hands together, palm to palm, without interlacing his fingers. Sara Jean got up, holding Selve's bowl in her left hand. Layberg stared at her, expecting her to say something. "There couldn't be any mistake," he went on. "She was, Keyliss was sectioned like a plate from an anatomy text."

Sara Jean sat down on the other arm of Layberg's chair. She covered her husband's hands with her own free hand. "I thought that must be it," she said. "That we couldn't be their ancestors, whatever they said." She smiled wanly. "Even Selve."

"Now how in Hades would you know that, Jeanie?" Dr. Layberg demanded in a tone of frustrated sadness. He had gripped his wife's hand greedily. Now he drew it toward his chest as if he could physically prevent the blitheness with which she seemed to be drifting out of his life. "It doesn't show from the outside, not when they're wearing clothes. I don't know how many thousand chests I've looked into and I never said, 'Oh, nine true ribs on these so-called time travelers.' "

The woman leaned over and kissed Henry's hand. As she straightened, she held the bowl out between the two of them. It had the texture of parchment and a mottled pattern as delicate as the curves of an ammonite's septa. "This wasn't human, Henry. Not—a blood human, whatever. Selve and I are very much alike, I think, but—the way a bat and a bird are alike."

The fear of loss that had shocked Dr. Layberg a moment before was fading. He stretched out one arm to Sara Jean's waist while he continued to hold her hand with the other.

Now that he was sure that his wife was not mocking him, Layberg proceeded in a reasonable voice to correct her mistaken assumptions. "Remember, Jeanie, that they were supposed to come from the future. They of course might have equipment that does wonderful things. The fabric, the suit that bandaged Keyliss automatically, truly marvelous. You know, it might even save her life? If the base facilities are of the same quality, I'm sure they did."

Sara Jean shook her head gently.

Her husband caught himself. "Ah," he muttered. Then he finished. "This pot is very amazing, too, Jeanie, but it's the sort of thing that even a few decades—well, centuries—of current progress could very well come up with."

"As an industrial process, Henry," the woman explained ironically, "I'm sure we could do better right now." She gestured carefully with the bowl toward the ranks of her own pottery on the shelves above them. "There's better ways to make mugs than the way I do it, too."

"Well," said Henry uncomfortably, "I think your work is very, ah, tasteful."

"You're sweet," Sara Jean said. Her elbow squeezed his hand against her waist. "And that doesn't matter. What I mean is, this is a handicraft, just like my pottery is handicraft. Back however long ago—ten thousand years— what Selve did and what I do were necessary so that our, our cultures would have something to boil water in and store seed grain. But what I do with clay and a kiln was as different to Selve as this is to us, Henry. We've grown in the same directions, but we grew from different worlds."

Henry Layberg sighed deeply. He stood up and took the alien bowl from his wife in both hands. It did not sit firmly when he put it on the table. The desiccated remnants of the branch were still attached to it. "Jeanie," the man said, "do you think they still sell tickets to Bermuda? For a week, maybe?"

"Why?" Sara Jean said from where she sat.

"Because I don't understand," the doctor said simply. "Because I've been going through life as if I was on tracks, and it seems the tracks may not go anywhere." He paused, managing both to smile and to meet his wife's eyes for the first time since he stood up. "Or they do go just where I thought, but there's more interesting places out there, too."

Sara Jean rocked to her feet. She did not close the short distance now separating her from her husband. "Henry," she said, "you may not like the islands. We could go to the beach here, maybe, if—"

Layberg set one hand on either of his wife's shoulders. He did not try to draw her in, but it was his turn to shake his head in gentle demurrer. "Jeanie, I may be bored in Bermuda and I may burn myself like a lobster. To tell the truth, I've been planning to get in shape." He looked ruefully at the belly which overhung his belt even when he tensed his muscles. "The—the exercise I got this morning with . . . Anyway, it made a believer out of me."

"Swimming and bicycling might be nice," the woman said as she stepped nearer to her husband and pressed herself against him.

"But that isn't the thing," Henry Layberg concluded. "I may be bored and I may not, but I'll go to my grave knowing which. And . . . Jeanie, I think I've missed you."

"I've missed you, too, Henry," said Sara Jean.

"Arlene!" he called as he heard the hall door open. "Arlene, where the hell have you been?" As he got a look at his wife, Dave Myaschensky blurted, "Like that?"

Arlene closed the door behind her. She wore her shoes, her bra, and a towel that was a good deal less ample than the hips which it draped. "Upstairs at Laura's," she said. "She let me use her shower. We talked." The woman tossed the slacks she carried and the towel over the back of a chair as she walked toward the bedroom and her clean clothes. Bruises were particularly prominent on her shoulders and the wobbling inner side of her thighs.

"Talked about this, did you?" her husband said. He waved a fan of eight-by-ten-inch prints. They were still damp enough to sling water from their trailing edges. "Just come and have a goddamn look at what you did!"

Arlene paused in the bedroom doorway. She walked back to her husband. Her calm as she stood almost nude in view of the living room windows would have struck him as amazing if he had not been so upset himself. "Look at this!" Dave shouted. He slapped a print into her hands. "Or this one!"

The woman looked at the first print carefully and held the other in her free hand for comparison. It seemed to her to be surprisingly good, though she had never been able to accept black-and-white photographs as real the way color ones were. The subject was one of the winged insects against a tree trunk. The wings were slightly raised and enough out of focus that their veins were a suggestive blur instead of being the sharp pattern of lacework that Arlene had seen on the original. Still, the body was clear enough to show the ruffs of fine hairs at each joint of the abdomen and the legs.

The second print . . . well, it was a different insect, shot at enough of a frontal angle on its perch that the abdomen trailed off in a blur indistinguishable from the bark. Still, the creature's frontal parts including its side-spread wings had razor-sharp definition. Like the other, the photograph was much better than Arlene had hoped to achieve.

"All right," she said to her husband, "I think they're pretty good. What's the matter?"

Dave's face went white and his right arm drew back.

"Don't hit me, Dave," Arlene said in a voice which had no emotional loading at all.

Her husband swung open-handed. Arlene raised her left arm with the care she would have used to position a circuit board for hookup. Dave's wrist struck the point of her elbow, numbing his hand by the force of its own blow. Arlene's mind was a magenta blur of recalled emotions. She straightened her right arm, crumpling the prints against her husband's chest and hurling him back over a chair. The small man crashed to the floor with a look of amazement on his face.

"Don't hit me," his wife repeated as flatly as she had said the words before.

Arlene closed her eyes and shuddered from her neck to her calves. When she looked up again, she began to straighten the photographs against a sofa cushion. For the first time since her return, she seemed to be aware that the blinds were not drawn. The prints which Dave had not given her were scattered across the floor beside him. "What was the matter with the pictures?" Arlene asked without looking directly at her husband.

Dave Myaschensky got to his feet slowly. He touched his chest where Arlene had straight-armed him. "Look at the legs," he said. "Look at how many legs they've got."

His wife knew as little about entomology as the next person, but that was enough to understand the problem when it was directly stated. "Eight legs," she said. "So they can't be insects, they're spiders."

"They're not goddamn spiders," Dave shouted, "and

they're for sure not spiders with wings. They're *fakes* is what they are—goddamn fakes!'' His fists clenched, but he did not step closer and swing.

Arlene smiled coldly and unconsciously; then her face smoothed. ''They weren't fakes, Dave,'' she said as she looked again at the photographs. ''All of them were moving, were flying around. It was so long ago, a hundred million years or whatever. Couldn't they have evolved since?''

Pallid anger flared briefly across the entomologist's face again. It replaced itself with nervous surprise, a copy of his expression as he'd sprawled over the chair. ''They don't evolve into two fewer legs, Arlene,'' Myaschensky said in a perfectly reasonable voice. ''Any more than we could breed six-legged cows. It doesn't work that way.''

He picked up one of the scattered prints and stared at it. On this one, the wings of the subject blurred not from focus problems but because the wings were fluttering. ''Damn,'' Myaschensky said softly. ''If they're not fakes, Arlene, then something else is wrong. Because nothing built like this ever lived on Earth.''

The structure into which they threw Charles Eisley was cylindrical and about ten feet both in height and diameter. The diplomat rolled to a sitting position cautiously. Each of the dozens of aliens around him had carried a weapon. The ones which were not actively engaged in putting up the prefabricated structure kept their disk-topped guns pointed determinedly at their prisoner, even while he was firmly lashed to the tank carrying him. Either the eight-limbed creatures were ridiculously nervous, or something had occurred to give Charles a reputation he could not justify. Perhaps they thought the carnivore had been under his control when it tore into the first patrol.

The building, the cell, was solid except for its door,

which had disappeared as soon as it slammed shut, and the two fist-sized holes carved in its side walls. The building material had looked thick but spongy, like Styrofoam sheets, to Eisley when he watched the hasty construction. It was indeed foam; but now that Eisley could touch it, he found the material was as hard and unyielding as concrete. The tip of Eisley's pen scraped along the wall, scarring the metal without leaving a mark on the structure.

The door fitted flush without need of gaskets; there was no sign of a latch or handle on the inner side. The structure had obviously been intended to be gas tight: except for the two gun-carved holes in the walls, it still was. Charles walked to one of the air vents and fingered it. The hole was too small to pass even his hand. His skin began to prickle.

Eisley jumped back, instinctively connecting the touch of the dense foam with the tingle over his body. The tingle continued. Hope leaped high in the diplomat's breast as he recalled the similar feeling an instant before he and Sue had found themselves stumbling on a grassy slope. The tingling had almost been lost in the vibration which permeated the engineering building, but surely this was the same—and surely it meant that he was about to shift back to the world he had known that morning.

Nothing changed for seconds, for the minute during which Charles forced himself to stare at the digits flickering across the window of his watch.

A door opened outward with angry suddenness.

Eisley's mind jumped and his muscles all sprang taut, although his body did not move perceptibly. The diplomat's instincts were those of any man, but his formal training for years had been to wait, not act.

There was little that action could have accomplished anyway, except to get the captive dismembered by the six waiting guards who were standing in an arc outside the doorway so that their weapons could sweep almost the whole interior of the cell. Eisley stared at the aliens for a moment before the arc split to either side and the nose of a vehicle slid against the doorway hard enough to jar the structure.

The prisoner had no time to grasp the whole of the vehicle before a portion of its flat bow blocked the door opening and all real view through it. All Eisley could see was a black sheet similar to the viewscreens of the utility vehicles. This close, the material had a suggestion of internal pebbling like that of heavy stained glass.

"What's your name?" the black sheet asked in excellent English. The voice had a noticeably southern—even black—tinge to it.

"My name is Charles Eisley," the diplomat said. He crossed his hands behind the small of his back. It was a trick developed from reception lines, to keep his shoulders straight and his hands out of the way. "Who, may I ask, are you?"

The demands broadcast by the vehicles hunting him had obviously been prerecorded and mindless. Eisley was expecting the same situation here, though perhaps with an array of stock phrases which might be tailored to the situation. The bodiless voice chuckled and said, "Why, you can call me Vrage, Mr. Eisley. And you can forget about handing me a line of bullshit because you figure you'll snap back to where you came from in a few minutes. We're holding you and whatever all you came with right here. Feel the charge? We're using our own drive to stabilize you right here."

"I don't understand," Eisley said. It was intellectually the truth. The way his belly chilled and solidified hinted that his body, at least, understood very well. He took a step forward to increase the illusion that he had free will.

"How did you get here?" the voice asked.

"You're human, aren't you?" the diplomat said. For the moment it seemed better to act on a basis of assumed equality with his captors. "How did you meet these, these aliens?"

Torture of prisoners was a regular part of several of the political systems on which Charles had reported as a part of his duties. Like cotton production or voting patterns, torture was not a thing which had ever touched him personally. Feeling otherwise meant that the plainclothes police who escorted you were imagined attaching electrodes to a prisoner's genitals—as indeed might be the men's duty the next day. That attitude of detachment meant the burst of high-frequency noise which lashed Eisley was wholly unexpected.

He lost physical control and perhaps consciousness for a fraction of a second. The side effect of Vrage weapons firing had been gratingly unpleasant. This was deliberate and focused, enormously greater in both amplitude and range of frequencies. Charles received it not as a sound but as a blow across the entire frontal surface of his body. He fell to his knees. Even then he had to fling his hands out to keep from sprawling headlong.

"You're alive, Eisley, because it's quicker for us if you are," said the voice.

The world was pulsing around Eisley. He closed his eyes. The fluids in his eustachian tubes surged in time with yellow flashes across the back of his eyelids. He gagged to keep from vomiting.

"You don't have to be alive, it's just quicker—if you're willing to answer questions." The voice throbbed in a universe of lights and bile. Charles could hear it with perfect clarity, but it rose and fell against a background not of noise but of white velvet. "Raise your head, now, Eisley," it coaxed. "Look at me for a moment and you'll understand why you have to be reasonable."

Charles took his hands from the floor and slowly opened his eyes. His reluctance to do so was entirely subconscious, a certitude in his body that he would begin to vomit if he opened himself to the external world again. In fact, the hard outlines of the door and the seams of floor and wall damped his nausea and made a human being of him again. He rose to his feet, only a little wobbly. "You can do as you please, I suppose," he said with dignity, "but you have neither right nor reason to punish me. I—"

The blank, black plate filling the doorway went translucent. It cleared in a vortex like that of a toilet flushing. The interior of the vehicle became visible through a network of shadows. Charles Eisley had been logically certain that the Vrage who spoke to him in normal English had to be human—had to be an American, in fact, although the purple-suited creatures with the guns were neither.

It was no subconscious surprise, however, that the creature which sprawled behind the screen was a grossly distorted version of those in atmosphere suits. The eight limbs of what had called itself the Vrage were approximately the size of those of the others; the thorax to which both legs and arms attached was bulkier but still basically the same.

There parity ended. The abdomen of the suited aliens, each approximately the size and shape of a basketball, hung in the midst of the four legs and did not appear to affect the creatures' ability to run quickly. The abdomen of the creature speaking to Eisley was the size of a boar's carcass and contorted rearward. It must have weighed several hundred pounds, several times as much as the remainder of the Vrage's body. The creature could have moved itself unassisted only by dragging that dead weight like a broken-backed snake.

It wore no clothing within the sealed environment of its vehicle. The ellipsoidal pucker in the middle of its chest must have been the mouth which was missing from the low-domed head. The skin, baggy at the joints, was a variety of mottled colors with red predominating, giving it somewhat the effect of a fall woodland. On an animate creature the pattern looked diseased.

The Vrage was inhuman, but more or less as expected. The brain in a transparent vat beside the Vrage was not expected, and it looked quite human.

"We already met a couple of your friends, you see," said the alien. "This one was named Thurmond." No part of the creature from which the sound could have come was moving, neither head nor presumed mouth. One of the creature's arms did reach out to stroke the vat, however. The brain within stirred sluggishly. Transparent tubes running across its pink-white surface were barely visible because the fluids they carried had indices of refraction different from that of the supporting bath.

"We would have had to sacrifice them anyway," the voice continued, "to learn enough to be able to deal with you this way. It didn't matter, since somebody transported them to our homeworld, not here." Laughter, deep and resonant, rolled from the horrible tableau. "Not a good thing to do if you need to breathe oxygen, no. Somebody played them for fools. Played you for a fool, too, dumping you here for a decoy. You'd better tell me just what happened."

Charles Eisley stared at the scene. He was trying to pretend that what he saw was distanced by fiction, that it was a television picture. The shadowed clarity betrayed him and tightened his vocal cords.

The Vrage caressed its human remnant again. "You'll tell me what we need to know, Eisley," the alien said. "Either now or after we've sent you home—to our home— for more extensive treatment. And you'll still be alive, but you won't be quite as handsome, hey?"

The floating brain nodded in its trembling vat.

"So tell me, why did the Skiuli sent you here?"

Charles Eisley gave a grim smile. He had fantasized in Viet Nam and in the Moslem countries in which he had served later about how he would hold up under questioning by ruthless fanatics. He realized now that he really *was* willing to die rather than betray his country.

But he had absolutely nothing to protect in this situation, except his life—and Sue. Unfortunately, his very inability to tell the Vrage anything useful was apt to cost at least his own life.

"I've never heard of the Skiuli," the diplomat said aloud. "So far as I know, I was sent back in time because of a mistake by, by a Professor Gustafson. He was . . . His experiment may have been aided by time travelers from—I was told—ten thousand years in the future. Ah, the future of our present."

The statement, which was as truthful and circumstantial as Charles could make it, sounded absurd to him. It sounded more, not less, unlikely because he was speaking to something with four arms, four legs, and a human brain floating in a vat by its side. The least that he expected was another scorpion-tipped blast of noise. Only slightly deeper in Eisley's awareness was a vision of his flesh sloughing and then the bone itself being eaten away, until all that was left of Charles Eisley was a bundle of nerve tissue in a bowl of heavy fluid.

To Eisley's surprise, there was no gout of punishment when the Vrage stroked instruments below its prisoner's sight. Instead the alien said, "Describe the beings who told you they were time travelers." There was a flicker of lights reflecting within the vehicle as some hidden process took place.

The diplomat rolled his lips between his front teeth to moisten them. "There's a man and two women," he said. "One of them—the woman—is good-sized and very solid, like a Russian athlete." The simile's pointlessness struck him as the words came out, but he continued anyway. "Mu—my informant calls them travelers, the Travelers." Charles paused, then blurted, "I don't have any evidence to convince you, of course."

The Vrage laughed its human laugh again. The mental effect on Eisley was almost as unnerving as the blast of white noise had been earlier. "I can't read the thoughts I get from your mind, Eisley," the alien said, "but this can." He stroked the vat of brain once more. "Keep on telling the truth. It's better for you." Pale yellow light quivered again within the Vrage's vehicle. A bubble began to rotate up its helical path to the top of the tank in which the brain hung.

The Vrage thrust forward its flat, mouthless head. "They've been lying to you, my man," said its voice. "They're travelers, all right—from Skius. They're just as human as I am." The laughter rippled around Eisley and echoed in his cell. It peeled his doubt like the skin of an orange.

"Then I don't understand what's going on," said Charles Eisley. Unconsciously, he had set his feet half a step apart with the toes pointing on ninety-degree axes. His shoulders were set and his hands were crossed behind his back again. It was the posture he would have adopted as a junior officer being chewed out by his ambassador.

"What's going on," said the Vrage as it eased back

against the support of its abdomen, "is that you're all being used as cannon fodder by the Skiuli. Worse. They're putting your whole planet out front to stop the lead we're going to fire at them." The chuckle with which the Vrage punctuated his discussion was as humorless as a death rattle.

"The Skiuli know," the Vrage resumed, "that we'll send hundreds of cobalt bombs along to rebound with their assault force. Not a World Wrecker like they'll try to implant in the crust of Vrage, but enough to make the sky glow at night and burn away every scrap of life that isn't protected for the next century by a mile of rock. And they don't want that to happen to Skius, so they're probably planning to launch their assault through your Earth instead of attacking directly from Skius. We'll do the same thing, of course—from here. But first, we'll see to it that the Skiuli's plans are delayed."

There was a pause during which the Vrage dismissed Eisley as thoroughly as if the door to the cell had already slammed. The viewscreen went black and opaque again.

"Wait!" the diplomat shouted. He jumped forward and set his palm against the screen. Its material felt cool and waxy. "What are you going to do with me?"

The vehicle shuddered with incipient motion, then settled again into clifflike stability. Charles snatched his hand back as the blackness cleared from the viewscreen.

The eyes of the Vrage were nearly human. They stared at the captive with the interest of a laboratory assistant for a white rat. "I'm going to send you home, Eisley," the Vrage said. "Right now we're holding you by using our drive coils to counteract the tendency of all the mass you were transported with to rebound. That creates a strong residual field. I'm going to ready a little present for your Skiuli friends. When we turn you loose, it'll ride along on the wave of that field. And I don't think the Skiuli'll be using the hardware they built on your planet ever again."

The viewscreen went opaque. The Vrage vehicle backed an inch, then spun on its axis. The vehicle was huge, the size of the tanks which had captured Eisley. In shape and sleekness it was more similar to the small utility vehicles, though the egg had been planed flat on the front and bottom. The magenta armor shone almost wholly purple under the artificial light.

Even as the Vrage vehicle swung clear, the six alien soldiers thrust their weapons toward the path of the closing door. They were as silent as poised spiders.

But from the vehicle that slid away rang out a terrible simulacrum of human laughter.

Lexie Market's two-inch heels measured her paces down the aisle. The sound lost itself in the basement's volume and angles.

Mike Gardner was seated on a metal folding chair in front of the silent control panels, not so much staring at the dials as communing with them. He turned just his head when the door opened behind him, not even lowering his feet from a crosspiece among the instruments. As a result, he could not see who had joined him in the darkened room until she paused at the gate into the enclosure.

The pressure of Lexie's hand swung the gate open, surprising her slightly. She had come back to the engineering building without any specific agenda. The diamond-patterned screen pivoted away, and she met the eyes and half smile of Mike Gardner. The physics professor froze in her tracks.

The woman's surprise recalled Gardner to society and recollection that the intruder was a professor, albeit in a sister discipline. He jumped to his feet in a clatter of chair supports. "Ah, hi, Mrs. Market," he blurted. "Damn! Dr. Market, I mean. Will you . . ." The student's hand drifted, searching for hospitality to offer. The closest approximation was the single metal chair.

" 'Lexie' will do just fine," the physicist said. She had started life as an ugly duckling; handsome men generally made her nervous. This one, however, managed to make her feel sophisticated, and that was more than a matter of the years she had on him. "It would be 'Miss' if it weren't 'Doctor,' anyway."

"Ah, do you want the lights?" Gardner asked. He was standing with one hand on the chair back, like a debater clinging to the podium for support. Both of them were well aware of what had happened in this room the night they first met. Memories of confusion and death emphasized instead of hiding other emotions which stirred in both of them. "I was just sitting here, trying to figure out what I was. . . ." His tongue waited while his brain marshaled ideas and then made the decision to expose them to this stranger in dim light. "Sometimes," Mike went on, "I think I've spent my first twenty-three years screwing things up so badly that I won't be able to make them right in the next however-long I live."

Market laughed, and the silver beads of her earrings winked in the haze of street lighting through the windows. She was wearing a dark skirt and a matching long-sleeved blouse, its throat rolled loosely so that it gave the suggestion of a stole as the woman moved. She touched Gardner's hand where it rested on the metal. "I used to think that," she said. "Now I think it's thirty-two, when I get in that mood." Her face sobered. She dropped her eyes from the man's but did not remove her hand. "Which is a lot, lately," she went on. "Has there been any news about Barry Rice?"

"Something's coming," said Gardner. He lifted his hand and hers to point past the controls. There was a touch of paleness forming over the docking area.

"Oh, my God," Lexie whispered, her right hand clenched at her throat. She was determined to wait for the Travelers and demand to be told about Rice. Perhaps that had always been the plan her conscious mind would not admit.

"Come on," Mike said, grasping her raised forearm. The strength of the woman's resistance and the sudden taut look around her eyes were a shock to him. "No," he explained, "we've got to get out of here." He relaxed his grip.

"I need to talk to them," Market said, and took a deep breath.

"You don't understand!" Gardner cried. "There's something else out there, spiders"—Professor Gustafson's shocked description made the misidentification inevitable— "and they *kill*! Hide in the office."

Market nodded, then ran ahead of him with the care required by her skirt and footgear. The light infusing the docking area was not really perceptibly brighter, but heightened attention made it seem so.

Mike slammed the gate shut and locked it. The heavy wire would not stop the sort of weapons the returnees had babblingly described, but it would at least pose a delay.

Lexie waited in the office doorway. When the student joined her, they both instinctively crouched below the level of the windows and peered through the narrow crack the woman had left between the door and its jamb. She could feel the pulse in his thigh as they squeezed together to watch.

The glow winked out in a nonevent. The appearance of two figures and the angular bulk of the Travelers' locker in the docking area was less disconcerting than the eerie light had been. One of the figures spoke to the other. The words were only a murmur. Even the squeal of the locker was muted as the pair slid it beyond the painted circle.

"Selve and Astor," Gardner mouthed, though the names would have meant nothing to his companion, even if she had heard them clearly.

The locker opened. Darkness and the conspiratorial silence in which they hid kept Lexie from greeting the Travelers, even now that their identity was certain. They were donning the atmosphere suits whose orange color was empurpled by the mercury vapor street lighting. Astor was sealing hers. Selve stepped to the control panels and began to bring up the system. Phosphorescence from the computer terminal gave his face definition if not color.

"It's just what they were doing last night," the woman whispered. She rested a hand on Gardner's thigh to steady herself, physically and otherwise.

The building began to hum its insistent note. The office windows trembled, casting hinted shadows within because irregularities in the glass created minute lenses. Selve joined his larger companion in the center of the docking circle. Astor handed him one of the guns she held. Mike Gardner's chest went numb with remembrance of how Keyliss had been mutilated. A different weapon, of course, but the same unexpected conflict. . . .

"Look away," Lexie Market reminded him. Gardner closed his eyes. The flash was scarlet as it seared his retinas through the blood vessels of the eyelids.

Mike was moving through the door before the air had cleared of echoes. He was leaving the physicist behind, forgotten in his fear and sudden resolution.

Market uncoiled from her crouch with a gymnast's grace, hiked up her skirt with one hand to keep from being hobbled, and met him when he thrust the key into the lock of the enclosure. "What are you doing?" she demanded as fiercely as if she already knew.

Mike went through the gate. He could already see that the Travelers' locker was open, just as they usually left it. "Going to follow them," he muttered, half hoping that he would not be understood. "We've got to find out what's going on."

He unhooked the third suit from within the locker. Keyliss's weapon, bumped by the student's arm, slipped and clashed its butt loudly on the floor of the locker. "They're not going to tell us, so I'm going to look."

"You saw Barry," the woman said. She did not grab Gardner's wrist, as her strength and agitation made him think she would.

Gardner scuffed his shoes off without untying them: the atmosphere suit would fit over his jeans and polo shirt. "Professor Rice wasn't wearing one of these," he said. "Mrs. Market, I think *somebody's* got to do this. Please don't get in the way." Mike knew that the more he thought about what he was doing, the harder it would be when it came time for him to execute.

He stepped into the suit. The front of it was split down to the crotch. His hands fumbled as they tried to find a zipper.

"Here," said Lexie as she brushed his fingers aside. She had watched the Travelers opening their suits the night before. As she expected, the seam closed neatly between her thumb and forefinger as she slid them up the opening to the man's throat. She paused there, continuing to hold Mike as if she had caught him by the tie. "Now, wait," she said firmly. "You don't know what's on the—other side, and you can't. But before you do anything else, we'll close the hood and you'll breathe for a full minute to make sure that it's really functioning. Agreed? Before anything else?"

The young man nodded because he did not fully trust his voice. "I need to check the controls," he added, a statement without emotional baggage.

"Wait," Market repeated. She lifted the cowl over Gardner's head. The lower edge fell into a smooth join with the torso of the suit without even her touch to guide it. "If you can't function normally while you're wearing it, then you need to know that now."

"Right," he said. Though his voice was normal, it was an octave lower than before and came from his chest rather than the closed hood. "Hey, M—Lexie. This works!"

He was probably taking a deep breath in proof of his words, but Lexie could see no sign of it. The sheet covering Mike's face was slick and opaque to her. Presumably he could see through it without distortion, because he stepped decisively to the instrument panel and threw a switch. Just as Barry had done, the woman thought.

Aloud she said, "I wanted you to wait."

"It'll take more than a minute," Gardner explained, "for the charge to build, Keyliss says, but I—" He broke off with a catch in his voice. "I don't guarantee the mechanism, but it's true that it takes. . . ." He broke off, his faceless mask turning from the woman to the docking area.

Lexie held him by the inner crook of both elbows. Mike's head spun to her again. She raised herself on tiptoe and kissed the smooth covering over where she thought his mouth must be. "Go get 'em, tiger," she murmured as she released him.

Mike Gardner held his pose for a moment longer, looking like a statue of surprise sculpted by Henry Moore. Then the insistent buzzing that made the soles of his feet quiver reminded him of his decision. He jumped over the painted boundary of the docking area.

The flash came fifteen seconds later. Dr. Alexis Market was still within the fenced enclosure. Her back was turned to the drive coils and the circle. The arms that she had thrown over her lowered face were there to protect more than her eyes from what was coming.

Sue Schlicter had started to doubt that she would find anything, even the creek. Then her right boot sank in mud, and there was no longer a sprawling tangle of branches in front of her.

She had assumed that she could pick her way downhill easily enough, despite the dark. That had not been true even on the steeper part of the slope. The trees camouflaged the terrain surface with unexpected thoroughness. When she did suddenly splash into her initial goal, however, the ultimate goal was facing her. In the soft plants across the stream lay the corpse of the giant carnivore; beside it hovered the car from which the beast had plucked the first alien to threaten it. The vehicle's empty cockpit glowed the soft greenish amber of a sick man's urine.

Sue splashed toward the car determinedly.

The sky glow was not sufficient to make more of the carnivore than a bulk whose surface quivered. The motion was not that of life or even the creature's autonomic nervous system disengaging from the muscles it had served: the slayer had become carrion, and thousands of its lesser fellows were devouring their late lord. The chitinous buzz of insects was multiplied by the numbers of wings involved. It led to an unpleasant recollection of the time machine that had ambushed her and Charles.

Heavy insects lighted on the woman's blouse and face as she strode closer. Their touch was shocking, and their feet drew blood as they briefly gripped. Schlicter's cheeks were taut in fearful parody of a grin, but she managed to swat the creatures only with her left hand. Her right held the open knife, its three-and-a-half-inch blade her only hope against larger predators now that the dark foreclosed flight. The insects disliked the woman's odor as much as she did their touch. None of them gripped her for long or tried to slash or suck her flesh.

There was other alien wreckage and even one broken corpse sprawled near the water's edge like a patch of algae; however, only the one car seemed to be functional. Sue had not been sure the aliens would have left anything. It had seemed a reasonable possibility, however, since only one-person vehicles had penetrated the forest fringe. It was not surprising that the aliens, nervous and literally out of their element, had not dispatched recovery personnel on a hike through the trees in the dark to a site where numbers of their fellows had been slaughtered in broad daylight.

Anyway, the alien vehicle afforded the only possibility Sue saw for rescuing her lover.

Its cockpit was something of a scramble to enter. The aliens had not seemed particularly strong, but their joints were extremely limber. The car was apparently intended to be mounted by gripping the coaming with a combination of six hands and feet, then executing a quick jerk to swing the rider aboard. Schlicter grimaced as her right palm slipped on the four-foot-high coaming. She folded her knife, slipped it back in her pocket, and tried again to clamber aboard. Her boots first slipped vainly, then flailed outside the cockpit as her buttocks landed on a seat not meant for humans.

The controls were not meant for humans, either.

The cockpit was lighted, but there was a tiller instead of a steering wheel; no knobs or pedals; and no identifiable instruments. The pattern of lines in the dashboard's lumpy padding might at that have been the instruments, but the possibility could only be tested if Schlicter got the vehicle to do something in the first place. The cockpit had the warm washday odor of bleach, but there was no gush of chlorine to poison a human occupant as she waggled the tiller experimentally. Nothing happened.

Gingerly, she put her feet down, boots cocked sideways to make room for her toes, her knees raised almost to eye height by the low seat. Her feet did not shuffle onto hidden controls.

Running her right index finger along the dashboard, Sue found that what had seemed to be padding was in fact hard and slick. Therefore, the bulge over which her finger was tracking might—

The car dropped with a bump and a slurp of mud. The lights went out. The woman swore. On reflection, though, anything was better than still being stuck here in the morning. And if touching the top of the lump made the vehicle ground itself, perhaps . . .

Her finger tweaked the lower curve of the dash, very briefly, as if she were testing a hot stove. The touch was enough: the car rocked as it freed itself and balanced again a handsbreadth above the ground. The hidden cockpit lighting again cast its bilious glow over the interior.

Since the molding to the right of the tiller was the off/on switch, then the similar excrescence to the left must also be significant. Sue touched the top of the lump with more assurance than she had reactivated the car a moment before. Nothing happened. Frowning but still determined, she slid her finger down over the surface of the lump. The car lurched forward as if someone had let in its clutch with a bang. Above Sue, the open viewscreen flapped like a sail.

Experience with motorcycles kept Schlicter from the

panic reaction of snatching her hands away from the controls. Instead, she drew her left index finger fiercely back up the curve which had set the vehicle in motion. Her right hand grabbed at the tiller.

The car slewed to the right momentarily before it lost its forward motion.

A fan of light flooded from the curve of the vehicle's bow, illumination as clean as that of a halogen beam, but—like the interior lights—with a disquieting hint of yellow green. Schlicter had palmed the end of the tiller, a natural act for a human but not for the Vrage, whose hands had more of an elbow joint than a palm. The light switch, out of the way of its normal users, had been thrown by human accident.

Sue Schlicter paused. She was cramped into the alien vehicle like a fat man in a basket chair. The car's lights glared out at the tangled forest. Beneath her, the stream bubbled frantically. She took a deep breath and drew the viewscreen down. Her vision through it was as clear as if it were optical-grade Plexiglas without the differing refractive indices of air and glass to contend with. The screen hung where she released it, its bottom edge a finger's breadth above the coaming. Whether or not chlorine would flood the cockpit when the screen latched, the seal would certainly cut off the outside air the human herself required.

"Dear God, Charles," Sue muttered. Then she touched the speed control and began to pick her way through the vegetation.

The dome rattled, as it always did when someone transported to Base Four from an oxygen world. The volume balanced. The slightly higher pressures within the shed before transport, however, meant that the flimsy structure shuddered at the shock of partial vacuum.

The door flew open before Selve could reach for it. Selve and Astor had expected to be greeted by one of the Monitors. There were six figures waiting. All of them were anonymous in their suits until Deith spoke. "Come to beg us for another chance when the Directorate won't give you one?" the stocky Monitor said, gesturing the Contact Members out of the shed with a brusque hand.

The Monitors wore holstered handguns. Unlike the shoulder weapons which Astor had insisted she and Selve carry, guns were not issued to Monitors as part of their working equipment.

"Do you like wearing atmosphere suits, Deith?" Astor said as she strode out of the docking shed without looking down at Deith. Selve followed his colleague more deliberately. He knew that his own physical presence would not prevent jostling in the doorway. None of the Monitors would permit themselves to be in Astor's line when the tension was this high.

"If you don't," the big female continued as she walked away, "then let's keep this till we're inside. But hold the thought, it's important."

The cruel atmosphere made an underwater scene of Base Four. Vision was not impaired more than it would have been on Skius—or Earth—in a light haze, but the distorted colors were more unpleasant than was the actual constriction of the atmosphere suits. Vehicles for internal ground transportation in this hostile environment snapped along the guides set in the streets when the base was laid out. There were no aircraft. Anything more than a few feet in the air would be suicidally vulnerable in combat of the sort the base's architects anticipated. So far as the planet itself was concerned, there was nothing anywhere on its surface of interest to the Skiuli except for the staging area they had built for their assault.

Of course, the Vrages must have made similar assumptions when they equipped their own staging area.

Deith muttered a demand to one of her colleagues. That Monitor, at her order, abandoned dignity and ran ahead of the party, which Astor continued to lead with her long strides. The Monitor pulled open the outer door of the airlock and stood holding it, as if he feared that the Contact Team would slam it shut on their hosts. Astor halted at the opening without looking around, blocking the others until Selve stepped by her. The big female then followed Selve regally, making room for the Monitors.

"Not what we're here for," Selve muttered disapprovingly. Pumps began to ram the local atmosphere out through vents.

"Neither is breathing," said Astor. "But we have to breathe, too, if we hope to succeed."

The Portal Four control room was in a wing devoted solely to instrumentation and living quarters for the Monitor Group. Deith and her fellows were nearly as isolated from the remaining base personnel as the Contact Team was from the local populace of Earth. The Monitors were to remain behind during the assault and holding action which would mean death for very nearly everyone they sent through the Portal. The circumstances *could* have made Deith what she was . . . but Selve, for one, believed the pattern of the Monitor's personality had been set long before.

The remaining half of the Monitor Group waited in the control room. They did not wear atmosphere suits—or guns. Astor and Selve stripped back their hoods as soon as they were out of the airlock. The Monitors escorting them stayed masked and faceless until Deith had closed them all within the control room.

"We have a proposal," Selve said as if he were not aware of the psychic atmosphere.

"The Directorate has already turned it down," Deith said from where she stood in front of the door.

Selve and Astor were in the center of the room, near the main console. Selve abandoned the fiction that all members of the Monitor Group were equals. He turned to Deith as he continued. "The Directorate has taken it under advisement. We want to explain it to you so that you can add your agreement to ours."

"Advisement," Deith sneered. "Rejected and you know it."

"I know it's the best chance we'll ever have to end this war without more of our own being slaughtered!" shouted Astor as she whirled toward Deith. The Monitor stepped back by reflex and bumped the door panel.

One of the suited Monitors started to draw her gun. "Wait!" Selve shouted.

"If we wait," Astor said, "half a million of the people out there are dead." Her voice was loud but controlled. Instead of simply waving, she accompanied her statement with three full-armed chops in a short arc toward the outside wall. "Luck's given us a chance to smash the Vrages. You can't throw it away."

"It isn't really luck," Selve broke in quickly as his companion sucked in a breath. "The Vrages were bound to offset their staging area just as we did ours, so that they won't lose their homeworld to the bombs sent by rebound. They didn't need to separate their base from their bridgehead, because they were willing to sacrifice the whole assault force. It was natural that they'd have set up on one of the most Skius-like planets in the direct Skius transport column."

"Then what matters," retorted Deith in a deadly voice, "is that we attack at once, that we set up a perimeter on Vrage, that we emplace a World Wrecker, and that we blow their foul planet to ions!"

"But there's a better—" Selve began.

"There's no better way than following orders!" the Monitor bellowed over Selve's words.

Astor pointed her long arm straight at Deith. She said, "There's better than losing more like Keyliss! Listen to us, Deith. It could be everyone *you* know next."

"What advantage is there to fighting the Vrages at Portal Thirty-one instead of their homeworld?" asked a Monitor wearing her ordinary uniform instead of an atmosphere suit. "The only way we can win is to destroy their planet once and for all. They're—Vrages."

The question cooled the tension. It also made it clear that Deith's gibes had been based on more than guesswork: the proposition which Selve and Astor had gasped to the Directorate while Keyliss was being hooked to life support and replacement systems. That proposition had already been relayed to Base Four in accurate detail. Supply and communications channels from Skius to Portal Four were closed to the Portal Eleven Contact Team. That the Directorate had chosen to use those channels now, when the traces they left could be a signpost to Vrage attackers, showed desperation at the highest levels.

Astor swallowed. She crossed her hands to the opposite collarbones and gave herself a firm hug. With her eyes closed she said, across Deith's attempt to reenter the discussion, "The base is here at Portal Four so the troops could live and train under the conditions of the assault. How would you like to fight a battle here?"

"They aren't fighting a battle," Deith snapped. "They're going to take and hold a perimeter on the Vrage homeworld for three hours until a World Wrecker can be dug down into the crust. Nobody claims we need to overrun Vrage!"

"The Vrages spotted us this time at Portal Thirty-one," Selve said. "Where their base is, their assault force is training in oxygen just the way ours is stumbling around out there in the chlorine.''

Deith opened her mouth to interrupt. Selve made a quick, one-handed gesture with his palm up. ''We slaughtered them, Deith. Astor did. I did, *me*.'' He slapped his slung weapon in an attitude of disbelief. ''The same way they'll do to our troops on Vrage—or would *here* if they could find us. No matter how well trained our people are, they can't fight the Vrage on a Vrage world. Not for three hours, not for one hour. We won't end the war that way.''

''Something's come through!'' called a Monitor who had stayed bent over his console while arguments over the future existence of Skius rattled across the control room. ''A few minutes ago, from Portal Eleven.'' The readout bloomed in sapphire light above the Monitor's instruments as he separately polarized the display to face every person in the room.

''You're an idiot!'' Astor said. ''That's us.''

''No, he's right,'' said Selve. He alone of those scanning the data could interpret it with assurance. ''Somebody riding our flow, Astor. Again.''

He and his colleague broke for the doorway with such abrupt determination that instinct threw Deith out of their way before her natural hostility could try to block them.

''I'll get Security!'' cried one of the armed Monitors.

''You won't!'' Deith shouted back. ''Come on, we're going to check this out ourselves and make sure the Directorate hears!''

She caught one of her suited fellows by the elbow and dragged him with her through the doorway to start the pursuit. Deith's right hand was fumbling with the flap of her holster.

                        *   *   *

This time, the second occasion the drive coils had sent Mike Gardner through what he thought was time, the sensation was that of stepping into a bath of cold water. Then he spread his legs for the sake of mental, not physical, balance and blinked while his brain finished correlating the real world with his terrified imaginings.

He was in a domed shed whose door was quivering. The light had an unpleasantly chemical appearance. It slanted through the translucent walls strongly enough to fling Gardner's shadow onto the door panel.

Mike dared fate with a deep breath. The air he drew in had a tinge of plastic and low humidity. There was none of the chlorinated lethality that he had feared. The student wet his lips and stepped briskly through the door, out into a world as bleak as an army base in winter.

The purulent yellow green of the air did not so much soften lines, the way fog would, as dissolve them in acid. Even without that, the two- and three-story buildings were stark and windowless. At first glance, the area was a single structure, like the snakes knotted behind the statue of Laocoon. Ten broad avenues leading to the hub where Gardner stood were overarched by covered bridges which managed to suggest an oil refinery rather than a willow-pattern plate.

Mike walked faster. He had begun by bending his neck stiffly toward the ground as if by not looking he would not be seen. That was foolish; his whole purpose here was to see. One thing immediately obvious was that this was not the planet Earth, however many years into the past or future one might go. The Travelers had been lying—arrogant Astor, sensitive Selve, and Keyliss, whose arm had flopped back onto the concrete at her feet that afternoon.

The pillars of the transport equipment—here black and so tall that Gardner could not pick out their tops at sunset in the turgid atmosphere—were set over a hundred yards apart. The shed in which the human intruder had appeared was at one apex of the isosceles triangle formed with the drive pillars as a base, an arrangement quite familiar to Mike Gardner. The scale at which it was constructed, however, was stunningly unexpected.

Toward Gardner slid a vehicle very nearly as broad as the entire avenue. It filled the arches over the roadway like a train through a subway tunnel. Though it was still a thousand yards distant, the engineer's mind translated scale into objective reality: thirty feet high, minimum; a hundred and fifty broad; and at least that length for stability. At least. The domed surface was studded with antennas like convex shields, too numerous to be microwave dishes and of unguessable purpose. The tubes beneath all the antennas were too like the muzzles of the Travelers' shoulder weapons to be intended for any other purpose.

There was some traffic on the others of the ten radial avenues. Vehicles the size and shape of the front half of a motor scooter zipped past or even between the central pillars. They and their orange-suited drivers were more noticeable for their motion than for shape, like flies glinting from cow to cow in a pasture. No one seemed to notice Gardner, though he was the only pedestrian in sight. Sara Jean's description of the city like a giant termite mound recurred to the young engineer. This time the words were colored by his near certainty that the city, the Travelers' home, was not on Earth, either.

Dear God in heaven.

Mike walked toward the nearest building at a pace just short of a run. The bow of the oncoming tank blinked each time the vehicle slid under the shadow of an arch. The tank was as awesomely fast as it was huge. The ground was beginning to rock. Though the whole surface was either covered or stabilized, there was enough grit to rise in a gray haze around the bow and sides of the vehicle.

A one-story appendage of the sprawling buildings reached to within thirty yards of the point at which Mike Gardner had materialized. The structure would be dwarfed by the tank, but at least it would be noticed and avoided. A lone interloper in the path of that vehicle would be swatted away as certainly as a sheep strayed onto the railroad tracks.

Mike halted with one hand flat against the wall of the building to reassure himself that it was there and protecting him. The tank slid into the circular plaza around the pillars, and what had been a parklike expanse looked suddenly like a cul-de-sac with the rusty, jagged mass of a garbage truck using it. The tank was much longer than Gardner had dreamed, four hundred and fifty, possibly five hundred feet. The dust it raised seemed to expel the vehicle from the boulevard into the hub like smoke from a gunshot. The tank passed between the pillars and, without slackening the speed which its size made seem less than the real forty-five miles an hour, bent its course up another of the radial streets.

In shocked amazement, Mike Gardner watched nine identical vehicles follow their leader. Their scale was naval, not military, and the array of weapons with which each bristled had been equaled by nothing on Earth since the battleships which took the Japanese surrender in 1945.

Gardner tried to press his left fist against his mouth and bite his knuckles through the forgotten face mask. His mind staggered with the thought of those tanks and the thousands more implied by the size of this encampment: cities blazed and fell to ruin before them, and all the screaming victims in his mind were human as their destroyers surely were not.

The sound of the airlock opening beside him was lost in greater thunder, down the boulevard and in Gardner's mind.

Someone shouted an interrogative in no Earthly language.

Mike jumped before he glanced around. Astor's fingers slid off the shoulder of the borrowed suit. Like Gardner himself, Astor was unrecognizable, with a reflection instead of a face. The intruder could see himself as an orange distortion in the rippled mask of the figure confronting him.

Beyond the person who had called to Gardner was the shorter, equally anonymous form of Selve. Selve's weapon had not been slung securely. When he stumbled through the airlock, the gun had slipped and tripped him. Now Selve carried the weapon in both hands. He was thinking only of keeping the unfamiliar burden out of his way, not at all of where the muzzle pointed.

Mike Gardner dodged around the corner of the building to avoid the unintentioned threat.

"Wait! Who are you?" Astor cried in English as she ran after the intruder.

Behind her, the airlock sprang open again. If either member of the Contact Team had thought the situation through, they would have wedged the outer door open to prevent the inner one from being used. The suited Monitors spilled out. "Grab him!" Deith ordered.

It was not until two Monitors tackled him that Selve realized he, rather than the fugitive, had been the object of the command. "No!" the Traveler said for the instant he thought that Deith had made a mistake. Then one of the Monitors wrestled the weapon away from Selve while the other one threw herself across his chest to pinion his arms and upper body.

Gardner ran down the side of the low building which

had sheltered him from the traffic. It was no shelter now: the wing that thrust out into the central plaza housed a control room which stood in much the same relationship to the drive coils as did the instrument consoles controlling the lesser units on Earth. The walls were smooth and opaque with no door alcoves, window ledges, parked vehicles, or even litter to give the illusion of cover. The main building from which the wing was thrown blocked Gardner's path a hundred feet in front of him, featureless and three stories high.

"Are you trying to get killed!" Astor shouted. The step Mike had paused when he realized there was no escape gave his pursuer the opportunity she needed. Astor tackled Mike from behind, using her bulk to topple him beneath her to the ground.

"Astor?" the engineer gasped. Her voice was recognizable despite the suit and the circumstances. "What *are* you?"

"Mike? Mike?" the Traveler said as she shifted into a kneeling position. "You shouldn't have come here, you fool! Look, you'll rebound in a minute or two at the most. Stay here, wait for us, we'll—"

Four more figures in orange pounded around the corner thirty feet away. One of them had a pistol cleared.

"I've got him!" Astor shouted. She raised her left hand in prohibition. Instinct rather than conscious direction made her right shoulder twitch. The sling fell away. The gun slid down the inner curve of Astor's arm till her hand on the grip caught it.

The four Monitors stopped. Three of them clumped beside the wall. Deith stood a step apart and called, "Get away, Astor! This isn't the business of somebody who's blundered as badly as you three!"

Selve cried something, the words muffled and unintelli-

gible to his female colleague. They could have been
". . . few seconds!"

"Deith, *we'll* take care of this!" Astor said. Her mind
was lost in a sea of icy needles. There were no good
choices. Even the questions were only amorphous horrors
to her. She was not fit to decide this, that was for Keyliss
or—

"You chose," Deith snarled as she raised her sidearm.

Pure reflex is not enough for a gunfight conducted
within the matrix of civilization. There must be go/no go
decisions programmed by the intellect. Otherwise the ground
is littered with dead hostages, dead allies, and dead children who opened a door at the wrong moment.

Reflex would have snapped Astor's shot into the center
of mass, damn the consequences to the shooter and to the
proposal she had endorsed. Astor fired instead at Deith's
hand and gun while part of her brain correlated data which
no one else present had fully gathered as yet.

The beam was choked tight. There was a white flash at
the point of impact. Fractured molecules from Deith's gun
and hand were combining with chlorine much as they
would have done at similar temperatures in an oxygen
atmosphere.

One of Deith's fellows released his equipment belt and
flung it away, gun, holster, and all. Deith herself staggered sideways, toward the missing hand. The atmosphere
swirled at the end of her wrist.

"Get a clamp on it, you idiots!" Astor shouted as she
rose to her feet. The muzzle of the weapon faded back to
neutral gray. She waggled it above the heads of the Monitors. "And get her inside. How much atmosphere do you
think these suits hold?"

Behind Astor but by no means forgotten by her, Mike
Gardner disappeared from the world of Portal Four Base.

There would be repercussions from what Astor had just done. Perhaps Selve could handle them, perhaps Keyliss was well enough by now to handle that task which would normally have been hers.

Right at the moment, Astor was feeling wryly glad that she had been offered a choice in terms she could fully comprehend.

Sue Schlicter's body kept telling her that she was fully in control of her mount. Intellectually, she knew she was not. For the first week on a vehicle, there is always something new to learn—normally at a bad time. Her first ride in the parking lot on a motorcycle had been exhilarating until she tried to remember which of the levers and switches controlled the brakes.

Still, the alien car appeared to be of idiot-proof simplicity. There were no major obstacles to contend with once Sue nosed out of the forest. That experience had left her palms sweaty and her knuckles aching with strain, but scrambling through the trees had been awkward on foot as well. The animals she came upon were all herbivores, stragglers from the majority of a herd which now snorted and splashed in the creek—startled but not panicked or enraged by the bright lights.

The car was traveling at over twenty miles per hour, faster than was prudent, when it topped the grassy lip of the crater. Sue's lights shot off into empty space, then sprayed the ground as the vehicle plowed dirt with its nose—the car had almost no axial stability when its front and back ends were at significantly different heights. Sue's own attempt to compensate by throwing her weight back had no effect. Luck alone prevented disaster, and that only as the bow scraped wickedly.

Schlicter dialed back the power, overcorrected to a halt,

and finally brought the speed back up to a fast jog, hoping her inept driving had not drawn the attention of any of those tens and hundreds of thousands of aliens in the encampment below.

The great pool of lights hid signs of particular interest as completely as absolute darkness could have done, but she could see some vehicles moving among the maze of buildings. More important, there were still a few other fans of light on the inner crater wall, vehicles traveling to or from the encampment just as Sue was struggling to do.

Though the slope down which she now drove was not dangerously steep, it was studded with frequent outcrops of rock whose abrupt lower faces could tip the car as thoroughly as the crater rim itself had done. The care required to steer around those dangers when they appeared in the lights was actually a benefit to Sue. It kept her from worrying about what she could do if she did reach her lover. Charles might fit in what seemed to be a storage compartment behind the seat—but that would mean folding the seat back, and she had no idea of how to accomplish that. Even if Charles were still in there. Even if she reached him, even if she released him from what was clearly a prison.

Those were the medium-term questions. The larger and still less answerable doubt was how they would ever return home, since the time machine was not snatching them back the way Mustafa had said it did for others.

Almost abruptly, the alien camp became an obstacle course instead of a goal. Buildings with wrinkled walls and no apertures replaced the grass. The headlights became a fan of greater intensity in the area lighting. Leaves no longer whickered along the surface of the car. The alien presence of the buildings restrained any impulse to speed up on the smooth surface.

Schlicter entered the encampment on a causeway which was not straight and which might not have been a street at all, though it was brightly illuminated. Walls wobbled to either side of her vehicle. Occasionally, a structure overarched the road. The feeling of driving down a tunnel was weakened by ten-foot-high standards that threw out polarized floods of lime-tinged light. Nothing could really be seen above them anyway, so the fact that there was a building rather than sky overhead could be put out of mind.

Now that it was too late to determine, Sue realized that she could not remember where on the roadways—right, left, or middle—the aliens had themselves driven. The only thing she could recall with certainty was the image of the troop which captured Charles: the lighter vehicles had been scattered in the wake of the tanks. Since the tanks were as broad as the street, that provided no real answers. There was no traffic control evident at intersections, so the question had possible consequences worse than simple detection. The tall woman could only stick to the center of whatever roadway there was, swiveling her head with taut determination at every cross street or kink substantial enough to suggest a cross street.

No other traffic was now visible, a blessing but a threat to someone who feared to stand out. Occasionally the texture of a wall would change abruptly as she slid past it. Porosity became mirrored smoothness or a pattern of waves. Schlicter could not tell whether that was chance, a trick of the light, or a challenge which she, presumably, was not answering correctly. She kept moving.

Five minutes after she had entered the camp proper, although the road had twisted too many times for rational certainty, Sue remained convinced that she was coming close to the center and her goal. She had expected the huge drive coils themselves to orient her, but they were invisible because of the roof of light, even in those rare instances where the structures were far enough apart or low enough to permit a decent view upward.

When an avenue eighty feet wide intersected Schlicter's path, it gave her almost as great a shock as would the cul-de-sac she had been fearing all along. Her thumb twitched down on the speed control over which it had been poised. The car slowed sharply enough that Sue's head bumped the lowered canopy. In front of her, and as unexpected as the avenue itself, sped three trucks like those which had transported infantry across the valley. These were empty, but they were moving at over fifty miles an hour. If surprise had not stopped her, Sue and her car would have been centerpunched into wreckage as complete as anything that the carnivore had wreaked in the stream bed.

She let the car glide forward again, more slowly than she would have walked had she dared to dismount. There was no other traffic moving. A quarter mile to her left rose the globular drive coils, the nearer one superimposed on the sphere beyond it. The bulk of the units had ghostly presence above their brightly illuminated lower curves.

The small building she hoped still held Charles was nearer still—and it seemed unguarded.

Schlicter was clinging to the tiller with all the strength of her right hand. She was not afraid that the car would snatch control away from her, but rather that her trembling would cause her to lose it.

Expecting a bellow of authority as the car moved into the open area, her mind threw up images that normally hulked just below her consciousness. Her father stood there with his belt looped in his hand. Beside him was her onetime lover, the paratrooper who would beat her with anything but his bare hands when he became angry.

The fear did not keep Sue from acting, but it did keep her from looking around for real dangers because of her subconscious certainty that the past was about to savage her again.

She was as alone as a skater practicing in an empty rink.

When that realization struck her, Schlicter's tension drained out with a sudden giggle. She was alone, she was being ignored, and her car was tracking across smooth pavement in silence. There was danger, of course, but nothing that would be made better by letting her chemical terror overwhelm her.

Driving around the cell at an ambling pace, she was close enough to touch the building had she wanted to raise her canopy. The two vents she had seen being cut into the sides with guns were too small for escape routes. The aliens had probably stripped Charles before they locked him in, but it still seemed doubtful that Sue's knife could significantly enlarge the holes. She would try, if needs be, but the door seemed to be a better option.

Only she could not find a door, a handle, or a seam of any kind in the surface of the building.

She circuited the building again but achieved the same nonresult, then touched the speed control and slowed to a halt beneath one of the vents. So far as she could tell, the viewscreen was not degrading her vision in the least. Nonetheless, she seemed to have no alternative but to get out of the car and feel her way around the structure until she found a door. Or was found herself.

Then she remembered Charles might be present, albeit not visible. She swore under her breath and raised the canopy by an additional handsbreadth. Light—or images—passed through the unfamiliar material, but for all she knew it still might deaden sound. "Charles!" she called.

Her voice cracked. "Charles!" she repeated, furious with herself.

"Sue? Have they caught you, too?" floated Eisley's voice through the hole in the wall.

"I'm here in one of their cars," Schlicter said. Until her lover spoke, she had not been aware of how alone she had felt and how much that bothered her. "I'm all right—there aren't any of them around. I can't find a door to let you out through, though."

"Sue, this is very important," Eisley said. He spoke with the care of a parent whose child has just crawled out on a high ledge. "I can't be sure where the door is myself, even though I've seen it open. The edges must grow together. But it's very important that I get away from here. They're using their—their matter transmitter, it's not what we were told—to hold me here. When they—let go—I'll snap back with a bomb. A, ah, at least a fusion bomb, from what they implied. Can you move the whole building with your car? I think maybe just a few yards will do it, get me out of the focus of their machine. Otherwise, I . . . I don't want you to die, Sue, or me to die, either. And I'm afraid it's going to be much worse than that, back on Earth."

Schlicter did not try to absorb most of what the diplomat was saying. Two things were important: Charles did not think the door could be opened; and moving him like tuna in the can of his cell would achieve the same result.

"Move you away from the balls, you mean?" she asked as she examined the cell from a new mental perspective. She knew her vehicle was flimsy from the way the carnivore had shredded similar ones. That did not mean the—engine, whatever—was not powerful. By the same token, the cell could be light even if it were very strong. "Which way?"

"I don't think it matters," Eisley was responding. "It

must— I hope it's a point, an area, the way the docking area Mustafa explained was. If I get out of that, we'll be all right.''

Sue had not learned how to make her commandeered vehicle back up. She cramped the tiller hard away from the cell and touched up the least possible amount of forward speed. The car began to describe a slow, tight circle. When its nose aligned with the cell, Sue centered the tiller again. She let her vehicle coast against the small building with no more impact than the doors of an elevator closing.

"All right, Charles," she called. She fingered in slightly more power.

The car began to twitch with increasing anger. The cell did not move. Lines of white light began to pulse on the dashboard.

With the suddenness of bear traps firing, doors opened in half a dozen of the buildings in sight of the plaza. The aliens who scuttled out were the first ones Schlicter had seen walking on the ground.

Sue chopped the car's throttle. There was no audible alarm, but she felt a nervous tingling in rather than on the surface of her skin. Neither the cell nor the car had budged visibly while the one tried to push the other. There was enough energy stored somewhere in the combination, however, to fling the vehicle back ten feet when the car stopped thrusting forward. The elastic effect surprised both Schlicter and the alien whose beam slashed the wall of the cell where the car had been nosing.

When in doubt, gas it.

Sue slid her thumb fully down the lump controlling the car's speed. The acceleration was not the kick in the pants of a cammy motorcycle; the car's speed built at a linear rate but with quickness bespeaking an enormous power-to-weight ratio. Wind roar beneath the cocked viewscreen and the blur into which objects dissolved to either side of the axis of motion proved to Schlicter that she was aboard something even hotter than the 1,100 cc pavement-rippler she had parked back at the engineering building worlds away.

Human retinas have the capacity to react only to gross inputs during high-speed driving. Sue dragged the tiller hard toward the major avenue, knowing she could not hope to maneuver through a narrow alley at a rate that could get her clear of the alerted encampment.

Two of the eight-limbed aliens ran into the throat of plaza and avenue. There was plenty of room to avoid them, but both were raising hand weapons.

One of the aliens fired as Sue essed toward the avenue. The guide beam might have missed behind her—for a moment or two—if the car had continued its high-speed circuit. As it was, the beam ticked the flank of the car and shut down all systems as thoroughly as distributor failure does a gasoline engine. The car had been rock steady at short-radius turns on the unbanked plaza. Now it skidded and spun like a hockey puck. The alien gunner continued to waggle his beam, but he did not hit the car again.

Sue's hand flailed at the part of the dashboard which had started the vehicle while she was experimenting with the controls. Despondent without speed to exhilarate her, she had no hope that the car would restart. She slumped, visualizing the damage which the beam that missed her was doing as it slid across the cell and Charles within.

Control and the interior lights returned simultaneously. The rush of joy was as much of body as of soul. Schlicter's hand stabbed down on the speed control.

The alien who had not fired at her now cut down the alien who was firing.

Charles had been in Sue's mind and in the potential line of

fire, but that was surely no concern of the aliens themselves. Their own spherical drive coils were equally at risk to a wildly flailing beam, however. There was a fraction of a second during which a blue-white arc connected the alien gunman to the suit of his target. During that moment, Sue reacted and cramped the tiller again. Her car spun in a curve as tight as a yo-yo's.

"Move the building," Charles had directed, but shifting the drive coils would achieve the same result—and all *they* had to be shifted was off.

The acceleration was like a slingshot's. The aliens now running into the plaza from all sides might have been embedded in amber for anything their legs could do to match her speed. How long would it take to summon vehicles from other parts of the camp, tanks or trucks or even another car which could end Sue's run in a suicidal collision?

Longer than the aliens had left.

Another one fired. His aim was off, far behind, because the angle must be safe: a quarter frontal shot with no chance of slashing one of the spheres. Training kept the other massing aliens from shooting. They would have thrown their bodies into the car, hundreds of them, but they were too far behind and she was too fast.

She had always wanted to be a hero. She wondered if Charles would know.

At the last instant, all the lights in the camp were shut off. The final thirty feet of empty pavement arrowed back at Sue in the fan of her car's beam, but all her brain saw now was its own construct—the huge drive coil seemingly balanced on the ground without a pedestal or bracing.

The world snarled in a coruscant arc.

"Mike, they're here," Lexie Market called. From where she stood at the door of Professor Gustafson's office, she could see Gustafson and Ike Hoperin just entering the basement through the back door.

"That's all right, Mrs. Hitchings," Gardner said to Gustafson's housekeeper on the other end of the phone line, "we've found him. Thank you." He was already turning and slamming the phone down as his mouth uttered that last courtesy.

"Dr. Gustafson, Ike," Market called in greeting. Mike had blurted to her a description of what he had just seen. The shock of that information kept the physicist from being self-conscious as she had been when surprised the night before.

"Ah . . ." said Professor Gustafson.

Isaac Hoperin was wearing casual clothes, unusual for him in public, and carpet slippers on his feet. "Lexie," he remembered to say.

Mike Gardner burst out of the office. "Sir," he said, "I've been trying to get you. Selve and the others aren't building a time machine at all, it's—it's got to be something else, where we went just *looked* like Earth two hundred million years ago."

"Dr. Layberg just called me," Louis Gustafson agreed, frowning in puzzlement as if trying to decide which of two frozen dinners to warm in the oven. Mike Gardner was not fooled by the abstracted look or the mild tone in which his professor continued, "He and his wife say the same thing. I asked Isaac to pick me up and bring me here"—he nodded to the male physicist—"so that we could try to learn what has been . . . Michael, what in *goodness* are you wearing?"

"Sir, I followed them—through tonight," Gardner said. He waved an orange-gloved hand toward the enclosure across the aisle. "I wore this, Keyliss's suit, and it's not *Earth* through there."

"Louis, I think your apparatus is running," broke in Isaac Hoperin. "Is this something you've programmed it to do?" he added with a glance toward Gardner.

"Negative, negative," the younger man said. He made a dismissing sweep with both hands.

"It does that on the ret—on the rebound," Lexie said, walking across the aisle with firm, quick steps. "Mike, they didn't come back before you did. Maybe they're coming back now. The Travelers."

Gustafson and, a step later, Hoperin strode after the woman. From the door of the office, Mike Gardner cried, "Look, they've got guns. Sir, there's a whole *army* on the other side of things there."

"Then we'll ask them what they're doing," Louis Gustafson called back over the growing level of vibration.

Market paused, but the two men stepped past her into the enclosure. Dr. Hoperin seemed to be interested solely in the readings from the control panel. As the coils built to full potential, Louis Gustafson could be heard saying, "I built this for peace. I will not have it used for war!"

Freed by rebound from the Monitors who had tried to hold him, Selve and his gun appeared separately in the docking area. The male Traveler stripped his hood back and met the eyes of Professor Gustafson. The fact that the weapon lay ten feet behind him impinged neither on Selve's interest nor on his memory.

By contrast, Astor's weapon was an extension of her intellect: it swung with her eyes as she pivoted to take in her surroundings. Only when the big woman had recognized all those around her in the basement did she relax enough to unmask. Even so, the muzzle of her gun jumped when the Laybergs entered through the door Gustafson had deliberately left unlocked.

"Hello, Sara Jean," Selve called as he walked toward the analogue recorders, his expression unreadable. With one hand, the Traveler gathered in the formal and angry Louis Gustafson and guided him along. "This is a cross-over station between two linear matter transmission systems," Selve said, letting true details stand in place of the apology for which he had no time.

"Astor, what have you done?" asked Mike Gardner as he walked stiffly toward the enclosure fence.

Astor glared for a moment at the young man in the suit he should not have taken. Then she remembered Keyliss and the urgency of the situation in which she felt herself to be drowning. Her snarl cleared. "Selve," the big female begged, "what are we going to do?"

The two members of the Contact Team had had no time to plan during the violent confusion at Portal Four Base. They could have spoken here in confidence using Skiuli, but it was a measure of Astor's training and automatic discipline that she spoke clearly and in English.

"It's running again," said Lexie Market. "The apparatus is about to transfer someone else, Dr. Gustafson."

Astor again had duties with which she felt comfortable. She crossed the painted circle in two strides and scooped up Selve's gun. After slinging her colleague's weapon in the locker, she continued to hold her own as she returned her attention to the docking area. Selve would have said something if the transport had been programmed from the portal. If the flow were the result of meddling or error, there was no way to tell what would be appearing in a moment's time. Astor shifted so that her field of fire covered both the normal area and its reciprocal on the other side of the woven wire.

Selve kept glancing up at the area in which some one or thing would momentarily appear. Meanwhile he ran a sort of private race, scrolling from hand to hand the analogue tapes, checking for evidence of some transport for which this could be the rebound. The answer was not available from the data, and the exercise was in any event a pointless one . . . except that it was a part of Selve's conviction that he could solve any problem involving the programming of portal apparatus.

Most of the humans in the basement remained fixed where they stood at Market's warning. Henry Layberg had paused. He resumed walking toward the gate of the enclosure after cool consideration that there was no reason to do otherwise. Sara Jean followed him. She looked at and past Mike Gardner. It was only a look, the look of an erstwhile lover, and it did nothing to disturb the serenity of the person she thought she had returned to being.

For the first second of silence after the flash, no one—human or Skiuli—recognized the couple who sprawled at the reciprocal point outside the enclosure.

Astor shouldered and pointed her weapon, more because there was no reason not to than that the situation required such preparation.

As the kneeling man stood and the woman untangled her long legs, Gardner shouted, "It's all right! Selve, they're the people that got caught this afternoon. Mustafa's friends, do you remember?"

The woman who had just appeared was lifting what seemed to be the remains of a leather jacket. Not only had the garment been ripped, the leather gave the impression of having been tie-dyed—or rather, tie-bleached—from the action of powerful acids as it lay wadded in the carnivore's stomach. The man with her looked distinguished though disheveled. He eyed Astor with guarded suspicion even after the Traveler had lifted her gun to port when she heard Gardner's identification.

"Right, I remember that," Astor said as she turned to Selve.

"Thank goodness!" the professor said, his concern for the project transiently outweighed by his relief that this small-scale disaster had been averted. He trotted toward the newcomers, oblivious both of the docking area he was crossing and the fact that Astor's weapon had swept the area only seconds before. "Madam? Sir? I'm Louis Gustafson, and I'm afraid responsibility for this accident is mine. Are you all right?"

"Astor, this is—" Selve began. Another possibility occurred to him. "Michael," he snapped; there was no time for pleasantries, "are you *sure* this is the couple which was transported—five hours thirty-three and a half minutes ago?"

Gardner touched the fencing with one hand as he peered toward Schlicter and Eisley. The instant confusion made him revert to the assumptions of the past several months— that this was a colleague rather than an alien who had hidden enormous military power from him. "What? Yeah, I think—" the student said. "Charles and Sue?" he queried, calling the newcomers by the names he recalled Mustafa using.

Sue Schlicter looked up, eyebrows raised, when she heard her name called. Charles was talking through the fence to Professor Gustafson, warning the project director about the Skiuli in a voice he hoped Astor could not hear.

Sue was still too amazed at being alive to find anything about the future to be a matter of present concern. She walked up the long aisle, carrying the remnants of her jacket. Her first thought had been to abandon the ruined garment as a thank offering to the gods who had preserved her from a like fate. Then she realized that she really had to keep the jacket, to hang it over the TV set in her living room. Otherwise she herself, come next year or next week, would never be able to believe what had just happened.

The fact of the leather being dry explained her survival. She had expected, had intended, to die as her car shorted the coils of the great sphere. At the instant that happened, she and Charles—and presumably the volume of air transported with them—had rebounded to the present a moment before Sue would have been crushed into the hardware she was destroying.

Momentum did not transfer on the rebound. Sue had simply sprawled on the concrete without her dignity. If the coils had fried a half second later, she and her jacket would have been matched in their degree of mutilation.

"That's wrong," Selve insisted, "that won't fit the output or"—the tape bunched and slid expertly through his fingers to extend the section which had just come out of the pens—"the input side, either. They can't . . ." He looked up to face Sue Schlicter, who was sauntering through the enclosure gate.

"The spiders in the purple suits had Charles in their—" the tall woman said. She pointed in a gesture made theatrical because she used the hand which held the jacket. Behind the wire, Eisley glanced up, thinking the gesture was meant for him. To those who had heard what Schlicter was saying, it was obvious that she had indicated the drive coils. "Only theirs were round, not long like these," she concluded.

"Selve, a bomb," Astor said. She spoke loudly but with a clarity which made the words a command instead of a hysterical outburst. Schlicter and Eisley were to either side of the female Traveler. By instinct, Astor pivoted so that her weapon would bear—needs must—on the woman first. A human gunman would have made the opposite choice. "Shunt them into a test Portal—"

"Twenty-nine," Selve said as he let the tapes fall and lunged for the controls.

"—*fast!*"

"Selve!" cried Sara Jean Layberg, and touched the Traveler on the arm as he would have passed her.

He looked aside and met her anguish. She knew less than many of the others, but she must have guessed more. There was no choice or time to lose, however: if the Vrages had sent these prisoners back, they had done so with a bomb, however concealed. It would destroy the apparatus at Portal Eleven. With the apparatus would go the life of every human for miles around, and any chance for the maintenance of life on Skius.

"No, they escaped," said Louis Gustafson with unexpected firmness as he turned from his whispered conversation with Eisley. The diplomat looked through the fencing past Gustafson's shoulder. Charles began to stride up the aisle to join Sue and whatever awaited them.

"Right," Schlicter was saying. In her euphoria at present survival, she had not grasped the threat implied in the Travelers' exchange. "There was *going* to be a bomb when they got it ready, but I drove a car into their"—her free hand mimed in the air—"their things, the balls, and they let go of us."

Selve pivoted toward Schlicter with the grace of a pitcher turning to throw out the runner at first. "You drove a vehicle into the Vrage transport coils," he said, "and you did enough damage to affect dynamic stabilization?"

Dr. Layberg and Hoperin had been drifting toward Astor with different thoughts in mind.

Layberg had seen the accuracy and ruthless speed with which the big Traveler used her weapon. He had no idea what the aliens were planning now, but the way Astor's gun moved as a part of her showed what she expected.

Henry Layberg intended to jump the female at his first safe opportunity . . . though logic warned him that her strength and speed gave even the best opportunity an element of risk.

Isaac Hoperin was reacting at a deeper level to the disinterested command in Astor's voice. That the Travelers were indeed alien was a matter of wonder and interest to the physicist, but no more than what he had already felt at the evidence they were time travelers. Astor's willingness to treat humans as beans to be shuffled carelessly from pile to pile was not a sign of her own nonhumanity. Hoperin had heard the same phrasings, the same tone, often enough over the years. In his undergraduate days, many of the beans were being piled in Viet Nam. Hoperin, stalking toward Astor as he had years ago stalked toward a police line, did not even realize that his hands were clenched.

Almost none of the nouns Selve had used in his question made individual sense to Sue Schlicter. But taken in context, and aided by her ebullience at being alive, she could understand enough to answer. "I hit it going, hell, I don't know how fast. A hundred and forty? Faster'n I've ever gone on the ground, that I know. I hit it at the bottom, but there were sparks all over hell, and I don't think it was all in my eyes. I mean—we're *here*."

Selve covered his face with his hands in an attitude of worship which the watching humans misconstrued. There were tears of joy in his eyes as he took his hands away. "Sara, Astor . . . everyone!" Selve said. "We've won. Even without the Monitor Group's concurrence, we've won. We *have* to attack the Vrage base now while they're out of communication. They won't have a chance!"

Astor stepped past Isaac Hoperin and hung her weapon in the locker. Dr. Layberg blinked at the unexpected action. It was the sort of care with weapons to be expected of

Astor before what she did next—shout and stride to her colleague with her arms open to embrace him.

The big Skiuli's enthusiasm infected everyone in the basement with the exception of Louis Gustafson. All around him, people were clasping one another, despite general uncertainty as to what the good news had been. Selve, feet off the ground, was spinning in a circle, supported by Astor's arms. Those two were the only ones who understood that Earth's death sentence had been surely countermanded. The others simply reacted to the Travelers' relief—and it was enough.

"Why do you have to kill with it?" Professor Gustafson demanded loudly. "Destroy a planet? How can you think of that? And if they're chlorine breathers, dear God, even if there weren't an entire universe out there—what possible reason could there be to fight them?"

"Well, Louis . . ." temporized Dr. Layberg as his body shut down the systems which had been preparing him to grapple with Astor. At his present nadir of relaxation, the thought of resumed conflict between the parties in the lab was peculiarly horrible.

Simultaneously but from a different viewpoint, Charles Eisley said, "I don't think it's profitable for us to assess the merits of decisions made by sovereign parties in their own spheres, Professor."

The words were rote from his past training. The image in Eisley's mind was that of the thing which called itself the Vrage . . . and beside it, the thing which still housed a human mind, coupled now into machines and—like a machine—useful only for its function. The thought of bombs sweeping across the planet from which came that creature and its fellows was not something that troubled Eisley. "So long as our own interests are safeguarded, of course," the diplomat's tongue added.

Astor's mind had run a path parallel to that of Eisley. "They aren't like us, Louis," she said as she lowered Selve to the floor again. "I don't mean that they have more legs. Only. They won't share—not the universe, and certainly not the principle of transport."

"*You* aren't human," Henry Layberg said bluntly. He did not want to say the words, but the situation demanded that they be said.

Both Travelers turned to look at the doctor. Before either could speak, Sara Jean laid a palm inside her husband's crooked elbow and said, "I think they are, Henry. For good and bad. But I think they are."

Layberg glowered in exasperation, thinking that his wife misunderstood him. Sara Jean forestalled her husband's explanation by kissing him at the corner of the mouth. Then she turned back to meet Selve's smile.

"Louis," said Selve, "I think you may have been right about the chance for peace, not so many years ago." Astor glared in amazement at her colleague, but the look only tugged Selve's expression a little more wryly askew. "There's no chance now, even I am certain. The—pistol hammers are falling. For either party now to pause, to turn aside, Louis, would be only suicide. You would not be better for the Vrage surviving."

"That will not happen!" Astor said.

"That will not happen," her colleague agreed. He stepped to the terminal and began keying in a set of commands to replace those he had begun minutes before.

Lexie Market had watched Mike step back among the instrument chassis to strip off his atmosphere suit. That was fine for the moment, anyway, though the night wasn't over. Shunting her thoughts into a different track, the blond physicist said, "What do you propose to do to them now that you wouldn't have done before? What changed by their—drive coils being damaged?''

Neither Traveler responded to the question. Even the humans in the room seemed more concerned with their own thoughts or whispered conversations. Louis Gustafson was holding his glasses in one hand and slowly rubbing his eyes with the other.

Market walked into the enclosure. Selve was quite obviously busy with the computer terminal, but Astor appeared only to be waiting to take the orange suit from Mike Gardner when he got it off. Lexie touched the female Traveler's wrist. In a clear voice she repeated, ''What are you going to do to the Vrage that you couldn't while their tr-transport apparatus was working?''

Astor's ingrained habit of secrecy stiffened her back and her face at the question. The big female would not have been part of a Contact Team had she been wholly inflexible, however. The notion of treating procedure as a god minutes after she had shot a Portal Four Monitor seemed so obviously absurd that Astor clapped out a laugh. Then she said, ''These''—a wave toward the twin pillars dominating the room—''are a focusing device. They're controlled and fed from all this''—a wave toward the hulking transformers and instrument frames stretching to the far end of the enclosure—''but act only as a lens to shape a bubble in the planetary magnetic field.''

All eyes but Selve's were on the big Traveler now. Isaac Hoperin held the cigarette which his fingers were now steady enough to light. Professor Gustafson listened with the grim interest of a man being told the details of how his cancer has spread. The old man was not angry, but his hurt was as obvious as his resignation.

''That's true of every Portal in the column,'' continued Astor, ''except for Skius itself. The magnetic field of Skius drives every transport. All this or any other set of drive coils does is tap a path for that channeled power to sweep through.''

''And Vrage is the same?'' prompted Charles Eisley. The military implications were more clear to him than they were to the others in the room.

Astor nodded, a gesture to which she had been trained for her duties on the Contact Team. Out of her human persona, she would have flicked up a thumb and forefinger to signal assent. ''We both had located the other's homeworld. We both had built an assault base, to hold a few square miles of the other planet just long enough to be able to implant a bomb between the mantle and the core.''

''But that would take years,'' blurted Mike Gardner in amazement.

''Hours,'' corrected Astor, ''and I'm sure too long even at that. We can no more fight them on Vrage than they could fight me at Portal Thirty-one.''

Selve made a last entry. ''They put their base at a crossover point,'' he said as he stepped back from the control panel. ''In transport column both with Vrage and with Skius. Ours—Portal Four Base—is in column only with Skius. Our crossover point is here, more work but much safer; they couldn't have stumbled over our base the way we did theirs. Of course, there are disadvantages.''

''We were the bridgehead for your attack on Vrage,'' said Eisley. ''Whatever happened to your own planet, whatever happened to your base, the bridgehead itself was going to be destroyed. Wasn't it?''

''There would have been rebound attacks, Charles,'' Astor replied with a candor which was more disarming than evasion could ever be. ''That won't happen now.''

Selve squinted and bent closer again to the oscilloscope, part of the instrument panel's array, as it began dancing

with a pattern of signals. They were not, as he had first
hoped, harmonics of the transport he had just programmed
into the school's mainframe computer. "Astor," he called.
The situation was suddenly outside the realm of Selve's
own special competence.

"That's not enough," said Lexie Market. Astor had
glanced away from her, but the physicist's hand recalled
the Traveler to the question. "Why is their base so
important?"

"Because," said Astor, giving the flat answer she would
rather have avoided in front of Louis Gustafson, "it's their
only way of striking Skius directly. If we destroy their
base, we can take as much time as we need to blast Vrage
till it glows—and then set the World Wrecker."

"Astor, we're about to get company!" Selve shouted.

"I don't—" began Isaac Hoperin, then realized that the
factors included human survival as well as the morality of
war and peace. His mind wavered from death camp to
napalmed baby to a world shattered into asteroids. In a
universal scheme, it would not have mattered whether that
last image were of Earth or some world unimagined by
men until this moment. In fact, and despite his repugnance
at the realization, Isaac Hoperin did care very much that
the broken world not be Earth.

Hoperin looked at Louis Gustafson, who whispered,
"None of this would have happened here, except that I
made it happen."

Astor was only two steps in a straight line from the
locker and the guns she had put away—a straight line that
would have taken her through the docking area. The banks
of fluorescents hid the faint excitation glow, but the Traveler's skin tingled even beneath her suit in warning that the
circle was indeed the target area. The turn and extra step

meant that Astor was still reaching for the door panel when the six Monitors appeared.

The newcomers faced out from a common center like the petals of a flower, each Monitor with a pistol raised. The Monitor closest to Astor shouted at the Contact Member in Skiuli, *"Freeze! Freeze!"*

Deith whirled and fired across the circle. One of her fellows screamed and dropped his own gun. The shot had passed close enough to melt and blacken the sleeve of his tunic against his right arm.

Astor slumped. The pistols had a thirty-millisecond burst control to keep their miniaturized components from melting down. The white flash was too brief for the onlookers' comprehension, coming as it did without warning and on the heels of the Monitor Group's appearance. The energy transfer might not have stopped a Vrage in armor, but it was quite enough to burn a fist-sized hole in the back of the Traveler's atmosphere suit.

Astor's fingers scrabbled at the front of the locker. They found no purchase on the smooth synthetic to keep her from sliding down. Bubbles in the gray panel at chest height showed where the locker had stopped such of the blast as Astor had not.

"Wait, don't move!" Selve shouted in English as the humans in the basement reacted each in his or her own way.

Charles Eisley reached for Sue with both hands to shunt her behind him. The tall woman was fractionally off-balance because she was reaching for her hip pocket and the knife folded there. Her mind had gone white, and she had no idea in the world as to what her next step might have been.

Dr. Layberg reacted in accordance with his training. He swung around and knelt beside Astor, just in time to keep her face from striking the concrete. The shot's intensity was a violet dazzle across his retinas, forcing him to blink and use his peripheral vision to examine the wound. It did not matter, except to Layberg himself. The charred edges of the suit were exuding their protective film, just as Keyliss's suit had done, although there is nothing important to protect when the victim's heart has been burned away.

Sara Jean stepped sideways, putting herself between the guns and her husband. Her eyes were panicky and on Selve, though one of her hands reached down to Henry's shoulder to reassure her of his presence.

Gustafson and Isaac Hoperin were within arm's reach of the Monitors, both of them too shocked by Astor's final statement to make split-second decisions in the present. Mike Gardner had just stepped forward with the orange suit held out. Market saw him poise to spring back behind an instrument cabinet. "Mike!" she screamed, for she saw also a pair of Monitors taking final aim at the motion. Gardner froze.

The Monitors were not wearing atmosphere suits. Mike knew that meant they had not come through Portal Four, but the fact carried no implications for him. Only Selve realized that if the Monitors came by way of Skius, then the present madness was not merely some aberration of Deith's.

It was madness all the same.

The Skiuli in pastel-patterned uniforms herded Selve and the humans together against the enclosure fencing. Deith watched, grinning like a crocodile, her pistol held slanted across her chest in her remaining hand. Two of the Monitors holstered their weapons and walked to the controls of the transport equipment. One of them was pursing and pushing out his lips, the equivalent of a worried grimace in a human.

Isaac Hoperin looked across at the body of Astor. Minutes before she had been his personal symbol of overbearing authority. He said, "Who are these people, Selve? Are they arresting you?"

In Skiuli, Selve said, "We've got to report home at once, Deith. The Vrage base is not only located at Portal Thirty-one, their coils have been knocked out of service. If we attack at once, they won't be able to warn Vrage itself."

"We've reported to the Directorate," Deith said. She laughed, a sound beyond the edge of tittering madness. Her right arm waved. The sleeve was neatly capped below the elbow instead of being pinned. "I should thank your friend for this," the stocky Monitor went on. "It was the proof we needed that you were quite mad and far too dangerous to be entrusted with the safety of the race. Quite mad."

She walked over to Astor's body and kicked it. Muscles spasmed. Astor's back arched and her throat drew a grating breath. "Thank you, Astor," Deith said.

The Monitor with the shot-burned sleeve pawed for his gun on the floor for a moment. Then he threw up on the concrete.

"Deith, you don't know how to use this equipment," Selve begged in Skiuli. "We'll go back together and explain to the Directorate about the Vrage coils. Deith, it isn't *us*, it's *Skius*."

The female of the pair of Monitors at the controls glanced up before resuming her work. She and her partner spoke in low voices as they checked and keyed instruments. The two were awkward, but they were clearly familiar with their task. Their three fellows with guns trained on the captives seemed a great deal less certain of themselves.

"I knew you'd screw up," Deith gloated. "I knew I'd have to take over." Selve wondered if shock from her wound had driven the Monitor over the edge, or if Deith had always been madder than any of the Contact Team had dreamed. "You filed complete plans of this—tangle—at home. We built a mock-up, so Sehor and Kadel could practice on it every day for the past month. Practice for this." She waved the stub of her arm toward the controls and the pair at work setting them up.

Isaac Hoperin stepped forward, his mouth slightly open and his eyes on a future far beyond Deith. He did not understand the language or any of the details of the situation. But while the humans with him feared and waited, the physicist's own mind had connected one fact to its unstated corollary. The fact was that Selve and Astor had a plan which would prevent the destruction of Earth as a side effect; the corollary was that the plan had been countermanded by someone utterly ruthless. Hoperin would *not* stand by and watch that happen, even though his death would not stop it.

Professor Gustafson caught the younger man in a bear hug even as Hoperin's foot lifted for his first step. The project director wrapped Hoperin up with a strength not far short of hysterical, crying, "*No*, Isaac, you mustn't make me have killed you!"

The shock of contact and his colleague's words jarred Hoperin back to the present. He gaped at the Monitors. Their gun hands were tight and their faces frightened. Embarrassment at being manhandled by a fellow faculty member subdued the physicist as the guns could not have. "It's all right, Louis," he mumbled. "It's all right."

"When they rebound," said Selve in English, "set the

apparatus for, ah, the Mesozoic, Portal Thirty-one, and engage it at once. In case I'm not here to do that. Don't make any trouble now, please don't, it'll be all right." He could not help but stare at Astor whenever his eyes fell from Deith's. Selve could not help the tears, either.

"We're ready," said one of the Monitors at the controls.

"Go ahead, then!" Deith snarled in a return to her normal style of interaction with her colleagues. It was in triumph, however, that she added to the prisoners, "Perfect timing, two minutes before we rebound."

The main switch slapped into its live position. The pair of Monitors sidled away from their handiwork, glancing first at the controls and then toward their one-handed colleague.

"Did you think you were going to reset the Portal after we were gone, Selve?" Deith asked through a smirk.

Selve sidestepped once, then again. He struck a brace as he waited for the blast that would kill him. He was standing far enough from the other prisoners that none of them would be caught by the shot as well. He knew that the Monitors—that Deith—could not afford to leave him to undo their own settings. What Selve hoped and prayed, for the sake of Skius and of Earth, was that Deith did not realize the locals could save the situation.

Even if Selve had already gone the way of Astor.

"The Directorate isn't going to change plans now on the word of madmen," Deith continued in grim echo of Selve's own thoughts as he watched the hand and watched the gun. "The assault force will attack as soon as we return to tell the Directorate that Portal Eleven is open and tuned." The nervous buzz of the coils rose through a set of blackboard-scraping harmonics. The Monitors were all keeping carefully clear of the docking area.

"Deith, you're sending them all to die," the Contact

Member said. "We can win the war if you'll just direct the force to Portal Thirty-one. Even without warning the troops, they'll be able to slaughter the Vrages instead of being butchered themselves." His voice rose of necessity to be heard over the vibration. There was no doubt that strain was forcing it into a squeak as well.

"You've forgotten your duty," the Monitor sneered. "We haven't forgotten ours."

The drive coils tripped in a blue flash as stunning as the pistol bolt Selve knew would follow in the silence.

Deith turned and fired into the center of the left-hand pillar. The Lucite shell dimpled away from the bolt in concentric circles. The superheated plastic ignited in a ghostly red flash, a sphere two feet in diameter. Only at that point had the wave front broken up enough to mix with the oxygen needed for fire.

The coils themselves died less obtrusively than the cover sheet did. The circuits carried ultrahigh voltages, but their current was too low for spectacular arcs. There was a violet lambency, almost a fluid drifting from the sagging ruin. Copper burned green in the direct path of the shot. Some of the insulating lacquer smoldered for a moment or two afterward.

Deith licked her lips in satisfaction. The glowing muzzle of her weapon waggled for a moment toward the other pillar.

Mike Gardner had invested over a hundred hours of coil winding in each of the pillars. The destruction of the first had been a shock greater than Astor's murder. The student had never seen someone killed before, so the murder was an act without any real-world referent. When the gun pointed toward the other half of his laborious construction, he lunged into Lexie Market. The physicist had set and braced herself, knowing that Mike's instincts would drive him toward the weapon.

Market put her arms firmly around him. "Hold still," she said. The blond physicist had always been good at anticipating irrational behavior . . . except when it affected her directly. "Got to work on that," she muttered. She stepped aside when Mike relaxed, keeping her right arm around his waist.

The one-handed Monitor did not bother to fire into the second pillar. The first set of coils had been pierced through the phenolic mandrel on which it was wound. The odor of carbolic acid was bitter and overpowering, even among the other effluvia of destruction. That deterred Deith from a needless follow-up shot.

"We'll see you back home in the half hour or so it'll take you to rebound, Selve," Deith said. She smirked. It was notable to Selve that the other Monitors did not speak aloud, except in terse reply to Deith. How had the Directorate ever listened to this mad thing, who terrified even her closest colleagues? Were the best minds on Skius so desperately afraid?

They were right to be afraid. It was their decision which was so tragically wrong.

"You'll be arrested there," Deith was saying. "Treachery affecting the state. Unless they choose to dismiss the charges because of the victory celebrations."

"Twenty seconds," called a Monitor who until then had been only a guard with a trembling gunhand.

"I know that!" Deith shouted.

"Deith, you can't let them jump into disaster on Vrage," said the single remaining Contact Member, although he bowed his head in full subservience. Selve was not one to let hierarchy affect the survival of worlds. "Trust Astor's judgment at least on that."

"The assault force will be well on its way to destroying Vrage utterly, before you even rebound to explain your team's actions," Deith taunted.

Selve had thought Astor's name might goad the Monitor to fury if it did not shock her into reason. Selve's own death might have resulted from that fury. Death was blind. Selve saw Astor's body when his eyes were open. He saw hundreds of thousands of other Skiuli dead uselessly on Vrage when his eyes were closed, his imagination free.

But Deith was as untouched by the memory, the flash of her hand and arm vaporized, as she was by the logic of what Selve said. Her smile was beatific as she and her fellows vanished. That smile soured air that reeked already with the burned residues of plastics, metal, and flesh.

With the Monitors and their weapons gone, Mike Gardner lunged for the pillar, though its total ruin had been obvious from twenty feet away. The thermoplastic covering was frosted and wrinkled a yard above and below a hole the size of a dinner plate.

Mike jerked the warped panel open. The metal's high thermal conductivity had spread and dissipated much of the bolt's effect, though not enough to avoid total destruction of the apparatus: the pit through the multiple layers of copper was conical, tapering down as it plunged deeper. For the first time, the implications of such energy release on a human target became real to Gardner. He turned and stared at Astor's corpse. Lexie Market guided him away with a hand on the student's wrist and another on his suddenly pallid cheek.

The equipment for which he had risked his honor was only part of a nightmare to Louis Gustafson now. He knelt at Astor's side, hoping that the obvious was not real.

Dr. Hoperin looked at Selve and opened his mouth to

speak. The Traveler had sunk into a crouch when the Monitors disappeared. He covered his face with his hands.

Hoperin swallowed and joined Professor Gustafson. Henry Layberg did not bother. The Monitor who thrust a gun in his face had moved him from Astor without argument. He knew there was nothing he or anyone on Earth could do for the victim. A day earlier, Dr. Layberg might have been more interested in the structure of an unusual corpse than he was in the fact that the corpse had been someone he knew. For whatever reason, he no longer felt that way. He put his arm around his wife's shoulders and looked at Selve. The living Traveler might need help as the dead one did not.

"Selve," said Sara Jean Layberg, "aren't they going to—invade through here?" Nothing that had occurred or been spoken just now made any sense to her. She knew enough to be afraid. She knew also to keep the quaver out of her voice as she forced those around her to deal with the real problem and not its side effects.

"No one would have been appearing here anyway," said the Traveler as he rose wearily to his feet again. "The drive coils at Portal Four command a volume beyond the capacity of this unit to accept when energized. What this will do is redirect the transport to the current focal point of this Portal. To Vrage."

Professor Gustafson's face was averted from the corpse by which he knelt. He was rubbing the flats of his hands against one another, although he had not actually touched the body. "There is no focal point," he said. "The coils here have been destroyed." He spoke without frustration. The old engineer had lived and taught too long to become exasperated when someone missed an obvious factor.

"Louis," said Selve in the same tired voice as before, "the hardware isn't the Portal, it opens the Portal. The planetary magnetic field does the real work. By destroying the apparatus, Deith has seen to it that the focus can't be changed until it dissipates naturally." The Traveler had been speaking audibly but toward an angle of the room with no one in it. Now he rotated his head to face Professor Gustafson. To do less would be cowardly. "By the time the Portal has closed, a Vrage counterstrike will almost certainly have rebounded along the transport column. To here."

"Do the little coils upstairs still work?" Sara Jean Layberg asked unexpectedly. "The ones that—the other day, took Danny and me to the city?"

Selve was alert and fully alive for the first time since the Monitors had ended the moment of triumph. "Michael," he said, "were the coils destroyed or just disconnected?" He thrust up a peremptory hand to still the gasps and inchoate words from the others nearby. This crisis was Selve's meat.

"Keyliss separated the coils so that they couldn't harmonize with the big pair," Gardner said. He was already striding for the gate. There was a toolkit in the bottom drawer of the desk on which the test unit sat.

"Wait, we'll need communication between there and here," the Traveler snapped.

"Well, the phone," said Professor Gustafson. "The labs all have phones."

"I'll get it," said Lexie Market. She did not run directly after the engineering student. Instead, she ducked from the enclosure into Gustafson's office to check the number on the phone dial there. It was faster than trying to find a university directory in an unfamiliar lab. Only then did she dart up the stairs calling, "Mike! Which lab?"

Selve was at the computer terminal. A quick pass cleared the settings in force. He began to key in new ones from memory. "Louis, disconnect the main coils, even the damaged one," said the Traveler as his fingers flashed. "They won't function properly, but there are infinite ways they could malfunction enough to interfere."

The phone in Gustafson's office began to shrill. Isaac Hoperin exchanged glances with the Laybergs before scurrying into the office. A moment later, he stuck his head out the door again, holding the phone at the limit of its cord. "It's Dr. Market," he called. "Mike is hooking up the equipment and she's standing by to give him the phone when necessary."

"This is done," said Louis Gustafson, rising from between the pillars. He held the socket wrench with which he had just disconnected the bus joining the two sets of concentric coils. "I'll go up to the laboratory to help Michael."

"No," said Selve without looking up from his own work at the instrument console. "I need you here on the phone, Louis. When I give instructions, I want them passed on by someone to whom they're more than gibberish. Michael knows more about the unit upstairs than you do, anyway."

Henry Layberg was bending back his interlaced fingers to have something to do with his hands while others worked. "I'll go upstairs," he said abruptly. "In case they need somebody to, to hold a retractor or something." The big man moved at an accelerating pace, as though he feared that if he hesitated, Selve would call him back to further nervous inaction. In fact, Selve had no present use for the doctor and therefore no concern about where he went.

The slim Traveler completed his own task by loading the program he had just written. He did not throw the switch. Selve's body was dried comfortably by his body suit, but sweat had beaded at his hairline. He wiped his face with both hands as he called, "Isaac, are they ready yet?"

Eisley and Schlicter were outside the enclosure now, uncertain but ready to be directed. Hoperin and Professor Gustafson stood together in the office doorway. The physicist still held the phone. "No," he said without having to relay the question. "Dr. Market will tell us when they are."

"They're going to have to modify the cyclic rate at which the signal is fed," Selve said. "We'll start at thirty hertz, but they'll have to vary from that depending on what readings I get here from Skius. Tell them that."

Isaac Hoperin pursed his lips. He handed the phone to Professor Gustafson. The physicist could not imagine what terms Selve trusted only the engineer to transfer correctly, but there was no time now to argue about absurdities. The Traveler seemed to think he could save Earth. As much as it offended Hoperin's personal code, the stakes this time were too high to refuse to bow to authority. It was at least possible to believe that Selve, unlike human soldiers and politicians, had the world's best interests at heart.

Louis Gustafson murmured distantly into the handset while the Traveler rubbed his face again.

"Selve," said Sara Jean Layberg, "won't it already be too late? They left here before we . . . even started, after all."

"That crew," Selve scoffed. "You saw how long it took them to align this." He caressed the raggedly functional instruments before him. "They're no more familiar with the main unit that they'll have to set also. These aren't"—he gestured with his palm up and fingers splayed—"plastic cups from an extruder. Each set of Portal controls is as truly unique as anything you create, Sara, or I do."

"He's connecting the lines from the signal synthesizer,"

called Isaac Hoperin. The engineer still held the phone. "That will be the last."

Selve watched a dial quiver. He snorted as it moved a quarter of the way around the scale and hung there. "All this time and they're only now tuning the carrier," he said.

It was a moment before Sara Jean realized that the Traveler was not referring to Mike and that woman with him upstairs. Varied thoughts drifted through Mrs. Layberg's mind, some of them involving relief. Aloud she said, "Selve, you—are you going to be in serious trouble because of what you're doing here?"

The Traveler stared at her. Sara Jean's lips were pressed firmly together and her hands were folded, one over the other, across the cloth-covered buckle of her skirt. He doubted that Sara Jean knew exactly what she was suggesting, and exactly what the consequences would be for Earth if Selve abandoned his present course. Though perhaps she did.

"My duty is to Skius," Selve said. "Certain decisions were our responsibility to make, the Contact Team's; others were not. If the fate of the war and our planet rests on a difference of opinion between Deith and Astor . . . Sara, I will not sacrifice a half million lives and our chance of winning the war simply because the Directorate accepted Deith's judgment."

"Michael is ready now," said Professor Gustafson. "Should he engage?"

"Don't let them touch it!" Selve said sharply. "I'll control that. Michael is to stand by at the oscilloscope to beat the signal at his end. *When* I direct him."

Gustafson spoke quickly into the telephone, his eyes still focused on Selve, twenty feet away and separated by the heavy mesh. "They're clear now," the professor called almost as soon as he finished talking to the phone.

Selve threw the main switch. His whole control panel was by now alive with signals from Skius and the beginnings of his own attempt to control the Portal. The Traveler stepped to the other half of the panel. "Sara," he said, because she was near and his soul ached to tell someone, "it won't have enough power. It won't be able to stand the strain."

He looked through the fence and across the aisle. "Louis, divide the signal at twenty-eight hertz. The fools can't even plot synchrony with their own programmed transport!" Selve glanced at another gauge and moaned again. "Sara," he whispered with no sign of his earlier official harshness, "they mustn't close down upstairs no matter how badly the coils overload. No matter what."

"Twenty-eight hertz," Gustafson relayed.

"Louis, twenty-eight five!" ordered the Traveler.

Selve's words to her had been a prayer, not an order. Sara Jean nodded and ran out of the enclosure anyway. The eyes of the other humans tracked her briefly. She had nothing to tell them. Their heads rotated back toward Selve even before the woman disappeared into the stairwell.

The air outside the basement proper was cool and a surprise to Sara Jean. She did not notice the undertone of vibration until the fire door closed behind her, either: in the basement, the sound of the coils had been lost in the noise of other equipment and the general atmosphere of tension. Small as it was, the tabletop unit was making the whole building sing to its note. "It's enough," the woman muttered. "It took Danny and me to Skius." The difference between that accident and an army of a half million or more was too obvious to bear consideration.

The fluorescents in the upper hallway were on, the ballasts of some of them harmonizing with the buzzing of the drive coils. The result was less nerve-racking than the sound of the coils unaugmented. Sara Jean's cork-soled sandals were loose enough to slap her heels as she ran to the open doorway of Laboratory Three.

The tinny noise was so obtrusive within that Dr. Market held her hand cupped between her mouth and the receiver when she spoke into it. Henry Layberg stood between her, at a desk along the side wall, and another desk in the center of the lab on which the apparatus was running. When his wife appeared in the doorway, Layberg looked surprised but went to join her. The room was hot. The insulation odor, unpleasant in itself and for its associations, was already a burden on breathing.

Mike Gardner leaned forward in a heavy wooden chair, one finger and thumb teasing a control knob in gentle fractions of arc. The oscilloscope before him was in series with the feed from the signal generators in the basement. A grid was etched across the instrument's small, circular screen. Mike was eyeballing the peaky saw-edge which the phosphor bead traced across the grid. It was faster than any other method of matching cyclic rate to the relayed orders. He hoped to God that it was also accurate enough.

"Twenty-nine five," Lexie Market shouted against the background of white noise. "They may rise to thirty again."

"Twenty-nine five," Gardner repeated.

The coils themselves trembled, then froze; trembled again. Their lower ends were bolted to an aluminum chassis. When the harmonics were just right, the foot-high coils pulled enough play from their base that their tops described visible circles in the air around their axes. The electronic struggle going on within the apparatus was much more violent than what Sara Jean had seen the previous day. Even then it had been enough to frighten her—and the Travelers, when they learned of it.

Sara Jean put a hand on her husband's forearm as she waited for an opportunity to relay Selve's message. Henry was trying to say something to her. Her hand, while affectionate, was angled to fend him off.

Gardner took his right hand from the tuning knob and leaned back as if he feared his breath might disarray the stasis he had just achieved. Sara Jean stepped close and bent to her former lover. "Selve says not to shut down no matter what," she said.

Mike risked a glance around. His long forelock was dark and plastered over his forehead by sweat. Taut cheek muscles had drawn his lips into something between a smile and a snarl. Nevertheless, there was a smile in Gardner's eyes as he said, "He's got it!" Fate had given the student an opportunity to act in a fashion for which he had been trained. He liked it, pressure and all.

"Thirty and rising!" the physicist shouted.

"Thirty!" Gardner shouted back, and touched his dial.

There was an active, palpable silence that gathered in all sound from the lab and heaven knew how much farther away. The room was a pool of light that owed nothing to the fluorescents. Everything glowed the lime green of light reflected from vegetation when the sun is low and its beams are polarized by a cloud layer. There were orange-suited figures in the soundless ambiance, superimposed on the reality of tables and hardware. They stretched far beyond the tiled walls of the laboratory, as if the green light were a hologrammatic simulation of a huge army. The tanks were too huge to be other than camera trickery . . . save that Mike Gardner had seen them roar like freight trains through the chlorine mist.

Looming over all, even the tanks, were cylindrical drive

coils that could have been paired office buildings. They blazed with an effulgence which seared its reality through the matter of Earth.

The dial and front of the telephone disappeared in a spray of plastic. The small electromagnet in the ringer had explosively melted everything around itself. Congealing droplets gleamed against Lexie's skirt as she threw herself to the floor.

Henry Layberg seized his wife and the graduate student from behind by the collars. Gardner had already started to get up, but haste jammed his knees between his chair and the top of the desk well. Layberg jerked back with as little ceremony as he would have shown in cutting clothing from an accident victim. Mike and Sara Jean flew backward as the drive coils vaporized.

The surge that sublimed the copper wire involved greater potential energy than could have been supplied by all the generating stations on the Southeastern Grid. The coils' failure was so sudden that virtually none of that potential was actually released. The great coils in the basement would have gone gaseous just as certainly, and they would have taken most of the engineering school with them.

In Laboratory Three, copper vapor recondensed wherever the globular shock wave hurled it. From desk height upward, the walls and ceiling were gray with shadows in negative wherever some object had earlier blocked the gaseous metal.

Sara Jean was on the floor and protected by her husband's bulk. The forearm Mike Gardner threw up to cover his eyes was black on the side facing the catastrophic overload. The copper was divided too finely to have any color but black. It glittered on the student's hair and chin, but the wide swath including his eyes and nose had been protected.

There was sound again—normal sound to the extent that it is normal for small electrical fires to wheeze and sputter. There was a dry chemical extinguisher clamped to the laboratory wall. Lexie Market took it down and blew two short gusts into the chassis which had supported the coils. The spluttering died in a dance of white crystals.

Sara Jean Layberg was starting to get up again. Henry held her steady for a moment for a quick visual examination. He kissed the tip of her nose in dismissal before he turned to Mike Gardner.

"Jesus," the young engineer muttered as he stared at his left arm. Cracks appeared in the sooty coating and the skin beneath when he tried to ball his fist.

"Wait," said Lexie as she dropped the fire extinguisher and stepped toward Gardner.

"I'm all right," he said. His eyes were slitted in a face scrunched tight with pain.

"You'll be all right," said Dr. Layberg as he snapped out his clean handkerchief, "as soon as we get you to some burn cream and wrap you up against shock." He laid the linen diagonally over the arm and hand and began to knot the free corners. "I've got a proper first-aid kit in my car," he said to the two women, "but I think it's simpler to run him over to the emergency room. One of you phone ahead and tell them I'm bringing in a patient with second-degree burns on arm and face. Use my name."

Sue Schlicter burst into the laboratory. The air currents she stirred reminded the quartet of how good fresh air smelled. "Are you all right?" the tall woman demanded. "Are you all *here*?"

Professors Hoperin and Gustafson were right behind her, Hoperin limping. The phone he held had gouted hot plastic also. Though his hand had been spared, the dial had lain against his right thigh when it boiled away.

"Michael, you're all right?" said Louis Gustafson, echoing Schlicter's more general concern. Gardner was the professor's personal responsibility.

"What happened downstairs?" asked Sara Jean as Lexie Market helped Layberg tie the makeshift bandage.

"One of the transformers melted," said Charles Eisley from the hallway. The door was filled with those who had already entered the lab. "Nothing serious. Not in comparison to what had already happened."

Eisley rubbed his hands and looked down at them. When he raised his eyes, he continued in a louder voice that cut through the babble, "Professor Gustafson, everyone. I'm going to make some phone calls to Washington as soon as possible. I want you all to realize that. The—responsible authorities must be informed."

Isaac Hoperin sniffed. Without personal rancor, however, he said, "And much they're going to believe now, aren't they, with all the apparatus destroyed and Skiuli gone."

"Professor," said the diplomat, "this isn't over. It's important that State and not the Pentagon make the next decisions—how much to make public, whether to make anything public. But the decision won't be made here." Except, Charles Eisley thought incongruously, he had decided that he was going to remarry.

"Gone?" Mike Gardner asked as he lowered his bandaged arm. It throbbed with every pulse. He was beginning to feel dizzy.

"Selve disappeared just as the equipment overloaded," muttered Professor Gustafson. "Rebounded, I presume. The—" He coughed. "Astor is gone also."

There was a brief stir in the doorway. Hoperin eased aside to admit Arlene Myaschensky with a sheaf of photographs in her hand. "I hoped you might . . ." Arlene said. She held the pictures toward Louis Gustafson, though her eyes widened as they took in the state of the lab and the people in it. "The— We haven't been going back in time. These pictures . . ." She broke off as she realized that only Charles Eisley, whose gaze sharpened, was paying attention.

"It's too early to worry about what the government may do," said Sara Jean Layberg in a clear, distant voice. Her eyes were focused beyond the walls of the room. "Any moment now the—counterstrike, they called it? Any moment now we may all be dead on a dead planet. They must have defenses, but *we* don't, the whole *Earth*."

"It's all right," said Sue Schlicter as she laid her arm across the other woman's shoulders.

"It's *not* all right!" Sara Jean said. She tossed her head so violently that tears sprang from her cheeks to glister through the air. "It burned up, it *didn't* work. They're going to die on Vrage, Selve's people, and we're going to die here. . . ." She flung herself, not away from Sue, but into the arms her husband spread to receive her.

"No, it's all right," the tall woman repeated into the waiting silence. "Your friend was smiling when he disappeared. Your friend Selve was smiling."

Sue reached out with the object which had dropped to the concrete when Selve's pouch disappeared from around it. It was the goblet Sara Jean had given the Traveler, unbroken despite its obvious fragility.

"He wouldn't have smiled if it hadn't worked long enough, would he?" said Sue Schlicter.

Their fingers touched as Sara Jean took the goblet from Sue. The faces of both women glowed with hope and trust.